SATYRDAY

"The ravens surrounded her."

SATYRDAY

a fable by
STEVEN BAUER

Illustrated by Ron Miller

Published by
Berkley Publishing Corporation
Distributed by
G. P. PUTNAM'S SONS

Eight lines from "Sunday Morning" by Wallace Stevens, copyright ©
1923 by Wallace Stevens, renewed 1951 by Wallace Stevens. Reprinted
from *The Collected Poems of Wallace Stevens* by permission of Alfred A.
Knopf, Inc.

Library of Congress Cataloging in Publication Data

Bauer, Steven.
　Satyrday, a fable.

　I.　Title.
PZ4.B3375Sat　1980 [PS3552.A8364]　813'.54　80-13534
ISBN 0-399-12533-7

Printed in the United States of America

The author wishes to thank the Fine Arts Work Center in Provincetown for a Fellowship in Writing, during which this novel was written.

*for Bonnie,
and Michael*

Contents

Illustrations

We live in an old chaos of the sun,
Or old dependency of day and night,
Or island solitude, unsponsored, free,
Of that wide water, inescapable. . . .
And, in the isolation of the sky,
At evening, casual flocks of pigeons make
Ambiguous undulations as they sink,
Downward to darkness, on extended wings.

— "Sunday Morning,"
Wallace Stevens

"I have you!" the owl said.

SUNDAY

It was just past midnight and the air was filled with wings. An army of ravens came out of the west like a cold black storm. Leaves rustled in the deepening chill, and over the ground a wind rolled, a darkly visible tumbleweed of air.

But in the sky was a rumble such as a distant earthquake might have made. The moon was startled by the sound. The night had been peaceful, its curved sweep studded with stars. Above her, their sharp sparks bristled. She had followed this course forever, her bright edge unfolding until a pale medallion hung full in the sky. Balanced between the earth and the pincushion of stars above, she remained pleased with herself, the axis of night, the interlocutor. But now she was waning, past half, growing weaker with the loss of light. And this rumble behind her was frightening.

Over her shoulder the moon watched the ravens approach. They came like a rippling sheet, its slow waves caused by unseen hands, the fury of its organization apparent even at this distance. In an instant the ravens were cawing. The first hoarse streaks of sound reached the moon and multiplied until their monotonous echoing rattled the night. *Crauk. Cr-r-cruk.* It came from everywhere, its hard consonants scratching at her, and under the surface a denser noise, the violent reverberations of their wings.

13

The moon thought the whole of creation was screaming. The earth disappeared. Ravens swooped under her, so thick she could see only her own dim light flung back at her by their glassy blackness. Thousands still flooded from the west, a turbulent stream of feathers unfurling from the horizon. Beneath her, the stream curled in a sudden arc and the bright red darts of the ravens' eyes pushed past her face, in front of her.

Only then did she see the net. Hooked in the ravens' talons was a fine gauze, black as their wings, hardly visible in the reflected light. As the birds whirled around her, the net caught the horns of her crescent and stuck, drawn ever more tight. She was imprisoned by layers of gauze; she was strangled by them. The hoarse screaming of the birds grew, pulsing through her until the cawing seemed to be coming from inside.

She could see nothing more. She felt herself stiffen, the sudden onset of vertigo releasing into the certainty of fall, and she groaned as the ravens wrenched her free from her path over the earth. Her fire went out. The night filled with a horrible rush, the dissonant flapping of thousands of wings, the hollow suck as she left her orbit, and the creeping cold of the wind which took her place.

The satyr stood under the leaves of an ancient maple, out of breath. He scratched his hindquarters, put his hands on his hips, and panted. His two horns glinted in the moon's spare light. He bent at the waist and let his torso hang until his fingers brushed the ferns and moss of the forest's floor. It was summer in the meadowlands and his chest filled with the fragrance of leaves, rich dirt, the rank smell of his body. Then he straightened and yawned and swatted at a mosquito which had landed on his shoulder.

Matthew swayed and abruptly sat down, his back to the tree. His tangled hair caught on the bark and he grunted in annoyance as it tore loose. And then the pain, like the itch, was behind him, with nothing before him but the two tapered legs, covered with goat fleece, stiff with dirt and twigs. He pressed the heels of his hands against his eyes to stop the reeling; red suns exploded in his head, the aftermath of wine.

Not even he knew how old he was. For him the past was a blur. What few memories he had were focused against the succession of seasons, a rhythmic celebration the world held, tension and release. Instinctively he'd known these warm indolent nights would soon be upon him when he noticed skunk cabbage jutting from the forest's mulch. Then its leaves untwined, the willow's furred blossoms appeared, the day lingered in the sky.

Matthew heard a noise in the stand of saplings to his left, his body tensed, and he scrambled into a crouch. From the underbrush a six-point buck stared at him. The animal's eyes were wide, its flanks quivering in the moonlight. The satyr was an awesome figure to the other creatures of the meadowlands, and he was never completely trusted. He had a strange smell, and wilder eyes, sparked with a cunning beyond them. Perversely he leapt at the stag, his arms outstretched. The animal bounded deeper into the forest, crashing through a brace of trees, leaving only Matthew's rough laughter in its wake. The satyr threw back his head again and looked at the moon's horns through the maple's translucent leaves. She hung suspended in the night sky, a paring of her fuller self.

Tonight he'd drunk himself senseless by her light, run through the forest almost soundlessly, in search of the nymphs who had vanished from the meadowlands years before. He had never abandoned hope that one night he would round an oak and there, glimmering like foxfire, she would appear. She would glance over her shoulder, toss her long hair, and run away from him again. It might have been yesterday, but he didn't remember. Now, still slightly muddled, stirred by his encounter with the stag yet ready for sleep, he thought of her.

A noise began to build in the forest behind him, a noise no animal might make, a distant sound like the steady crash of waves against a cliff. He whirled around, could see nothing but the retreating welter of trunks and bushes. Yet the noise grew until he saw what appeared to be a wall of darker air move toward him. Twigs jumped from the ground, the maple began to creak, and its leaves rattled as if someone were shaking the branches.

It happened quickly; a pool of blackness gathered around his hooves. He turned sharply and looked at the sky. The moon was gone. And then he heard the noise. It was like river ice cracking in a spring thaw, like stumps being pulled from the earth. Stepping to the side, he ducked around the maple's trunk and the wind's full force almost knocked him over. Leaves flew into his face like the wings of bats. He struck out at the whirling air as if he could brush it away.

He had to get back to his ledge. If the wind were this strong, what would the rain be like? But he was drunk, unsettled by the onslaught of this storm, and he stumbled away from the maple in the direction of

home, cursing as the wind rushed him along, howling as it threw him
against trees or tumbled him into a briar patch. He'd known only one
night to rival this. It had been long long ago, and he'd almost—
almost—forgotten.

The boy was hunched by a fire when the moon disappeared. He had
gathered wood in the late afternoon, dragging it from the forest surrounding the meadow. He'd kindled the fire as the sun's last rays faded
around him and ate his supper by its warmth. He was waiting for Matthew, but the darkness thickened and the satyr never arrived. It seemed
he was often waiting for Matthew, whose arrivals and departures had
no pattern, who could not be counted on.

The moon appeared in the east over the fringe of trees, rose higher in
the sky. Derin grew tired and fidgety and bored; when he finally
allowed himself to sleep, he slept fitfully. A twig cracked and he awoke,
expecting Matthew, but it was only a squirrel come to share the fire's
lingering heat. He looked up again and saw what seemed to be a solid
black sheet move from the west. It swept across the sky, bringing with
it a subtle thunder. He stared, transfixed, as it slipped over the moon's
horned face and the light around him disappeared. The stars to the east
still shone, more brightly now, but the moon and the western sky were
dark.

Around him, the trees circling the meadow writhed in a heavy wind.
He was suddenly very cold. The wind bore down on him and its chill
damp entered his shirt, crawling over his chest and back. In a panic he
threw himself on the ground and rolled. The wind passed over him,
harsh as sawgrass, and when he slowly stood again his fire was out,
stone dead.

Everything had disappeared. His arms went out in front of him as
though he were suddenly blind. He tripped and broke his fall with his
hands. It was no use. He would be better off where he was. Pulling his
knees to his chest, he decided to stay where he'd fallen and try to warm
himself, hoping to wake from this nightmare which seemed so much
like the truth.

The moon thought she would never breathe again. Down, down she
went through an air so liquid she knew she'd been dragged under
water. Then the falling stopped. The wings surrounding her beat them-

selves to a halt. She felt a slight pressure on her side and it terrified her. Whatever was under her was moist and chilly, the touch of decay.

Out of the darkness, through the gauze which trapped her, she heard a voice. It had nails in it, the sharp glitter of quartz, the bruising force of unquestioned power.

"Unwrap her," the voice said.

She felt the net unwind, and as the layers grew thinner, dark forms materialized. She could breathe again, and her light returned to her, only a little, but enough to see by.

"And gag her when you're through," the voice said.

She lay in the clearing of a huge forest, amid dirt and rotting leaves. All around her stood trees, leafless and gaunt, their angular branches reaching into the dark air. On every limb for as far as she could see perched the ravens who had captured her. They hunched deep in their lustrous feathers, their beady eyes bright with malice. In the clearing in front of her sat a huge black rock the shape of an egg.

To her horror, the rock began to turn. It wavered from side to side on the enormous gnarled claws at its base until it faced her. She gasped and caught her breath so sharply she glowed for a moment and then went out again.

In the brief light she cast over the clearing, she saw a great horned owl. Its slow breathing ruffled its feathers. Its beak was hooked, like a sickle. Its eyes, yellow as jaundice, were the size of gold ducats. And on its neck and chest, where its bib should have been, was a wet swatch of red the color of blood. The owl fastened the moon in his somnolent gaze and held her there.

She was about to cry out when two of the ravens standing guard clamped a gag over her mouth. It was made of a linen so tightly woven that only the most sustained effort pulled air through it. As she breathed slowly, she seemed to herself ridiculous, trapped, blinking on and off like a firefly, a small curved flicker in the night. From the owl's maw came what must have been a laugh, but it was ugly as a mauled animal. The ravens hunched deeper in their feathers until their red eyes disappeared.

"Let me look at her awhile," the owl said, "and then we'll fasten her in the tree."

The owl stared at his captive, his great eyelids drooping. Behind her, the moon heard a rustle high in the treetops, and turning, saw a small group of ravens readying a series of ropes and tackle. They were nearly hidden among the twisted branches of an ancient oak, one of the tallest in the forest. Its upper reaches did not move in the wind.

The ravens were preparing a cage, tying back the branches at one side with great effort. In the center of the oak was a hollowness around which the branches naturally tightened.

"I have you," the owl said. "You are not mine, but I have you. The nights will be very dark without you."

He laughed again. As before, the ravens sank in their feathers, all but one who sat on a branch near the moon. This raven was preening herself, pecking under a wing for fleas, and as the moon watched, amazed at what seemed a display of sheer arrogance, she couldn't help imagine that the raven looked straight back at her and winked.

As Derin slept, strange noises filled the meadow. The sound of water from the stream stopped, and the whole world of night was changed. Everywhere diurnal animals woke from their sleep. A badger stuck his snout from the mouth of his burrow, hurriedly looked around, and disappeared. A squirrel ran up the trunk of a maple, sat on one of the higher branches, and chattered as though she were dying of cold.

Still Derin slept on. He trembled in the grasp of troubled dreams. In one, his friend Matthew was a great brown bear who lumbered through the clearing on all fours, ripping everything in his path with his curved claws. The animal was not frightening, nor even particularly vicious, but he was so unlike Matthew, yet had Matthew's face, that Derin cried out in his sleep.

The squirrel quit her chattering and swayed on the branch. The badger did not reappear. Above the clearing, the sky was dark and thick, a solid cloud. Like a fine rain, dust began to filter through the air, falling on everything, on the leaves of trees, the stones in the brook, on Derin as he slept.

His cheek twitched as though a fly had alighted on it. Had he been awake and had he the ears of a great horned owl, he might have heard a very distant noise, days distant, faint as fingernails on slate, stopping and starting, very like the noise of a heavy object being raised off the ground with the aid of blocks and tackle.

The ravens had fastened ropes to the moon's cusps, and she felt ashamed hanging upside down and powerless, a foolish golden bowl. They used the dead truck of an elm as a weight, and in fits and starts she was jerked into the air. The overhanging branches jabbed at her, but she could make no noise, being tightly gagged. Her usual weight-lessness was gone, and she strained as the earth tried to pull her back. She was afraid she might break and crash to the ground in pieces, or if she didn't break, she might bend until her horns were joined and she was a crazy lopsided circle with a hole in the middle.

After what seemed a very long time, the moon found herself hanging opposite the clearing in the oak's branches. Ten ravens flew at her, pushing, and ten more maneuvered the ropes. She swayed into the mid-dle of the cage, and with a crash the branches closed around her. The ravens gnawed at the ropes holding her, and one by one they snapped.

From below her came the laugh she had heard before. The ravens returned to their branches. And then responding to a summons never openly given, the animals came.

From dry bushes among the dead trees, from the recesses of darkness, from the branches of forest hidden from view, they came in double file, quartering the globe, the reptiles, black snakes and puff adders, rattle-snakes and copperheads. Toads and scorpions hopped and slithered into view. Timid field mice followed a band of rats with yellow teeth. Behind them came rabbits and woodchucks, skunks and opossum. She saw deer, squirrels, wolves and foxes and boars. And from the air, like the descent of snow, came the birds.

They'd been hiding since darkness had fallen and now, gathered at the owl's command, they cowered before the moon. All their lives she had crossed the expanse of night above them; now she was sequestered among them, caged, a symbol of his power.

The owl sat in absolute stillness, his fierce yellow eyes surveying the assemblage. In concentric circles, far beyond the reaches of the clearing, the animals encompassed him. Slowly he turned his head from side to side as if to say, *This is good.*

"I have been successful," the owl said, "as you can see." With a powerful flick of a wing, he loosed a feather which floated up toward his prisoner. "The moon no longer rules the night. That is my domain now, all of it. Every creature of the Deadwood Forest, every citizen of the Outer Lands, will pay homage to me."

Not an animal made a sound, but even from where the moon hung, it was as though the air had soured. "Does anyone have anything to say?" the owl asked imperiously.

A small band of rats suddenly broke for the forest. Their squealing, the startled noises of the other animals they attempted to push aside, cracked the hush which had fallen over the clearing. The owl puffed up his chest and gave two thundering hoots. From the trees behind him, a squadron of peregrine falcons, their talons gleaming, swooped from the sky and surrounded the rats. Each of the birds wore a slit leather hood and out of that darkness their eyes and beaks shone.

The owl stretched his wings until they almost covered the clearing. Under him the animals huddled in his shadow, but the moon doubted they felt protected by that outstretched canopy of feather. Slowly the owl folded his wings. "Bring them here," he said. As if in deep thought, he surveyed the trembling group at his feet. He lifted one of his claws; talons as long as the blade of a boning knife closed around one of the rats. "Do not try that again," he said, and tossed him back to his fellows.

The owl's eyelids drooped, as though he were about to fall asleep, as though the power of the moment had exhausted him or made him drunk, but nothing moved in the clearing around him.

The moon looked down with awe upon that fur and scale. From the air above her, she heard a noise, a faint flapping, like wings. She strained to see, but could make out only a blur in the darkness. Whatever it was was headed east.

A look of pure pleasure shone from the owl's round face. If he had heard what the moon heard, he gave no sign.

"You may show your love for me," he said. "You may prove your fealty."

So, one by one, the animals kneeled and then rolled over, baring their throats and stomachs, their softest, most vulnerable parts.

Derin woke at what should have been dawn. The sky was a milky grey. The trees circling the meadow were ragged and badly in need of water. Their lowermost branches almost touched the ground, and the leaves were parched and dusty. The air was curiously still, as though it had never moved, had always hung heavily, pressing the earth.

He knew, even before he was fully awake, that everything was wrong. All the sounds he was used to, bird song and river song, the low sweep of wind across the meadowgrass, were missing. He sat, rocked to his knees, and hunched down, peering around to see what was threatening him. But he was totally alone.

Seeing nothing to make him flee, he stood up. His movements were quick and angular, and his thick blond hair was matted with burrs. His eyes stared out of a face marked by an expression almost feral, as though he had been hunted all his life.

The grass ebbed around his knees, the only movement in sight. Still cautious, he waded through the meadow to the creek. Water, brackish and warm, hung between its banks as though suspended, more like a puddle than a stream. A dead lizard lay belly-up on the bank. Derin splashed some water in his face and wished he hadn't. It felt slippery, left a slimy film on his hands.

From across the meadow, Derin heard a familiar noise, the faint grumbling morning song of the badger as he made his way through the thick grass. Most days Derin avoided the lumbering slow-witted animal, but today his approach felt like a gift. The boy could see the meadow part and close as the badger made his way toward the stream. But well before he reached Derin, he went underground, burrowing. Finally he arrived at the edge of grass by the water and surfaced again.

"Morning, badger," the boy said, but instead of the rough greeting he expected, Derin heard what sounded like the clicking of tiny teeth and the animal stuck his head from his burrow only long enough to motion to him. Puzzled, Derin walked closer. "Get out of there," he said. "I like to see who I'm talking to." But all he got in reply was the click of the badger's teeth. He got down on his hands and knees and peered into the burrow.

"That's better," the badger whispered. "I don't want anyone to hear us."

"Who can hear us?" Derin asked, quickly looking behind him. "There's no one around but the two of us. Where is everyone?"

"I don't know," the badger replied. He hunkered further down into his hole so that Derin could hardly see his snout. "Something is terribly wrong, Derin," the badger said. "Something is terribly wrong." The blond hairs on the back of the boy's neck twitched. For all his faults, the badger was not an alarmist. "It's been this way for two hours now," the badger said. "Grey as doom, grey as a wolf's coat in winter."

"The sun will be up soon enough," Derin said.

"I'm not so sure," the badger said. "She should have been up hours ago. It's later than you think."

Derin looked at the sky suffused with this unfamiliar light. He thought of the trees, drooped and dusty, of the brackish water in the brook.

"I had the weirdest dream last night," he said. "A sheet slipped over the moon and a wind put my fire out."

"A sheet of what?" the badger asked.

"I don't know. I thought I was asleep and awake at the same time."

"I wouldn't know anything about that," the badger said. "I never dream. I never hoped to dream. But now, today, for the first time in my life, I hope this is a dream and that I'll wake, come out of my burrow to find the sparrows flittering in the maple by the pond and the sun hot and silky on my coat." He slunk still deeper into his burrow until Derin couldn't see him at all. The boy had never known him to go backwards, and it seemed a bad sign.

Without waiting to see if the badger would return, he got up from the ground, started to run, and soon reached the woods at the edge of the meadow. The trees were silent as he passed through, and he thought of the soughing they made when the wind aroused them. The woods were dark and quiet. None of the animals seemed even to have awakened. If they had, they'd gone back to their nests or burrows to wait for the true day to begin, not this false dawn.

He had to find Matthew. Matthew would understand the silence in the meadow and forest, the badger's paranoia, the prickly sense of dread he'd awakened with. The satyr slept under an overhang of rock, a granite ledge about a mile from the clearing. Derin made good time. Today there was no one to stop and talk with, and the trail was well-trampled and clear.

Matthew was still asleep when Derin found him. Out of breath, the boy stood over him with clenched fists, stared down at the body which changed so suddenly from man to goat. He had expected the satyr to be awake, but Matthew lay unconscious, one arm thrown over his eyes, blocking out what little light there was. "Get up!" Derin said urgently. He knelt and shook the satyr's shoulder. Matthew stirred, groaned, rolled on his side. "Wake up, I said," the boy repeated, shaking his friend again.

The satyr uncovered his eyes and looked at the boy. "Stop yelling, damn it," he snarled. "You sound like something bit you."

"What's going on?" Derin demanded.

"I'm trying to get some sleep, you fool. Go away, will you? Come back this afternoon."

"It's late, Matthew. Something's wrong."

"I know something's wrong," the satyr said. "My head feels like it's coming apart."

"Were you drunk again last night?" Derin asked.

"What business is that of yours?" the satyr asked. "If you think talking to you is what I want to be doing . . . ."

Derin felt a tide of panic rising in him. He stood and gave Matthew a kick which almost raised the satyr's hindquarters off the ground. Matthew howled in pain and instantly was on his legs, his face twisted in rage. "You monster," he yelled. He swung at Derin, missed, howled again. He sunk to his hocks and cradled his head in his hands. "There are bats flapping in my skull," he said. "Termites destroying whole forests."

Above Matthew the branches parted and a dark shape filtered down, across the edge of Derin's vision. It was a bird, unlike any he had seen before, black as midnight, its beautiful glossy wings outstretched. Without making a noise, without a flick of its wings, it landed above them, light as a milkweed seed, disturbing not a single leaf.

Derin was startled. Even Matthew was amazed enough to remove his head from his arms and stare at the bird.

It sat on the limb, slowly folding its wings, until it was still, its red eyes intent on the two of them. "*Corvus corax*," it said, simply. "I have come from the Deadwood Forest, beyond the Outer Lands."

It was not, of course, the first time Matthew had been drunk, nor the first time Derin had struck out at him. As the boy had grown older, he'd become more silent and withdrawn, would erupt in flashes of anger which Matthew didn't understand. He would suddenly pick up a rock from the ground and dash it into a lake, throwing a rainbow of water high in the air. He smashed his fist against the trunks of trees. And occasionally, for no apparent reason, he struck out against his friend. The satyr was prankish, sly, given to perverse twists of humor—he trampled the first leaves under his hooves, he stole from the nests of birds—but he was neither vicious nor vindictive.

Derin had known Matthew all his life, and the satyr was the only creature in the meadowlands even vaguely like him. The boy had grown up learning the language of hawk and deer. He'd swum in water so cold his toes had turned grey. He'd climbed to the top of the highest tree in the forest and stayed there all day, watching night fall over the country like a flat hand. He had grown tall and thin and muscled, fierce, strong-willed, silently proud. His body was scarred, strong, impervious to weather. His skin was darkened by the sun and wind, his feet crusted with calluses.

And though he was now Matthew's size, he knew he was not yet Matthew's equal. The satyr's power in the forest was unimpeachable. Too many times the boy had seen the respect given the satyr by the other animals, a respect he'd never known from them, being too foreign, too strange. Matthew bridged the gap between him and the animals; he had his hooves in two worlds at once, and though the boy would never have admitted it, he was in awe of that fluid grace.

So why wouldn't Matthew tell him who he was? There could be no reason for holding that back; it seemed another of the satyr's jokes. Why was there no one around like him—only badgers, opossum, skunks, this impossible satyr? Derin had the growing sense that the answers to his questions lay elsewhere, not in the meadowlands. And then the bird dropped down like a blessing, a sign from another place.

By the time light first reached the Deadwood Forest, the clearing was empty except for two ravens left to stand guard. The moon, though exhausted, was unable to sleep. The gag bit into her mouth and the effort of breathing filled her chest with pain. In the darkest hours of the night, after the animals had left, she had strained against the gag, pulling as much air as possible through it to keep her fire from going out. She needed light to see by; she was looking for an avenue of escape. But try as she might, she couldn't find the slightest weak spot in the oaken fortress.

She wondered where the owl had gone, would have considered asking one of the ravens if she had been able to talk. The forest lay below her and stretched in all directions as far as she could see. There was no sign of life, no bird song, no rustle in the underbrush, nothing but the two ravens who sat opposite her like stone totems. But most astonishing to her was the total absence of the color green. In the dark, she hadn't been able to distinguish much except the clearing itself. Now, in the milky light of what seemed a very unpromising dawn, she could see beyond the clearing, but there was nothing to see. The few leaves on the bushes were brown and dry, and tree after tree lifted bare lifeless branches. There was no water anywhere.

Season after season, year after year, the moon had watched the world below her change from spring to summer with its vibrant greens, to the fireworks of autumn and winter's bare sticks. But here in the Deadwood Forest, the moon had the strange sensation that time had stopped. This was not a winter forest, holding deep in its sap the promise of another spring. If the trees here grew at all, they simply grew taller and more threatening, their branches spidering across a landscape like a sudden jolt to clear ice.

This thread of thought alarmed her. If there were no time, if it were fractured, she might never grow older, trapped in her cage. Things would always stay the way they were, and she would never be free.

As she hung there, she waited impatiently for her sister, the sun, to appear. The sun could burn into this forest, remove the shadows. If need be, the sun could destroy this whole place with a well-aimed ray. What was this but a graveyard of trees and bushes?

The moon closed her eyes and began to wish. In her mind, she saw a huge conflagration, the flames reaching over the tree tops, consuming them, their embers falling away, leaving an imprint on the air. She saw black billows of smoke obliterate the sky. She saw the spirits of birds and small animals ascend to heaven. And then, she saw herself, red-hot, glowing furiously, before she, too, crumbled into ashes and joined the general destruction on the forest floor. Well, she thought, if that is what it will take to be free, so be it.

But as she waited for what seemed hours and hours, the sun did not appear. All was suffused with the same deadly pallor. Great round tears rolled down her face and soaked her gag so that the wretched linen began to cut even more deeply into the corners of her mouth. There seemed no end to this and no beginning. What light there was was simply light, nothing more, a poor and subtle separation of the great blanks known as day and night.

Opposite her the two ravens sat, unblinking, staring at her with cold and lifeless eyes. There was no wind.

* * *

Derin glanced at Matthew, who stared upwards at the bird as though he saw a ghost. It sat on the branch, its throat and breast covered with short black feathers, its beard giving it the appearance of great age and strength.

"*Corvus corax!*" said Matthew with awe. "I haven't seen one of you for years."

"*Corvus corax?*" Derin said.

"My formal name," the bird said. "I'm a raven."

"But you don't live in the meadowlands, do you?"

"Does a peanut have whiskers?" the raven said. "No, not for many years. And what are you, if I may be so bold?"

"He's a boy," the satyr said quickly.

"*Boy*. A boy," the raven said, intrigued. "A new species to add to my life-list. I'm pleased to make your acquaintance. I was wondering what happened to the fleece on your shanks and where you'd misplaced your hooves. Never seen anything like you." Derin blushed. "I'm familiar with satyrs, of course, this one in particular," the raven continued. "No shock of recognition in that horned head of yours? Your name is—don't tell me—Martin, Mason . . . ."

"Matthew," the satyr said.

"Matthew. How absentminded of me." The raven pecked under a wing, a self-conscious gesture that made him angry.

"I'm supposed to know you?" he asked.

"I'm hurt you don't remember. I used to ride your shoulder when I was a fledgling. You were decidedly rambunctious, years ago."

"You're. . . ."

"Deirdre," the raven said. "Daughter of Orak and Ada."

"Of course," the satyr said. "That uppity little. . . ."

"Pardon me," Deirdre said. "I think the word is 'precocious.' "

"Wait a minute," Derin said. "What's going on?"

"I used to live here, you see," the raven said. "I was kidnapped from this place a long time ago. One night I was awakened from sleep by a noise like rushing water. I was huddled with my parents on the limb of a beech, and they slept on while the noise grew louder. I hadn't any idea what it was. I looked and saw a wall of darkness moving through the trees, and it seemed a waterfall but it was only wind. It picked up dirt and branches as it came until it was a landslide. My parents awoke, cawing, and we tried to fly, but it caught us and in that maelstrom were other animals, rabbits, and foxes, and all manner of birds. We rose in a black funnel. Over and over I tumbled until I lost my senses. When I came to, I was what seemed hundreds of miles west of here, in a place called the Deadwood Forest."

"It was before he was born," Matthew said.

"How old is the boy?"

"I'm fourteen," Derin butted in.

"Is that right?" the raven said. "Could it have been that long ago?"

"What's past is past," the satyr said. "I'd forgotten."

"There are things one doesn't forget," Deirdre said heatedly. "There are times which live on in the memory with the vividness of dream so that life becomes a simultaneity of past and present. Both my parents died that night. I saw them drop through the whirlwind's center, plummet to the ground. I remember every detail as if it were yesterday. I vowed then to avenge their deaths; I have dedicated my life to that."

The satyr stared into the woodlands, as though looking for a particular tree, as though he could fasten his life there and keep it earthbound. "It *was* a terrible night," he said. "Squirrels were taken, and ferrets. Foxes were thrown in the air like so many leaves. The wind stole every living raven from the meadowlands. The only ones left were dead or dying. I thought I'd seen the very last of them. In the morning the ground was covered with bodies. The water in the brook ran blood red."

"But why go on in grisly detail?" the raven asked brightly. "There's something of more immediate importance." She paused, and her red eyes glittered. "The moon has been stolen from the sky."

Matthew stared at the bird in stunned disbelief. "You're crazy. . . . "

"The Deadwood Forest is ruled by a great horned owl," she said. "Fourteen years ago he sent the wind which brought us west. Last night he abducted the moon. Before I flew here, I went to the great sea cliffs where I was born, the cliffs still farther to the east. The ocean is still as a dead rat's teeth, and the beach is littered with fish. The tides have ceased, and the vast hood of sky is blank as snow."

"You're lying," Matthew said. "These things can't happen. The tides never stop."

"A week ago I would have said the moon could not be purloined from the sky," the raven said. She was annoyed, her tone haughty. "But last night we were sent with a net. It was easier than you'd imagine."

"You helped steal the moon?" Derin asked. "You were there?"

"Of course I was there," she snapped. "What was I supposed to do? Sometimes one has no choice. I've lived in the Deadwood Forest nearly all my life."

"You might have done something," Derin said. "You could have stopped the owl."

"Tell me that again after you've seen him," Deirdre said. A shiver shook her from the point of her sharp beak to the elegant wedge of her tailfeathers. "He's cold and analytic, diabolical, preternatural. He means to rule the night. For years he's held the Outer Lands in his thrall. Now he's stretching his talons still further. But enough of this. I didn't come all these miles for the purpose of narrative exposition."

"You *have* come very far," Matthew said. "At least a week's journey." He reached up and covered his eyes with his hands, as if he were waking from sleep. In his mind, he stood in last night's forest as the pool of darkness gathered around his hooves.

"By air, only six hours," the raven said dryly. "It *is* a hefty flight. Yes. I will take credit for that. Now pay attention." The satyr bristled at her order. "Years ago," Deirdre said, "when I was little—mind you, I'm not prone to such emotional declarations—I admired you above all other creatures, excepting my parents. Because of those memories I've come here today. You've got to help. You're the only one I can think of. You've got to help me rescue the moon. You *do* understand how serious this is?"

"Of course," Matthew said, angry. He could feel the blood rising in his face. "You hot-mouthed condescending little. . . . " But Deirdre cut him off.

"Good," she said. "I knew you would. Now I've got to get back. I'm afraid they'll notice I'm missing. The moon hangs incarcerated in a tree in the middle of the Deadwood Forest. I'll be expecting you." Without another word, she ascended into the air and vaulted like a meteor toward the west.

"How do you like that?" Matthew asked. "The *nerve* of the bird. Not so much as a by-your-leave. And last night I thought we were in for a heavy rain."

* * *

Derin reached the edge of forest and entered the clearing. No one, not even the badger, was there. He looked to the sky but it was grey and empty. The raven had disappeared from view. The boy thought about the past twelve hours, wondering what had brought him to this point. He felt he had the beginning pieces of a puzzle, only the vaguest outline, and it nagged him as a splinter does when it slips more deeply into a finger.

He gathered his few belongings and put them in his knapsack. His woolen blanket. The carved stone, his talisman; his leather boots. He pulled the knife out of its deerskin sheath and ran his thumb along the finely edged bone of the blade, wondering if he would use it in ways he never had before. He picked up the two gourds he had played with as a child, the rattles Matthew had made for him, and he smiled as he let them drop. They would be of no use to him where he was going.

Where *was* he going? He knew as much about the meadowlands as anyone who lived there, but only recently had he given any thought to what might lie beyond. Beyond lay the Outer Lands. From what Matthew had told him, they were nothing like this. But had the satyr ever been there himself?

He pushed the last of his shirts into the knapsack and took off for Matthew's granite ledge. When he arrived, the small clearing was empty, though the smell of goat hung in the air. Where was he? Above the boy, the day seemed a well-worn piece of cloth he could put his finger through. The light was furred almost, feathered.

He thought of Deirdre headed out over that dismal landscape, tried to imagine it for himself. There were mountains, he knew, and a long stretch of arid waste, but these were things which had only been described to him, and they were as unclear in his mind as the owl was. *Tell me that again after you've seen him*, Deirdre had said. He remembered the wind of the previous evening, how it had surrounded him, rushing toward the center of the meadow from the periphery of trees, how it had left him in total darkness, blinded. He sat there, waiting for his friend, as the day seeped away entirely, and he imagined, his skin tingling, the faraway sound of a whirlwind churning across the forest, sweeping birds and animals, trees and bushes, into its hollow fist.

Matthew plunged through the forest wildly. His headache was gone, and this impetuous rush made him forget the raven, the boy, the journey before him. He was agile, graceful, dodging branches which loomed suddenly out of the air, threatening to brain him. Leaves whirled by, a tunnel of green. He loved to run like this, unfettered, with no destination, through an obstacle course altered by each change in direction. He was used to surprising the animals of the woodlands, but today he saw no other creature, not even a squirrel or bird.

He stopped, exhausted, and leaned heavily against a hickory, rubbing his back on the coarse bark. Sweat streamed down the sides of his face. He lowered himself onto the expanse of moss at the hickory's base, flung his fleeced legs in front of him, and closed his eyes. The only sound he heard was his own panting. There was no wind, no chatter, no song. He felt the muscles in his neck tense; the silence was odd indeed.

Suddenly sure he was being watched, he drew his legs back under him and crouched, one hand on the hickory for balance. He looked up into the overhanging branches, searching the receding trunks for a movement, a shadow, but he could see nothing.

Everything had changed. He took a deep breath. The sweet fragrance he had reveled in the previous evening was missing; the air itself was stale. Even the moss below him seemed rougher, its sheen tarnished. If the raven were telling the truth, there would be no escape from this degeneration. All the running in the world would only bring him full circle, back to this realization.

Who was this feathered braggadocio, wanting to rule the world? Matthew ruled the meadowlands—everyone knew that. The thought of its decline filled him with fury. But the owl was strong enough, perverse enough to kidnap the moon. He began walking back toward the granite overhang. Though he knew he had no choice, the idea of the journey he was about to undertake, necessary as it might be, angered him. He hated responsibility.

It had been fourteen years since the hooded creature had forced the baby upon him, a burden he had neither wanted nor graciously accepted. He'd known nothing of infants, their squalls of rage, their sudden fevers, and he's resented the attention the little creature needed. Fascinated by its grasping hands, its toes, its hairless skin with a smell like sun and windblown water, he'd still felt cramped, walled in by its relentless demands.

He'd been given no choice—either abandon the infant to a certain death, or attend to him as best he could. Derin had thrived, had grown as tall as Matthew, and sullen. Now, as the stranger foretold, a messenger had arrived from the Outer Lands, calling the boy home.

He walked until he reached the Rock, a protrusion of granite and shale, its natural steps leading to a pinnacle which cleared the highest branches of the forest. He scrambled up the Rock's side until he stood at the top. The wind was strong there, and he faced it, a lone figure brooding over the trees. If someone had seen him, they might have mistaken him for a natural outcropping of the Rock itself.

Matthew stood until the wind pulled water from his eyes. The sky overhead was dense and woolly, like the backs of sheep in winter, and clouds could be seen moving toward the west, unrolling in a single thick sheet from horizon to horizon as the air darkened. He remembered the stormy night he'd been summoned by a great blue heron from the swamp, who had guided him back to the banks of the Swollen River where the cloaked stranger had handed him the baby. He remembered Derin's first illness as he lay, bundled in furs by the fire, the flames throwing orange wraiths against the treetrunks. He thought of how he'd wished the baby would die so he'd be freed of its hold over him, and then his relief, a surprise, when the fever broke. The memories flooding him were all of Derin in danger; the time he'd broken through the thin ice on the pond; the day he'd fallen from the elm.

The years had gone swiftly, running into one another like creeks in a spring thaw, until they roared along, a river which was today. The cold wind whipped from him any last vestige of illusion. The time had come for Derin to leave.

It began to rain, a fine rain which slanted from the east and struck his chest and legs like thousands of needles. Meager and cold as it was, he took it as a sign to go. He had hoped for something more particular, but he was not in a position to quibble. In leaps and bounds he reached the forest floor and headed for the overhang.

Deirdre flew west as fast as she could. She was a large sleek bird and she made good time. She passed over the meadowlands with their patches of woods, their now stagnant ponds and lakes, and the swamp which stretched to the Swollen River. She flew so high the air was very thin, and she breathed steadily and deeply to keep from tiring.

Far behind her lay the cliffs where she had been born, the coast against which the sea no longer pounded. Earlier this morning, the beach had stretched below her like a tan bandage, its stillness interrupted only by the occasional flopping of a fish come on shore to die. Not a ripple was in sight; no whitecaps flecking the ocean's surface with foam, no crash of waves upon the beach. All the aeries were empty and crumbling. She had seen no other bird.

She flew over the Swollen River, its turbid width troubled by rocks, and over the Plain of Desiccation. Before her, the Mountains of No Return rose, blocking all view of the Deadwood Forest beyond.

She climbed higher to crest the mountains and then swooped down into the forest. Deirdre landed on a branch, immediately folded her wings, and stuck her head beneath one as if she were asleep. Furtively she glanced around to see if any creature had seen her land, but she saw nothing in the gathering darkness. She had arrived in time. Light was leaving the thick branches of the forest.

She thought how like a net the trees looked, how like a web. It was as though a spider had knitted the forest and moved on to another uninhabitable place to wield his malevolent magic. She imagined the light being held there against its will, trapped in the crisscross of twigs, but slowly it seeped upward and faded to the west, not with any fanfare or splendor, but with the tiredness of animals who lay themselves on the forest floor, breathe their last, and by morning are indistinguishable from the refuse of the woods.

And then the light was gone. Thick inky night filled all the branches and dripped from the heavens down, down until it seeped into her feathers, turning them a darker black. From beyond the grove of trees before her, the first hoarse gutteral croak of the other ravens filtered back. She answered wearily — *crauk, cr-r-cruk* — and went to join the others.

It was full night, though much too early, when Derin heard a rustling in the bushes behind the ledge. The sudden noise jolted him from his reverie. He jumped to his feet, his hand instinctively went to his belt and tightened around the knife's handle. Out of the gloom Matthew emerged, carrying a leather sack. Without a word, without even a nod of acknowledgement, the satyr went to the overhang and began to take apples and nuts and stuff them into his own knapsack. "Are you ready?" Matthew asked. "Have you packed?"

"Yes," the boy said. "I've been waiting for you. You startled me."

"I had a few things to think over," the satyr said. "I went for a run."

It's like that cheeky bird said. Everything's changed. Didn't see even a wood beetle." He turned and looked at the boy. "Put that knife away."

"I wasn't sure it was you," Derin said.

"Of course it was me. Who else would it be?"

"I guess I'm a little on edge." the boy said.

"Either give me the knife or put it away in your pack. I can't have you grabbing it every time you hear a noise in the underbrush." Derin placed the knife back in its sheath but made no move to take it off his belt. "When do we leave?" he asked.

"You're not listening to me. Do you understand?"

"I understand," the boy said. In one swift motion, he unsnapped the sheath and hurled it to the ground.

"No, you don't," Matthew said, picking it up. "I don't think you understand at all. You're not as old as you wish you were, but nothing I could tell you would make you understand better, so you'll have to find out for yourself."

"I don't need a lecture," Derin said.

"Maybe not," the satyr said. "Maybe you do. Just remember one thing. On this trip you answer to me."

"That raven came to both of us," Derin said angrily. "I have as much right as you have."

"Damn you, boy," Matthew said.

"I'm not a boy," Derin said. "I'm not yours to boss around."

They stood facing each other like sparring partners, and Matthew glared at this other creature who looked so much like him. What the boy said was true; he'd grown up. His chest had broadened, his voice deepened. And he had long ago begun to make his own decisions. When he was younger, he'd obeyed the satyr without question, but now he fought back at every turn, wrestling his life free.

Derin's face was hard. Without thinking, he struck out at Matthew, but his fist hit nothing but air. The satyr dodged, grabbed the boy's wrist and twisted, and Derin found himself on his back, his head throbbing.

"How many times have I told you?" the satyr said. "You're learning, all right. You're quick, but not as quick as you'll need to be. So listen to me when I tell you something. We're leaving tomorrow."

It had been Sunday all day, but the sun had never appeared. And now no stars broke the dense oppression of the sky. Derin and Matthew lay under the granite overhang, dim in the glow of a fire which had long since burned itself to embers. The boy slept fitfully. It was close to what should have been midnight when he awoke with a start. Matthew was beside him, his head resting on the knapsack, deeply asleep.

Opposite him, the darkness took shape, two bright gold eyes on either side of a hooked beak. On enormous talons the thing moved closer. "Matthew!" he yelled. "Wake up!" But the satyr slept peacefully to his right.

Derin rushed to the fire and stirred the embers. They scattered under his hand and slithered into the underbrush like snakes. He felt something in his hair and he recoiled in horror. He writhed, wailing, felt himself rising as if through layers of cold dark water. It was Matthew's hand in his hair, and when he opened his eyes, it was Matthew's face he saw. "So the hero has nightmares," the satyr said. "The hero is troubled by sleep."

And it was evening, and it was morning, one day.

"There was the badger . . . and the bluejay . . ."

MONDAY

The moon had not relaxed in twenty-four hours, and by midnight she was fast asleep. All afternoon of the previous day she had struggled against her bondage; the gag was no looser after her effort, no gap appeared in the oak's enclosure, and her need to rest became monumental. If nothing ever changes, she thought, why must I sleep? But she was too fuzzy to think out the finer points of a philosophical argument, and her eyes, heavy with worry and doubt, closed.

Deirdre, too, was asleep. She had feared her fall into that soft familiar darkness—she should have been sleeping all day, like the others, and wondered if any would suspect her if she rested while they were awake—but her need overcame her trepidation. In her dreams, she was flying, always flying, back and forth from the Deadwood Forest to the meadowlands, ceaselessly, buffetted by forces she couldn't control.

She awoke, exhausted. The forest was black as the ink of a squid. She blinked her eyes, trying to see if other ravens were about, but she saw nothing. She had joined them earlier, sat among them, invisible, listening to their idle vicious conversation, until she could no longer maintain a façade of wakefulness. And now she was alone. Where had they gone?

She understood more clearly one of the dangers she had taken upon herself. Doubtless, events had transpired while she'd been gone, things she had no knowledge of, and no way of discovering. She knew an offhand remark inquiring about the night's occurrences would create suspicion and distrust. The owl's plans were important for her to know, and right now, even as she sat there, attempting to clear her mind of the dust of sleep, he could be holding a meeting. Most troubling to her was the absence of the ravens. Wherever they were, she should be with them.

She climbed above the forest's branches to attain a better vantage point. Further to the west, she saw a faint glow, rising and falling, like breath; it must be the moon, she thought, and the meager quality of the light filled her with pity. She would be sleeping, poor thing, and there seemed little reason to fly in her direction.

Thus Deirdre, for the second time that day, flew east. She came to the edge of the forest and hovered in the air as if caught in an updraft. Before her, the mountains rose, formidable and bleak, and she could make out no movement below her on the short barren plain between where the mountains crashed to earth and the first wall of forest began.

Floating like a leaf, eddying on the currents of the air, she let herself drift to earth. She landed on a rock and listened. No sound greeted her, none of the noises common to the forest at night. She was filled with apprehension. It seemed as though the great wood were inhabited only by herself and the moon.

She rose again and pointed south. The trees passed beneath her in a blur. She flew until she thought her wings would give out, until the very thought of returning from where she'd come was impossible. Then, imperceptibly to an eye less trained than hers, the terrain began to change. This was a part of the forest she had never visited before. The trees were still the same, stark outlines of the splendid oaks and hemlocks which grew in the meadowlands, but the utter flatness of the familiar sections of forest gave way to a slight undulation.

The trees rose and fell with the rolling of the earth. Like waves, Deirdre thought, like the ocean. Her stomach felt queasy; she found herself rising and falling along with the terrain. Her head hurt and her breath came in short spasms. She was badly in need of rest.

As though she'd been hit, she arrested her flight, tucked her wings and dove on a diagonal toward the trees below her. Near the top of the forest, she spread her wings and softly landed. Immersed in that darkness, she cocked an ear and listened. It *was* the ocean, or something very like it, the faint roar of waves and the hollow sluice which followed their breaking. But the ocean lay far to the east. Was she hearing things now?

"Let's face it," she said aloud to nothing in particular. "I'm lost." There seemed no way around her assessment, but no panic either. She was simply on alien ground.

She began to laugh, filled with a sense of relief she hadn't felt in weeks. Perhaps she would stay here, eking out a paltry existence, far from the responsibilities she had placed on herself. Perhaps she had no choice.

She thought of Derin and Matthew whom she had visited — when? — the previous afternoon? It seemed ages ago, foreign as someone else's life. Even now they should be readying for the journey she had given them so little to prepare for. She didn't entirely trust them. The satyr was flippant and stubborn, the boy new to her. Still, they were her only hope. The animals in the Forest had been lulled into a passivity which bordered on sleep, and those who lived in the meadowlands would not understand. She would have to depend on those two upright creatures.

Too tired to think any more, she slept the uneasy sleep of the lost, a self-imposed exile. The ocean sounds grew fainter, and hunched in her feathers, it seemed she grew smaller, until she was almost a child again, until she sat on the great seacliff and watched her mother and father soar over the ocean on wings of steel, hunting food for her.

By the time Derin opened his eyes, Matthew was already up. The satyr whistled as he cleaned out his wooden bowl and stooped under the overhang to place his few remaining belongings in his knapsack. The boy's back ached from sleeping on the forest floor. He'd twisted in the night and an unfamiliar coldness had seeped into his bones, chilling him through. His neck felt stiff, and one of his arms was asleep.

He got up and huddled by the fire Matthew had built, stretching his hands toward it to warm them. His sleep had disturbed him, its rhythms still ruling his thoughts. The old dream had returned, the one which had haunted him as a child.

He was lost, wandering through an unfamiliar landscape, and everywhere he turned, the branches of trees seemed to close around him, to restrain him. The journey was endless, and although he was always moving, he never got anywhere. And then, just before he woke, a dark hooded figure loomed from behind a tree, a faceless apparition, reaching for him.

"Well look who's up," the satyr said. "I was going to kick you awake but thought better of it. How did you sleep?"

Derin didn't answer for a moment, stared at the flames. "I had that dream I used to have. I thought I'd outgrown it."

The satyr looked at him strangely. "Quite a night," he said. "Two humdingers. Always sleep so well?" He began lacing his knapsack closed with a strip of rawhide. "That's it," the satyr said as he finished. "We're almost ready. You must be hungry."

Derin admitted he was. "I've been to the meadow," Matthew said. "Look what I found." He showed the boy four duck eggs, pulled a large flat rock from the perimeter of the fire and broke the eggs upon it. They sizzled and spat, their edges curling up like dried leaves.

The boy ate quickly, without speaking. Matthew looked at him, trying to gauge his mood. "Friends of yours want to talk to you before we leave," he said.

Derin glanced up from his breakfast. "What do you mean?" he asked, his mouth full of egg.

"I told you I went to the meadow. Ran into two of your friends. Go ahead; I'll straighten up here."

The boy stood up, uncertain. "Go," Matthew said. "You're wasting time."

Derin handed Matthew his bowl and took off on the path to the meadow. It seemed like the day before. Overhead, the sky hung low and grey. The trees drooped, their leaves dusty. And the forest was deserted.

When he entered the meadow, he saw two animals by the stream, waiting for him. He approached, and the chattering he had heard stopped. There was the badger with whom he'd spoken yesterday and the blue jay he thought so beautiful.

"What's this about?" Derin asked. "What's on your minds?"

"We wanted to say good-bye," the badger said solemnly. "We heard you were going away."

"Matthew told you?"

The jay began to chatter. "He was here this morning. He stole some eggs from the duck. Said he was making breakfast. Eggs for breakfast? Worms for me, that's what I like, or grubs. Nice juicy white grubs. Said you were going on a trip. The moon is in trouble. *I'll* say she's in trouble. Been loafing, didn't do her job last night. Nowhere to be seen. What *I* want to know is. . . ."

"The moon really is in trouble," Derin said. "Night before last, she was stolen from the sky."

"A fine story," the jay said.

"It's so much trouble, traveling. Who knows where you'll wind up?" the badger said.

"Did you hear me?" the boy asked. "I said the moon's been taken from the sky. Kidnapped. Besides, we'll only be gone a few days."

"That's not what Matthew told us. I heard him. He said it. Gone, gone, gone. Right after breakfast. Right after those duck eggs. But what will you eat next, that's what *I* want to know. Me, I'm staying here, right here in this meadow. Lots of grubs, nice, white juicy. . . ."

"*Please*, jay," Derin said, smiling. "I can't listen to all that now."

"I've never trusted him," the badger said. "What's he up to now?"

"Matthew isn't up to anything," Derin said, growing angry. "You said it yourself, badger. 'Something is terribly wrong.' You told me that yesterday."

"Fiddlesticks," the jay said. "Balderdash. Poppycock, brouhaha. Bull-finch."

"It's just the weather," the badger said. "We're in for a drought."

"You may be able to fool yourselves," the boy said. "But I can't. A raven flew east from the Deadwood Forest to tell us about the moon."

"The deadwood *what?*" the jay asked. "A *raisin?*"

"Nothing good will come of it," the badger said. "I did say something was wrong. I'd have to be blind and deaf not to notice how odd things are today, but what can any of us do about it?"

"Who was this bird?" the jay wanted to know. "Some cockamamy crazy with a persecution complex. I've never heard of such a thing. Stealing the moon. What a story. I thought *I* had a vivid imagination. You'd tell me what to do with my tongue if I ever. . . ."

"But I *have* to," Derin said. "Can't you see? I've never left the mead-owlands."

"Seeing is believing," the jay said. "Now don't be long. When you get back, I'll throw you a party. I'll invite the world. And there'll be lots to eat. Watercress and mushrooms, filberts and pears. And grubs. Nice, juicy. . . ."

"Good-bye," Derin said. "I've got to go."

* * *

The light which reached the southern sections of the Deadwood Forest illumined a strange world. Deirdre still slept on her branch. But around her, the forest began to stir.

Covering some of the trees was a reddish slime, like mold. It quaked, rising and falling, sounding very much like a distant ocean. Moss blanketed the lower trunks of other trees, odd brown moss which sent out tentative streamers perpendicular to the bark on which it grew. The forest floor was thick with ferns, black and shaped like grotesque hands. Among them bulbous mushrooms sprouted, poking their poisonous white caps between the fronds. Frogs hopped under the ferns, and there were worms, long as the raven's wingspan and tinged a pale pink.

On the trunk of the tree where Deirdre sat, two starfish, or animals like them, slowly inched their way toward her. They hunched forward in a sickening roll, pointed long arms up, grabbed the bark, and pulled themselves along.

The starfish reached Deirdre's branch and began to slither toward her. They hung below it, gripping the branch with their five pointed arms, their bodies dim grey sacs. One by one, they extended a point, took hold, and perilously inched down the branch. Gradually they came closer until one was near enough.

It reached out, fastened itself to her far claw, and wrapped itself around the branch. With a snap, the second followed, moving with unexpected swiftness. And Deirdre awoke from her sleep with a start, both of her claws cemented to the branch, two round rasping mouths trying to swallow her feet.

Groggy with sleep, she looked below her. The ferns, black as her feathers, waved in the morning air. For a dizzying moment she thought she was about to fall into water, and then she made out their shapes, foreign and seductive, but recognizable. The mushrooms glinted in the grey light as if they were wet with sweat. And under this ground cover she saw the flash and glitter of the frogs and worms.

Her feet were being sucked and the sensation made her reel with disgust. She spread her wings and beat them frantically, but she couldn't move from the branch. The starfish held tight, their underbellies gripping with enormous suction. She cawed loudly, the ferns below her writhed in response.

She tried again. Slowly she began flapping her wings, attempting through sheer strength to pull herself free. She felt the starfish begin to release, but just when she thought she would leave the branch, they contracted and her claws were sucked back, so tightly this time she was afraid they dug into the wood.

Wings outstretched, she ducked her head and pecked at the fat stubby bodies. They were tough, rubbery, and the sharp point of her tightly curved beak bounced back at her. Shaking with rage, Deirdre stretched her neck as high as she could and brought her beak down in a tremendous blow. She felt the leathery skin break and her beak sink into the animal's body. A white ooze spread from the point she'd punctured. She pecked harder, her head jerking madly. The one grabbing her right claw let go, hung by one point from the branch, and then fell, somersaulting through the air until it disappeared among the ferns.

She turned her attention to the other. She pecked again, frantic, until she thought she'd given herself a concussion, but try as she might, she couldn't break its skin.

Deirdre breathed heavily, and her heart beat within her chest as if it had gone crazy. She spread her wings again, tried to fly free, but with one claw still held tightly she was lopsided, and almost lost her balance. She imagined hanging upside down from this branch, being held there by this animal. Perhaps then it would release her, and as she fell, she could catch herself and fly. Instead, she took her free foot, and with as much power as she had left, stuck the talons deep into its sluglike center, and all five points let go at once.

She was free! A shudder racked her sleek black body. She rose in the air, her wings flapping, the starfish gripped in her claw. When she was twenty feet off the branch, she realized she still held the thing and her leg twitched, shaking the starfish loose. It fell like the other, turning circles in the air. It hit a branch, its five wounded points wrapping themselves around the bark, and clung with prehensile strength.

Deirdre was filled with such revulsion she thought she would fall dead. But the idea of what would happen to her if she fell, plummeting beneath the ferns to make a meal for those flabby groping creatures, restored her. She soared above the trees. Below her the faint oceanic roar and suck of the slime receded. The undulation of the treetops continued to one side, and to the other the rolling fell away, became flat as the Plain of Desiccation. Remembering her exhaustion of the night before and her plan to live out her life in isolation, there in the southern forest, she wondered at herself. She must have been deranged.

And she knew her directions again. She flew as fast as she'd ever flown, in the upper reaches of the air where the clouds were beginning to settle. She didn't know what it was she was leaving behind; perhaps it was some place of punishment and purgation, some gratuitous prison the owl had constructed in his madness; perhaps she had merely imagined it. But no, she was awake, it was no dream, it had been real. As if to make valid that thought, she caught a glimpse of her left claw, now tucked tightly against the underside of her body. On it a drop of white ooze glistened like dew, and hardened there, a calcified knob.

The wracked trunks of the familiar sections of the Deadwood Forest soon lay beneath her. Never before had it seemed so much like home.

It was Monday, the moon's day, but she was utterly disenfranchised. It was truly the owl's day, she knew, and tomorrow and tomorrow would be the owl's as well. She felt calmer now that she was rested, but the new morning promised no more hope of escape than had the light of the previous day. She looked to the east for some sign of the sun, but there was none to be seen. The sky was a different color today, a different grey. It looked like the silver lining of a mussel. In its own way it was quite beautiful, but the moon would have given anything for a glimpse of blue, a hole in the clouds through which an arm of sun might streak like a battering ram.

Above her, the sky darkened and a large cloud descended. The air was filled with a deadly roaring. As she watched, the cloud took shape, its brown barred feathers furred in the grey light. The owl's head was bent, his beak pressed tightly against his bloody bib. Like a thunderbolt he fell to the clearing, thudding against the ground with such force he buried his talons in the dark loam. One by one, he extracted his claws and cleaned them. Behind him, a host of falcons settled, leaving him plenty of room.

"My one failing," the owl said to the moon, mildly staring up into the oaken cage. "I can't land without sinking in a bit. It's my imposing size, don't you know."

The moon struggled against her gag, but only muffled noises escaped her. "How thoughtless of me," the owl said. "You must think me a beast of a host. Ungag her."

Three falcons flew to the oak. Two of them separated the branches enough to let the third inside the cage. He flew around the moon until she was quite dizzy. On one of his swoops behind her, the falcon nimbly snipped the back of the gag and it fell to the ground. In a single motion, the two outside parted the branches, the third slipped through, and all three returned to their previous positions around the owl.

The moon groaned with relief. Her mouth was parched and sore and she swallowed painfully, trying to rid her throat of the dryness.

As soon as she found her voice, she let loose. The owl sat tranquilly, almost smiling, as she ranted at him. And when she finished swearing, she began with the curses. "May your talons curve in the night and silence your curdled brain. May you sink so deeply in the ground you suffocate on filth. May you live to old age a crippled one-winged toothless starving. . . ."

"Sticks and stones," the owl said, in a voice of the deadliest calm. "It is nothing for me to have my friends here gag you again."

The moon shut her mouth. Her chest was heaving so deeply the air around her glowed, a nimbus of fury.

"I thought you might be lonely and in need of conversation. After all, you're intelligent, I'm intelligent. I thought we could talk. Your rudeness wounds me deeply. I thought you might like to hear the news. So keep a civil tongue, if you will."

"I'm in no need of your conversation," the moon said.

"But I think you are," the owl said.

"I know my own mind."

"We are *huffy* today," he said and turned to one of the falcons who stood behind him. "How should I speak to her royal moonness? Perhaps her moonness is insulted by my diction. Perhaps I never learned the proper forms of address." The falcon stared dumbly at the owl. There seemed little reason to offer his opinion. "My flicker of light," the owl crooned. "My twin-horned lovely. Thou ghostly galleon tossed upon cloudy seas."

Emotions welled up in the moon she found difficult to name. She was enraged, of course, but the edge of her anger was muffled by the mortification she felt. Shame, yes, and a powerlessness, but there was something else besides.

"Stop your wretched poetry before I. . . ." she said.

"Before you what?" the owl asked, intent. "Before you spit? Not so genteel after all, eh? Finish your sentence."

"No," she said. "No, I will not. You make me forget myself. You may have humiliated me, but I shall not give you the satisfaction of watching me humiliate myself."

"Bravely said," the owl cheered. "Well put! Bravissima! But let me make one thing perfectly clear. Your courage will not get you very far. Your cooperation will. Do you understand me?"

"No," the moon said.

"That is your prerogative. You are ill-advised. I will never lie to you. To the others I will lie, if it suits my purpose, but never to you."

The moon tried to think of a comeback, some flippancy she could hurl at him, but nothing formed.

"You will have noticed the absence of the sun these two days past. You may count on her continued absence. Thick clouds cover the arc of heaven and the sun cannot penetrate them. She grows weak without you, you see, and in a few days, the earth will know only darkness. It is then I will send the falcons, my emissaries, to receive the world's acclaim. It will be a very different place to live, I promise you. And I need do nothing more than wait. You, of course, will remain my special guest. You should decide just one thing. If you want a stake in my imminent kingdom — and there are ways in which you could be useful to me — you have only to tell me this: I want to know where your sister spends her nights."

The moon was stunned, not so much by the news of her sister as by the thought of betrayal.

"I will leave you now," the owl said. "But be aware you will be watched. My falcons will return by nightfall to replace your gag."

He spread his wings and they began to shiver in the clearing. Small leaves and twigs eddied in the fierce air currents his wings created. They began to flap and he rose, straight into the air above her, with so little effort the moon was filled with awe. The falcons left with him, and she was alone again.

"Help!" she screamed. "Someone help me!" She screamed until her breath was gone and her fire was nearly out. The forest lay around her, silent as a cave. And yet there were presences there. If the owl said she was being watched, she knew she was being watched. Perhaps the trees had eyes. Perhaps this very oak had a life she didn't begin to suspect.

The smell of the owl hung in the clearing, an unclean odor that would not disperse. Suddenly she pinned it down, that inchoate feeling she had experienced before. There was anger, yes, and shame, and even a bit of awe. But there was also — could she admit it to herself? — a ripe plum of envy. In his way, he was magnificent and truly terrible.

And all these years she hadn't had a thought of competition.

Derin had no idea what time it was, morning or afternoon. The sky looked wet as a soaked blanket, and as heavy. The boy tried to figure out how many hours of daylight lay before them, but he had no point to start from.

They had long since left the granite overhang behind; they had crossed the meadow with its brackish brook. The jay had chattered madly at them from the elderberry bush near the oxbow lake, berating Matthew, but when he saw the boy and satyr would not be dissuaded, he wished them luck and let them go, giving Derin a touchstone to keep him safe.

They entered a section of the meadowlands Derin hadn't seen. It wasn't meadow at all. "Matthew," Derin said. "Have you been here before?"

"Not in a long time," the satyr replied. "Not since you were a child. Had no reason to."

The earth grew spongy under their feet as the trail began to descend. This decline in elevation excited the boy, gave him the first sense he'd had that his imagination's landscape might be met. They were readying to enter a new zone, and Derin, in the first flush of the journey, stared ahead with expectation.

"Do you know where we are?" he asked.

"We're nearing the Swollen River," the satyr said. "Still several miles off, I think, but we're getting there. If I'm remembering right, we're close to the swamp which borders it."

As they left behind the more familiar woodlands crowded with hickory and oak, the boy realized how little he usually saw of the world. Yes, he had *seen* — the maples by the oxbow lake, the beech whose leaves turned yellow as goldenrod in fall — but he'd become so used to them, he had ceased to look carefully. He simply captured them in his mind's eye, as if through peripheral vision, and moved absently on. But here, with so much of the vegetation unfamiliar, his eyes were cleansed. The world began to emerge from the fog which shrouded everyday life.

They passed through the edges of a marsh. Its tall thin reeds, bleached as weathered wood, were speckled and streaked with black. Cattails, brown and spindly, poked through the reeds. The dried empty cases of milkwood jutted in clusters from the ends of their thin stems. And there were other, stranger plants that Matthew knew—chokecherry, bullbriar, and sheep laurel. The air was filled with the rustle of their passing, a scratchy rasp like sand on rock, broken only by the ooze of displaced water which filled the little pockets their feet made. Derin bent and put his finger in the water. It was warm and silty and tasted faintly sweet, of mud and peat. The ground before him held two distinct holes, like half-moons, from Matthew's hooves.

Beyond the marsh, the ground rose slightly, became drier. They entered a forest of pine and oak. The soil was sandy, a flecked black which skittered under Derin's feet. The sand was blanketed with pine needles, and their resilience made the boy want to leap in the air, but the tree's branches hung only a few feet over his head. They passed bear oak and black oak. The pitch pine seemed stunted, reaching a height of only eight feet. It grew in stands of five or six trees, its dark split bark covered with lichen. Many were grotesquely twisted, pruned and pinched in fantastic shapes. Black huckleberry, broom crowberry, and barberry, all new to Derin, grew under the tree cover. Sphagnum moss was everywhere, its tiny furred stems reaching up at the boy.

It was an autumnal forest. Derin had the feeling he had entered a different time. It was summer in the meadowlands, the trees flush with large green leaves. Raspberries and blueberries made bushes droop under their weight. Before the moon was stolen, the land had been coursing with life. But here, a few miles from where they'd started, the leaves were brown and dry. The conifers still held their thin green needles, but the oaks were largely bare, except for the few ragged leaves still clinging to the branches.

As the trail fell again, the trees grew taller, sending their slender trunks higher into the grey air. It was the two of them who were descending, as though entering an excavation. The light dimmed as they continued. Derin, walking in silence, had the odd sensation of going backwards. The change in seasons was compounded by what he took to be a change in history. Matthew had explained to him the stories of the earth's beginning, and now he half-expected to see it for himself. His eyes were wide; every strange noise put him on edge. He looked above him, to the distant reaches of the pines and oaks, waiting to see a bird of prey eyeing them. But the forest was empty, the only noises natural, wind in the upper branches of the trees, the soft padding of their feet.

"It's very strange," Matthew said, almost to himself. "This forest was filled with birds. Swallows and goshawks, tanagers and kingfishers, every manner of bird lived here together. All day the trees were heavy with song, and the air was threaded with their flight from branch to branch. Where could they have gone?"

"Maybe the wind that took the ravens took the other birds as well."

"No, I don't think so. It's impossible that every member of every clan was either taken by that wind or died because of it. They must have left this forest for some reason; maybe there was danger here and they were frightened away. Or they chose to leave. But why would they do that? This forest. . . . Derin, it was as if music had been given a place to live forever and it lived here."

"But nothing lives here. It's not just birds. I haven't seen even a salamander or toad."

"It's the birds I miss," the satyr said.

"Have we passed into the Outer Lands?" Derin asked.

"Not yet. Not until we cross the Swollen River. Still, this seems like what the Outer Lands must be. It's as though they had a life of their own, a sickness, which leapt the river and poisoned the forest."

They walked in silence for several minutes as the trail fell below them. In the distance, Derin saw a wall of darkness rise from the forest floor. He sucked in his breath so sharply that Matthew whirled around in alarm. "What's the matter?" he hissed. Derin raised an arm and pointed.

"What's that?" he asked.

"It's the swamp," the satyr said. "Hurry. It's getting darker by the minute, and we don't want to be trapped there when night comes on."

Derin hung back. "Maybe we should stop here for the night, before we get there," the boy said.

Matthew thought for a minute, stroking the side of his face. "You're right," he said. "We got a late start."

He unslung his pack and put it on the ground. "But I can't say I like it much here either," he said. He quickly looked around for something which might serve as shelter, but forest stretched as far as he could see. No rocks, no possibility of caves. He shrugged. "We'll have to make do," he said. "Help me gather pine needles for our beds before it gets too dark to see. At least we can get a good night's sleep."

But when he looked at Derin, he realized the boy hadn't heard a word he'd said. Derin stared ahead of him at the place where the cedars rose like a fortress and the darkness began.

"Derin," the satyr said calmly. "I'm talking to you."

Deirdre flew east again, searching for Matthew and Derin. When she reached the meadowlands, it was close to nightfall. She had given up trying to be in two places at the same time, had decided simply to do what she had to do. For weeks, it seemed, she had flown madly here and there and back again. Now she was so tired she didn't care if the other ravens noticed she was gone.

With a thump, she landed on the granite overhang and tried to catch her breath. "I'm going to . . . uh . . . croak if this continues," she gasped to the thinning air, but nothing answered her. "I'm going to drop dead in midflight." It was crazy, crazy, crazy: from the Deadwood Forest to the meadowlands and back, and back to the meadowlands and back again, like a shuttle, a yo-yo, a spinning top. Just this morning, she had been in the southern reaches of the Deadwood Forest, and the thought of those starfish clinging to her claws made her shudder.

The forest was quiet. Derin and the satyr were nowhere to be seen. The ground below her still held the imprint of their bodies, but it was cold and damp. Hours, at least, had passed since they had been there. The scattered remnants of the fire were clearly from the previous night. So they had taken off, after all. They were on their way.

She smiled. "I've always thought I was a good judge of character," she said, and no one argued with her self-assessment. She flew to the meadow, thinking she might catch them there. But she couldn't find them anywhere. As she hovered in the light breezes blowing from the east, she saw the grass part below her and come together again. An animal was moving through the meadow. Perhaps it had some news.

Swooping down toward the moving grass, Deirdre landed in front of a badger who looked exceedingly alarmed at her swift appearance. He took off in another direction as fast as he could. "Wait," Deirdre said. "I just want a word with you." The badger didn't slow down. She flew again at the frightened animal who began to burrow with all his might, his claws flailing at the dirt. "I mean no harm," Deirdre said. "I only want some information." The badger stopped, half into the ground, backed out and stared at the raven.

"I'm looking for two friends of mine," the raven said. "A young boy and a satyr."

"You're a friend of Derin's?" the badger asked. "Why didn't you say so in the first place?" For the moment, he seemed to let down his guard. "He's gone, I'm afraid."

"Do you know where?"

"West," the badger said. "He's gone west with the goat-man. Messengers in the night. The moon caught in a tree. Nothing good will come of it, I promise you. They've headed for the Swollen River."

"Thank you, badger," Deirdre said. The badger looked at her with suspicion and a faint return of his previous alarm — how had she known his name? — and as he watched, she rose in the air and headed west. Who was that black bird?

"I hope you find them," the badger said glumly. "Nothing good will come of it, I promise. Not to any of you, I'm afraid."

But Deirdre didn't hear the badger's voice, nor did anyone else.

Matthew lay on one of the two pine-needle beds he and Derin had made. Soon he'd build a fire and see what was in the knapsack to eat. For the moment, he thought he'd rest. He took his panpipe out of the knapsack, sat up, and began to play. He imitated bird song and water music. He played until the melancholy forest echoed with his sound. And then he broke free on a flight of his own fancy, the notes cascading through the pine and oak like little stars.

To Derin, the distant music sounded more glorious than anything he'd heard all day. It was like light, like sunshine. It cut through the deepening gloom, a knife of pure feeling and release.

He had gone by himself to the edge of the swamp, leaving Matthew behind him. "Be careful," the satyr had cautioned before he started. "Don't go in." The advice wasn't necessary; Derin had no thought of venturing into that tangle alone. Behind him, the music rose and fell, but as he got as close as he dared and peered into the darkness, it seemed the swamp sucked all the music from the air, all the air from his lungs.

There was little light in the forest and less in the swamp. The cedars ascended before him, their tall straight trunks covered with a green bark, grooved as if by a chisel. Around them lay the water of the swamp. It looked cold, colder than it should have been, even in autumn, and Derin stared at the water covering a thin casing of ice.

"Everything's upside down," Derin said, and his words came back to him from the swamp's interior. They would have to walk through the water, their feet on the ice below. Hummocks of moss rose from the swamp's surface, but they couldn't spend their time jumping from one to another. They would have to grit their teeth and plunge in.

He stood looking into the swamp until the darkness was total. Behind him, Matthew should be making a fire, but when he turned to look, he could see nothing at all. He stumbled back in the direction he'd come. All around him the pines and oaks stood, looming out of the darkness when he was almost upon them. "Matthew!" he cried, but there was no answer. The silence oozed out of the earth. "Matthew, where are you?"

Could he have gotten himself lost in the few minutes he'd been apart from the satyr? He turned again and tried to retrace his steps, back toward the swamp. He'd expected the wall of cedar to jump out at him, a vantage point he could be sure of. But he had no such luck. He ran forward a few steps and stopped short. The ringing in his ears could only be his own footsteps. He called the satyr's name again, his voice rising in terror.

Wait, a small voice inside him said, just sit down and wait for Matthew to find you. So Derin sat and immediately stood up again. The sodden ground of the forest had seeped into his skin. He stood in the dark, his heart beating so quickly blood pounded in his ears.

And then he felt the hand on his shoulder. But it wasn't a hand; it had claws and the claws gripped him tightly, not sinking in, but fastening around him. He grunted in horror, jerked his shoulder, and fell to the ground, rolling away from whatever it was. He screamed, got to his feet, and began to run. He hit a bush, its branches tripping him, wrapping around his legs. And so he lay there in the darkness, breathing hoarsely, afraid to move.

"Derin!" Matthew's voice sounded behind him.

"I'm over here!" the boy screamed, relief flooding him.

"Derin," another voice said from the air above.

"Who's there?" the boy said, almost in a whisper, shielding his face with his arms.

"It's Deirdre," the raven said. "You almost broke my back with that inconsiderate stunt of yours."

Matthew came crashing through the underbrush to find the boy on his back, the raven perched in the branches of the bush in which Derin lay tangled.

All this the fox saw, but she never made a sound.

"His body felt dead."

TUESDAY

The fox had followed them, carefully keeping out of sight, from the time they first skirted the marsh. She stayed low, watching them as they slept. She waited. When it was time, she would join them, but it had been enough to see them push their way through the forest and stop on the edge of the swamp.

They were an odd pair, the tall boy with eyes the color of slate, and the satyr. From the distance, when she had first caught sight of them, they seemed identical, two creatures walking on their hind legs, threading their way along an overgrown path. She had watched them stoop and finger the leaves of shrubs, talking in low voices she couldn't hear. But as the fox crept closer, their differences became apparent. The older one had the hindquarters of a goat, and an air of wildness about him; his eyes were vibrant and his head twisted at the slightest noise. While he moved through the underbrush, he was constantly stopping to sniff the wind, alert to danger. He gave the impression of having full knowledge of the woods, as though he were a natural part of them.

The boy had the torso of the other, though thinner, less muscled. His legs appeared stronger than the satyr's, and were streaked with blond hair. He laughed when the satyr turned and talked to him. But when he walked in silence, his expression was fierce, hardening into arrogance. He seemed weightier, his intensity a cloak he never quite removed.

There was a strong yet subtle bond between them, a strange tenderness, a tension. Its surface was rough, full of harsh words, but in its deeper currents, where the two needed no longer to attack each other, it flowed untroubled. It moved her, yet she was disdainful of it. These male creatures would forever place one another in danger and then come to the rescue; they would move in and out of a circle of affection, the perimeter of which they couldn't find. They would clearly need her help.

Vera lived in a lair at the summit of the Mountains of No Return. She knew of the moon's capture, for her home was in the Outer Lands, close to the Deadwood Forest, and the owl held sway everywhere these days.

She was a snow fox, the last of her clan. Her fur was silver and soft as goose down. Her pale eyes shone in the dark, a flicker of flame. Like all snow foxes she was solitary, joining others only when the times demanded it.

And she had other traits which made her different from any animal who lived in the land. She was lightning, the flash of sunlight off a lake in full summer, the ripple of a trout's scales as he swims under cover of a snag.

She was magic.

Deirdre told them all she knew about the owl. It was past midnight before the three stopped talking and went to sleep. Derin and Matthew wrapped themselves in their blankets and slid among the pine needles as deeply as they could without touching the ground itself, for it was fearfully cold. The raven took up a perch in a pine over their heads, tucked her beak under her wing, and was the first asleep.

Matthew dreamed for the first time in weeks. The moon hung upside down, suspended by ropes from two ravens who flew back and forth across the sky, making a constant night. Sometimes the moon rose in the east and raced across the firmament like a haycart set afire and sometimes she rose in the west and traveled, a mocking grin, toward the place where the sun should rise.

A face coalesced out of the darkness, cruel, without a trace of kindness in it. Its large yellow eyes stared straight ahead, never blinking, surrounded by twin ovals, pale as dawn. A beak, hooked and powerful, jutted over the bottom of the face. And just above the eyes, two horns sprouted.

He twitched on his bed of needles as if the owl had him in his talons. The beak opened, and at the moment he would have been swallowed, Matthew woke. He lay in the dark, huddled under his blanket, sweaty though the air was intensely cold, and listened to the easy breathing of Derin, who slept in the darkness at his side. Above, he could barely make out the profile of the raven hunched on her branch, still lost in sleep.

"Only a dream," Matthew mumbled to himself. But in his half-dazed state, he couldn't shake the prickly sense of dread he'd awakened with. He was about to enter a place he'd never been before, and this antagonist had lodged in his mind before he'd even left the meadowlands behind. The owl, if Deirdre could be trusted, held power from the Swollen River to the farthest reaches of the Outer Lands. If he could command an army of ravens to capture the moon, what chance would they have against him?

Matthew stood and looked toward the swamp, a deeper darkness to the west. He strained to hear some evidence of life there, the throaty bass of frogs, the hum of insects. But the air was still. It was the swamp he had entered fourteen years ago, alone. He had stumbled in the darkness, seeing the heron's outline before him when lightning crashed across the sky, throwing its white glare down through the trees. Thunder rolled up at him from the dank water. At the river's bank, he could see nothing, swept up in the roar below him. Then the lightning flared again, and the hooded figure stepped from behind a tree, reaching out to give him the child. And had disappeared across the Swollen River, almost spirited away.

He had stood, looking out over the water, visible only through the sky's bolts of illumination, the water which roiled and bubbled like a cauldron, holding the child in his arms, the little boy who, even then, did not cry or scream, or shiver with cold, but looked up at him, eyes wide, no hint of a smile on his face.

Now a thin watery light began to seep from the east, until the upper reaches of the pines and oak were black and stark against the morning sky. While the boy and the raven still slept, he got to his feet and gathered wood for a fire. The pine needles, coarse and dry as dust, made good kindling and he soon had a healthy blaze.

He took an earthenware pot from his knapsack, filled it with water, and put it up to boil. He unwrapped some strips of jerky from the pack and slipped them into the water. Matthew brought the pot to his lips and took a sip, but the liquid burned his mouth and throat and he cried out in pain.

Above him, the raven's voice filtered down. "Old family recipe?" she asked.

Startled, Matthew stood up, knocking over the pot of water. It spilled into the fire, and a cloud of steam rose, scalding the satyr's arm. He howled and batted at the steam as if it were alive, while the fire hissed itself cold. "You shut up," he said in a voice which surprised him. He glanced up and saw the raven tilted forward, her red eyes peering at him. He was unaccountably angry.

Without thinking, Matthew picked up a rock and heaved it at the raven. He was deadly with a bow and arrow, and his aim was true. The rock came close to Deirdre's head, but she hopped deftly to a lower branch.

"What reason?" she croaked in a sore offended voice. "Watch who you're throwing at."

"I see who I'm throwing at," Matthew said, picking up another rock, but he stopped himself just as the raven flew into the air. What was he doing?

Above him, Deirdre landed again and danced from branch to branch, beside herself with excitement. "Blame the bad news, not the messenger," she said. "It's not my fault. I'm only the one who told you."

"I know," Matthew said. "I don't know what got into me." The air hummed around his head.

"Apologies are easy," the raven said. "They're only words."

"I'm sorry," Matthew said. "Calm down."

"Come *down*?" Deirdre sputtered. "Where you can get your hands on me? Not on your life. All these years I've thought nothing but kindly of you. I don't deserve this. I truly don't. *I* didn't kidnap the moon, *I'm* not responsible for the boy's. . . ."

He lost the raven's voice, though she continued to caw about indignity and danger, ungratefulness and salvation. Before him, Derin rose from the ground, unsteady, still half-asleep. The boy shivered, wrapped his arms around himself. "It's cold," he said. "What's all the noise about? And where's the fire?"

As the fox watched from a copse of pine, the boy and the satyr packed their belongings. Deirdre continued to hover above them, still petulant.

"Deirdre," Matthew said. "You're carrying on like a flustered child. That rock had nothing to do with you. You don't understand."

"What's to understand?" the raven asked. "I don't take kindly to slurs on my intelligence."

Matthew stood up and faced her, and she flew higher into the air as if he might try to do her more damage. "He's the one with the temper," Matthew said.

"Couldn't prove it by me," Deirdre replied.

"Listen," Matthew said. "Enough's enough." He stuck his arm out, turned his hand sideways. "Come here."

"Why?" the raven asked, suspicious. "Why should I trust you?"

"Because of all those kind thoughts you had about me. Because of those times you rode my shoulder."

Deirdre peered at the satyr, could discern no ulterior purpose in his expression. Cautiously she fluttered down and perched upon his finger, ready to fly off at a moment's notice.

"There," Matthew said. The raven was silent, her expression still peevish.

"Well," Deirdre said, turning her beak away. "If you can't trust your friends, who *can* you trust?"

The satyr laughed. He brought his arm around until he forced the raven to look at him. With his other hand, he reached up and stroked the sleek top of her head. "All right?" he asked.

"Just be careful," Deirdre said. "Remember you're about to enter the Outer Lands. Who knows what outposts the owl has there?"

The three of them, two by ground and one by air, approached the first wall of cedars at the swamp's edge. "Good-bye," the raven called. "I've got to go. I'll get back when . . . whenever I can." She left them, flying west. She dabbled in the wind above the swamp, did a loop-the-loop, and took off toward the Deadwood Forest in a straight line.

The fox crept closer, staying near the ground, keeping herself hidden from them. She thought of the trouble they would have in the swamp, for even the satyr had no idea how things had changed since the owl's power had penetrated east. She darted behind the cedars and approached them from its dark curtain.

"Stay behind me, now," the satyr said. "Can't tell what we'll find in there." He shielded his eyes and tried to peer into the gloom, but all he saw was water, the fallen cedar trunks, and the ooze which gathered at the water's edge before the earth heaved itself into moss-strewn hummocks.

Matthew looked up at the towering cedars before him. "Did you see anything in there yesterday?" he asked the boy. "Did you hear any noise?"

"No," Derin said. "Nothing but water."

The cedars stretched their tall grooved trunks so far above Matthew they made him dizzy. He contemplated their lacy reticulated tops. They were strange trees, without needles or leaves, with a network of thin green fingers which touched one another like feathers and filtered what little light there was until it fell around him in a dense web. The light was refracted as if through droplets of water, prisms suspended in the air.

The world was about to swallow them: they would pass through this curtain of cedar and the life they had known would close behind them. From this point, the future would be a series of doors leading from one strange room to a stranger one which lay beyond. It was like part of that dream — "A *dream*", the satyr said aloud — and the sound of his voice in that stillness heartened him.

"What?" Derin asked.

"I said, 'What are we waiting for?' We might as well be walking, as standing here."

He took a step and passed through the outer ring of cedars into the water. He left the solid ground behind, its outer bank a heap of dead leaves and matted dirt, held together by roots. Under the water, which was insufferably cold, lay the ice. His hooves slithered away from him, threatening to throw him, body and pack, flat on his back in the icy wetness.

Derin followed. He held his arms out to either side to give him better balance. There was no sound in the swamp but their sloshing. They didn't talk, using all their concentration on the task of staying upright. After a fifteen-foot passage which seemed to congeal his blood, Matthew reached a moss-covered hummock and climbed from the water.

"Look at my legs," he shouted, his voice too loud. Derin was astounded to see ice on the fleece above the satyr's hooves. "We're going to have to move fast," the satyr said, "or we'll freeze here. One step and our feet will hold fast to the bottom and we'll end it all, waving our fool arms and yelling at the sky."

He was about to strip some branches from a fallen cedar when he saw her. She appeared from behind a very large trunk, a hundred yards ahead of him. Her skin was white as milk and her soft silver hair thrown back from her shoulders revealed the most spectacular collar-bone he had ever seen. He was galvanized, standing there in the icy water. His eyes widened and he involuntarily grabbed for her, but she was so far away he smiled at the ludicrous move.

"After all these years," he whispered, letting his breath drain from his body. "I'm more deranged than I knew."

But what an apparition! She was lovely, pure grace, with a flirtatious pursing of her lips which made Matthew shiver with pleasure instead of cold.

He forgot the ice in his fleece; he forgot the treachery of the water beneath him. He was transformed. He took off after her like a bee in search of pollen. His legs sprouted wings. He danced above the surface of the swamp like a madman. Derin was astonished.

"Matthew!" he screamed. "Wait for me!"

As good as his word, the owl had sent three falcons back to gag the moon before nightfall of the previous day, and they came again at dawn to ungag her. They were respectful, and they left her alone after completing their errand. She sat in her cage, surveying the forest, the grey sky, the stark black trunks of the trees. How much longer could this go on?

The moon was beginning to feel slightly crazed. She had talked, for these past two days, only to the owl, and she had been cooped up here when before the wide expanses of sky had been her domain. She ached with disuse and (she had to admit it) with loneliness. She even would have welcomed another conversation with the owl, but she had not seen him since he had left her the day before.

The section of forest in which she hung was deserted, except for those unseen presences the owl had warned her about. But she wouldn't talk to an unseen presence; it would be like talking to herself, and she couldn't allow herself to slip like that. Not so much as a mouse had crossed the clearing below her. The air was silent, untouched by mosquitoes or flies, and except for the thin arrow of an occasional bird passing overhead, the moon was completely alone. So she was pleased when the three ravens descended from the sky and settled around her on the branches of her cage.

"Good morning," she said civilly, trying to keep her pleasure in the visit absent from her voice.

Two of the ravens looked at one another and back at the moon. The third, whose red eyes glittered with a wicked fire, flew to the ground and returned with a pointed stick. He circled the cage once and came up behind her. She whirled to face him, and the other two immediately began to chatter.

"Good morning," one of them said.

"A beautiful morning," the other said. "Wind from the southwest. Makes you glad to be alive."

The raven jabbed his stick through the oaken branches and feinted at the moon. She retreated to the furthest reaches of the cage until the harsh bark scraped her. The other two were breathing down her back, and for an instant, she thought one of them might try to peck at her, but instead their mindless chatter came pouring into her ears.

"The cage a little too close for comfort?" one asked, and the other answered, as if the question were addressed to him. The one with the stick jabbed repeatedly and flew around to join the others, and so the moon retreated again, more aware each instant of the closeness of her quarters.

There was no escape if they decided to take her on in earnest; she would have no chance if all three grabbed sticks and came at her. But they seemed to be enjoying the situation as it unfolded, and neither of the two who spat their inanities on the morning air were inclined to arm themselves, preferring to sit there and watch the third, who uttered not a word.

She tried to think of something clever to say, to alarm them or distract them, but her mind was such a jumble of fear and anger that nothing coherent formed.

She concentrated on the stick. It came at her from every interstice of branch until it was a blur and she was sick with dizziness. Just when she thought she wouldn't last another minute, the ravens began to tire of their game; the one who had taunted her dropped the stick. The three flew off, drifting in the air above her, throwing down a few more insults before they disappeared from view.

By the time the moon had regained her composure, and the knot in her stomach had reduced to a small displeasure, she was in an ugly mood. She raged at the empty forest, and if she had gotten her wish, destruction would have rained down around her. She called brimstone and fire, thunderstorms, tornados, every disaster weather could deliver. But the placid greyness of the sky did not change, the ground beneath her gave no evidence of a beginning rumble, and she finally fumed herself to silence.

She had reached the point of despair when the other raven arrived, wheeling in the air above her, dropping down like a silent black feather. As she saw the bird descend, she felt the words well in her throat again and she spewed forth venomous diatribes against all winged and feathered creatures, against all beasts which crept or galloped or slithered on the earth. The raven sat, patiently waiting for her to stop, but the very calmness of the bird further incensed the moon.

"You scurrilous, lice-ridden, winged contraption," the moon seethed. "You cowardly piece of fluff and bone. Wait until I am free of this cage. Pestilence will be visited upon this forest from that day until all ages have passed, and not one of you shall ever raise a brood again; worms will shrink from your beaks and you'll fall dead from hunger and thirst. Streams will dry up at your approach, and the other animals will kick your dead carcasses with disgust. You will be less than the rocks; you will rot to form leaf mold. . . ." The moon gasped for breath and reeled in her cage. She was so red of face the raven thought she might explode, and jumped to get a word in before the torrent of frustration continued.

"If you will hold your tongue for a moment. . . ." Deirdre said, but the moon ran ramshackle over her imploring voice. "Your bones will be used to pick the teeth of weasels and vermin, and wherever you die, ratsbane will rear its head. You will be known. . . ."

Deirdre fixed the moon with a deadly look, a gaze compounded of such long-suffering patience and slowly building violence that she stopped her ranting and waited for the bird to speak.

"And not a moment too soon," the raven said. "I'm not one to lose my temper, but you were sorely tempting me. I would have given you another minute before I flew away and left you to disintegrate in this forsaken place."

"Who are you?" the moon asked. "What do you want?"

"My name is Deirdre—not that it's of any use to you—and I am attempting to extricate you from this abominable situation. Now, no more questions, there isn't time."

"No, no," she said. "This is too much. I can bear your taunts and jibes, but please, I beg you, don't torture me with this. Just go in peace and leave me be." The moon drew a long deep breath and let it out so quietly it was like the breeze which ripples the highest branches of the firs at sundown. And she turned her back on Deirdre and closed her eyes.

Deirdre lost her temper. She flew into the air and made such a racket clattering her wings that the moon opened her eyes and looked at the bird. The raven seemed to be having a fit. Her eyes rolled in her head, her neck jerked, her wings beat unevenly in the grey silent air. But she landed again, close to the moon, and her voice had no patience left in it.

"I can't take this whimpering prattle. Self-pity infuriates me. I don't yet know how your rescue will be accomplished, but I'm determined that you shall be liberated. Right now, two . . . uh . . . collaborators—a boy and a satyr—are on their way to this forest to engineer your escape.

"I tell you this to build your courage. You're not alone in wishing for your freedom. You must take heart. I'll come again if I can. At the moment, I'm playing the role of a transcontinental carrier pigeon, and I have an entrance very soon somewhere else. So I haven't time to stay and chat. Just remember who you are."

The moon was astonished by this speech. No one had ever spoken to her so familiarly, without the slightest trace of respect. Even the owl in his hyperbolic poetical speech gave her some measure of her stature. But here this stranger sat and bid her keep her chin up.

"Do you have anything to say?" the raven asked. The moon could do no better than to shake her head. "Well, maintain your strength. Stay as cheerful as possible. Keep an ear open for anything you think might be helpful," Deirdre said. "And please. Don't talk to me again as you did a while ago. It has a vanquishing effect upon my determination to help you."

She was gone before the moon could offer apologies or thanks. But in the afterglow of Deirdre's visit, she practically beamed with joy. It was not even the possibility of her freedom which affected her so: it was more complicated. Never before had she needed the help of anyone, and now when she did, she felt a new emotion at the knowledge that there *were* creatures out there working on her behalf.

She felt both bigger and smaller than herself, as though, for the first time, she understood the outlines of her silver form when viewed from the earth. There was great value in that, and great understanding. She knew that when the falcons came again to gag her she would offer no resistance, but submit, as sweetly as possible, to their hooded smiles.

Several times he fell, slipping on the ice and drenching himself in the freezing water, but he picked himself up and ran on, chasing the beautiful creature who melted into the distance. He didn't feel the cold; it was as though all the contingencies of landscape and weather had evaporated, and all that mattered was the image he pursued, the steady healthy flow of his heart. Behind him, Derin's cries faded as the boy stumbled through the swamp, falling further and further behind.

Derin was so tired and cold he thought of flinging himself into the icy water and resting there until he froze, but he continued the mad chase after Matthew. The cedars ascended on all sides, tall and lordly, like druids. Derin's legs ached from the cold, but he dared not rest, frightened he would lose sight of the satyr, and then really be lost in the depths of the swamp.

What had gotten into Matthew? The boy had expected a slow and cautious trek across this wasteland, and instead, here they were, the two of them, rushing through it with as little thought as one would give who had thrown himself from a precipice. And this blind running was like that: the wind whipped Derin's face so that he imagined he was falling, and he almost closed his eyes and relaxed into the luxury of the dive, not having to do a thing but wait until he hit bottom.

He ran through a maze, constantly ducking and swerving; his face was scratched by the cedar branches he sought to avoid. Whenever he thought he saw a clear avenue to follow his friend's advance, a thicket of wild pepperbush got in his way. In and out of the water he ran, up one hillock and down again into the water. The swamp was crisscrossed by fallen trunks, and red maple and tupelo flared at him as he ran, reaching to put out his eyes.

In his haste, he became more careless. He vaulted a fallen cedar, his right leg stretched in front, toe pointed, his left trailing over the tree-trunk. On the other side, a stretch of water lay, the ice inches below the surface. His leg, the right one, hit first, and, coming down upon that ice from the vault's height, slipped out from under him. Desperately he tried to regain his balance, but he went down on his back, sending a wave of water in front of him, into a cedar root. It caught his foot and ankle, but the rest of his body would not be braked so easily.

Like flames, the pain raced up his leg and into his groin. He groaned and lay flat in the water as the wave he had started splashed against a hummock and returned to wash over him. The cold was forgotten, Matthew was forgotten. His eyes clamped shut, his teeth bit down on his lower lip with such force he tasted blood. He was afraid to open his eyes and look, afraid to see his foot no longer connected to the rest of his leg.

When he felt the ice begin to form in his hair, Derin knew he had to get out of the water. He raised his head, opened his eyes, and looked. The ankle was huge, a gnarled knot, part of the cedar root.

"Matthew!" he yelled. But the satyr had long since vanished from view and the only thing he heard, receding into the distance, was Matthew's muffled plunge forward. And then he heard nothing at all.

Derin was stunned by the density of the silence. It had a presence of its own, a thick, almost palpable texture, like fog. The trees guarded the stillness which magnified itself when he raised his head and looked around, until the sound of water dripping from his hair was like a cascade, a waterfall.

The disparity between that silence and the racket he made when he moved immobilized the boy. He was afraid to shift his arm, to sit up. Each time he jostled, the sound of water rippling away from him resounded through the swamp, echoing from the cedars and the hummocks until he was deafened by his own faltering movement. He couldn't speak, much less yell: the thought of his own voice calling out in that stillness filled him with awe.

Gathering his strength, Derin sat up, stretched forward, and put his hands around his ankle. An arrow of pain shot through his body again, and he groaned. The ankle and lower calf were so tender he could barely touch them. He closed his eyes again and settled back; the pain was increasing. It was as though some animal, a bear or panther, had him by the leg, tight in its strong jaws, and was holding fast. He imagined the teeth biting down, crunching through bone, severing his foot from his leg.

"Spirit of life," Derin said. Around him, the swamp whirled. In his delirium, trees toppled, sending walls of cold water over him. Beneath him, the earth opened, the ice cracked, draining all water away until he was in last night's bed of pine.

But the illusion didn't last. There was no use. He was being swallowed. He felt a great darkness in his ankle, a rush of night beginning to sweep up his leg toward his heart. "Spirit of death," Derin whispered. "Let go, let go!"

The hole in his chest slowly closed. He felt the darkness waver at his knee and ebb down to his ankle. The grip on his wracked foot subsided and then gave up altogether. He opened his eyes. He could feel nothing but the pain, and as his eyes moved over his freezing body, down his leg, he saw them.

Near his ankle, their heads sloping from the water, frogs had gathered. But they were larger than frogs. Their skin was a dull black, their mouths gaped open, and the section of underbelly visible above the water was mottled with dense blue spots like bruises. Their red eyes stared at him without blinking, glittered like rubies in the gloom.

Derin caught his breath, involuntarily pulling his leg toward him. The cedar root held fast and pain shot up his leg again. He moaned low in his throat, and for the first time, the frogs moved, slightly away. Where had they come from? The boy tried to calm himself long enough to remember if he'd heard anything as he'd run through the water, the croak of a frog, a bird's song. No, there had been nothing; if these creatures made a sound, they were hideously silent now.

When he lay still, they moved toward his ankle again, so smoothly they seemed to be floating. The water swayed away from them, a slight bulge in its dark surface, and as they approached, the boy thought he saw their mouths open further. There was no doubt: whatever these creatures were, they belonged to the owl. Their damp skin shone in the gloom, and their eyes burned, seven pairs of bright red embers coming toward him.

"Get away!" he screamed, thrashing, throwing water at them with his hands. They shrunk at the noise, and the churning swamp, so still before, kept them at bay. As soon as he stopped, the frogs inched toward him again. He began to babble, saying whatever came into his head, anything to keep noise alive in the air. He talked about the meadowlands, about his childhood, and his mind was flooded with memories he hadn't thought about in years. They hunched there, underbellies pulsing, patiently waiting for him to be quiet again.

He closed his eyes, bit down on his lower lip, and tried to wrench his ankle loose. The pain was so intense, the boy thought he would pass out. Instead, he gave vent to his terror and anguish and screamed. His cries came back to him, echoing off the cedar trunks, breaking the swamp's stillness. Derin sat up, grabbed his knee with both hands, and pulled again. This time he felt something give, as though he'd torn his foot loose. Close to his ankle the trunk of the cedar grew. Around it, roots spread out like mangroves, slimy fingers. And there in the water, free of the cedar, his ankle lay inches from the trunk.

Derin pulled himself up on one of the moss-covered hillocks, out of the water. His ankle throbbed brutally. He lay there, encompassed by pain, and watched the frogs approach. They crested the root which had caught his ankle, they surged forward to where his body had been, and stopped, several feet from the hillock, still in the water, and sat there staring at him. Derin looked behind him for a stick, a rock. "Stay away," he said, his voice low. "Don't come near me."

As his body began to thaw, he felt tiny fires being lit within him. He was like a dark plain on which battling armies had settled in for the night. Without taking his eyes from the frogs, Derin tried to massage some blood back into his legs. His body felt dead, the carcass of an animal he hadn't seen before. He looked in the direction he'd been running when he slipped. A vista of hillocks and cedar receded as far as he could see. In the other direction, past the fallen log he'd vaulted, the same landscape repeated itself endlessly. No variation in light gave a clue to direction; nothing looked familiar to him.

He'd taken no notice of his surroundings as he'd thrown himself forward. His only compass had been Matthew's back as he ran through the swamp. Above him, the trees disappeared into the grey sky, dwindling into sparser and sparser foliage until their spindly tops stuck into the air like spears.

The pain in his ankle spread until he was sure he could hear it in the swamp, like the ice's heartbeat. It grew out of everywhere. It was inside his skull and outside. "Stay away," he screamed. "Get away from here!" But this time his voice didn't stop them.

Matthew was unaware that Derin's cries of "Stop!" and "Slow down!" had ceased. He no longer heard the splash of water behind him, but that didn't slacken his pace. He was possessed. He would find her if it took the rest of the day, the rest of his life.

The nymph constantly eluded him. She glanced over her shoulder to see if he had gained on her, but every toss of her head threw her hair toward him, transfixing him, deepening his purpose in catching her. She darted under cover of pepperbush thickets, glided over the swamp's surface as if she ran on the water itself. She disappeared and reappeared with disconcerting frequency, so that Matthew never knew where his legs would carry him. He was breathless with anticipation; he ached to hold her.

She slipped among a copse of cedars. As Matthew splashed forward, he strained to see beyond the thicket to catch the next glimpse of her, and he saw nothing but the swamp. He was filled with elation. He had worn her out, and any moment, as soon as he rounded this tree he would have her, he would. . . .

Languorously perched on a hummock, her paws drooped over the edge, a silver fox stared at him. She sat there like a snow drift, placid and serene. For one second, Matthew considered asking whether the fox had seen a young woman pass this way, but Vera spoke before he could say anything.

"What have you done with the boy?" she asked. "I'm afraid you've lost him."

Matthew stood there, his chest heaving, overcome with disappointment at this unexpected conclusion. He should be wrestling with the nymph, her laughter filling the swamp like a company of bells. "What do you mean? I haven't done anything with the boy."

"Precisely," the fox said. "I'm sorry, but we'll have to go back." She got up, placed her front paws before her, and stretched. Her back rippled from one end to the other. She padded past the satyr and into the water, which came almost to her chest. "Come on," she urged. "We haven't got all day."

Matthew was dumbfounded. Where was the nymph? And how did this fox know about the boy? As he calmed, as his breathing returned to normal, his delusion hit him. There had been no nymph. He had run madly through the swamp, never looking back, and the boy, who had been thrashing after him, was now lost. He had left the boy behind. He cupped his hands around his mouth and shouted *"Derin!"* but fragmented syllables came back at him, an accusation.

"I don't think he can hear you," the fox said. "If my guess is correct, he's quite a ways back. I thought he'd catch up." As though there were nothing abnormal in her presence, Vera surged through the water. Her head was held high, and water rippled backwards making an inverted V.

"Now wait just a minute," the satyr said. "You?" he asked incredulously. "Was it you?"

The fox looked back over her shoulder and paused for a moment. "My name is Vera," she said, "at your service."

Matthew waded behind the fox, trying to put his information together. He and Derin had entered the swamp; the water was freezing, ice formed on his fleece and then, as in a dream, he'd seen the nymph. How long ago had that been? Where was he now? He'd lost all track of time and direction. He knew for sure only that he was still in the swamp, heading back where he'd just come from, looking for the boy.

Vera moved through the water with a power and grace that seemed otherworldly. The cold didn't bother her, and she never tired. For Matthew, it was much more difficult than he remembered. But then, he thought, he remembered only the image of the nymph. The cold returned to his legs and worked its way up his thighs and into his chest until his teeth were chattering, and he walked, hugging himself. He fumbled in his pack for the blanket, but he had drenched himself in his pursuit and now, in the slower going, he paid for his carelessness. Icicles hung from his hair; he stopped from time to time, lifted his legs from the water, and removed the small pieces of ice which formed in the cleft of his hooves.

Where was Derin? Ahead of Matthew, the swamp continued, drifting into the distance, an endless morass of pools and hummocks. Lichen grew on the cedars' trunks, turning the bark a deep green. In fact, everything looked green. The fox's white fur had taken on a pale sickly sheen, his own hands were stained, and the water eddied around his legs like algae-laden muck.

It was the light. It bounced off the swamp, reflected up to the cedars' tops and back again, a continuous mirroring of green.

They splashed through the water without speaking, or rather Matthew splashed; Vera cut through it smoothly. But he couldn't stop thinking of what had happened. If the fox could change her form, what else could she do? For the first time since he had begun to retrace his steps, he thought about what lay ahead. They had to get out of this swamp; they had to cross the Swollen River. And maybe, if the fox would go along with them, they would make it.

"Derin!" he yelled again, and this time thought he heard a thin voice raised in the distance. "Was that him?" he asked the fox. "Did you hear that?"

"I don't know. It could have been the boy. It could have been an echo."

They plunged in the direction of the noise, but when Matthew called his name again, there was no answer. "How long has it been?" Matthew asked the fox.

"Since when?"

"Since we started back."

"It's very hard to tell," the fox said. "Time's so slippery."

"How long has Derin been out there?"

"Perhaps you should have thought of that earlier," the fox replied mildly.

"But it was your fault," Matthew said, his voice sharp. He felt a hot knot rise in his throat.

"Now, now," Vera said. "Let's not point any fingers."

They found the boy on the hummock, surrounded by the frogs. Matthew and Vera saw him from a distance and stopped short. "What are those *things?*" the satyr cried.

The frogs sat silently, guarding the boy, their underbellies pulsing, their red eyes brilliant in the gathering darkness. When they heard the thrashing of the fox and satyr coming toward them, they slithered back into the water and disappeared under its opaque skin.

"Derin," Matthew yelled, spraying water in front of him as he ran.

The boy's face was a slight blue, tinged with the green light of the swamp. There was ice and mud in his hair, and his clothes were stiff with frost. His lips were tightly shut, thin as a dried reed, and his ankle was twisted sideways. The satyr knelt and took the boy's head in his hands, but Derin did not open his eyes. Wildly, Matthew looked to the fox for help, but she hung back as though what went on between the satyr and the boy was of no interest to her.

"What were they?" he asked again. "Where did they come from?"

"The owl," Vera said. "They belong to him."

"Derin, wake up," Matthew said. But if it were sleep which held the boy, it did not let him go.

The sun stared down at the clouds moiling beneath her and wondered what had happened to the world. For three days, she had risen in the east and looked down upon the same alien view. Gone were the meadowlands with their blue glints of lakes and streams. She could see nothing, not the wide river which cut the land, nor the tall snow-streaked mountains to the west. All was a grey turbulence, a fleecy mask of smoke.

She shone brighter, but the clouds did not disperse. Instead, they sent soft streamers up toward her, tentacles of mist. It was so odd. She had seen bad weather before, days of it, when the world disappeared beneath an impenetrable blanket of cloud. But this was different. She felt cut off from the world by these clouds, and she was growing weaker.

The sun did not understand exactly, but she knew how she felt. And where was the moon? She was used to being awakened in the morning by her sister, finished for the night, who would rouse her and send her into the sky. But for three mornings now, she had awakened alone, and late, and she was worried.

Without her sister, the sun felt her power dimming. They nurtured one another. She was afraid the moon was in trouble, but she didn't know what to do. The sun floated over the cloudy sea and racked her brain for an answer. There was *nowhere* her sister could be. The moon was so haughty and fickle, so impressed with herself, it was possible she had gone off somewhere—but where? There was nowhere to go.

The sun remembered the time when the world was forming, and the meadowlands seethed with mud, before the green sprouts of trees emerged. Then her sister had disappeared for several days as well. When she'd returned, she had said she was tired of shining and tired of being the same. Where had she gone? the sun asked, and the moon had said, "I traveled among the other suns to find another way."

And she had found one: elsewhere, she told her sister, there were places where the sources of light changed form. Sometimes they were round as a perfect circle, and sometimes thin and curved. She found great beauty in that, and fascination. "You may keep that dull round shape," she told the sun, "but I will be forever variable."

The sun, always the more steadfast of the two, had thought, "How vain!" But she'd consented to the new arrangement, and her sister had been happy after that. What was happening now? Had the moon grown discontent again, and traveled off in search of some new possibility?

If so, the sun wished she would get back soon. Even though she hated to admit it, she missed her sister. The sun forgave the moon her vanity, her haughtiness, with a condescension natural to older siblings. The moon would never catch up to the sun, would never be as bright. It was her lot to lag behind, to be paler, more beautiful.

But without her sister, the sun was incomplete, only half of what she was. The moon took great pride and some spite in saying she was the better half. Halves were just halves, and so the sun ignored the jibe. Now she was worried. Without her sister around, they were both in trouble. She, for one, was losing her light.

The fire blazed higher. Vera piled twigs and leaves from a fallen cedar, and strips of bark. Matthew knelt on the hummock, shaking the boy. Derin's arms hung backwards from his shoulders as if disjointed, and his legs bent at the knees and fell limply to the side. "Derin," he said harshly, and when the boy did not respond, the satyr cuffed his face. "You're not leaving me alone in this," he said. "Not after all this time."

He put the boy down and began to massage his chilled body. He worked up Derin's arms, beginning with the fingers, and then rubbed the boy's neck and chest. Vera took the earthenware pot from Matthew's knapsack, filled it with water from the swamp, and put it beside the fire to warm. When a faint mist drifted from the top, she brought it over to where the boy lay. Matthew rummaged in his pack for a piece of cloth and found the flask he had forgotten.

"Of course," he said. "Just the thing." He drenched the cloth in the warm water and wiped the boy's face. Then he lifted Derin's shoulders, tilted his head back, and gently opened his mouth. Derin's face had lost its blue tinge, and when Matthew put his ear to the boy's chest, he heard a steady heartbeat.

He poured a few drops from his flask into the boy's mouth. Derin's throat contracted, and the boy jerked forward, coughing. The satyr hit him on the back until the coughing ceased. Derin sat up and wildly looked around him. He threw his arms in front of his face, knocking Matthew backwards.

"Get away!" he screamed. "Get away from me."

Matthew struggled back to his hooves. "Derin," he said. "It's me. Cut it out."

The boy's eyes were full of terror. "Stay away," Derin screamed. "Get out of here."

"It's all right. *Derin*. Listen to me. They're gone. The frogs are gone."

The boy caught his breath and looked around him at the hummock, his arms still threshing the air. He calmed down by degrees, his head twisting until he was sure they were nowhere to be seen. The air stuck in his throat in little hiccoughs, until he covered his face with his hands and started to cry. "You did a job on this ankle," the satyr said. "You might have broken it." He pulled Derin's hands away and gathered the boy in his arms. Derin did not resist. He buried his face in Matthew's shoulder and sobbed. It had been years since the boy had allowed himself to be held, and Matthew felt the burden of all that time. His throat tightened. "You should have been more careful," he said gruffly. "You've got to take care of yourself."

"They came out of the water," Derin said. "I couldn't stop them. They were all around me."

"They didn't touch you," Matthew said.

"How do you know?" the boy said, wresting himself loose from Matthew's hold. "You weren't even here."

Vera, who had been watching everything, came forward. "Let's take care of his ankle," she said. "We've got to get back to the river."

"Who are you?" Derin asked in amazement. "Where did she come from?"

"Her name is Vera," Matthew said. "She's the reason I left you like that." He turned to the fox. "Can you get some wild sarsaparilla?" he asked.

Vera disappeared among the cedars. "She can turn herself into a nymph," Matthew said when she was gone. He shrugged his shoulders. "I ran after her."

By the time the fox returned, Matthew had told Derin all he knew of their strange companion. He made a poultice of warm water, wild sarsaparilla, and rotting cedar and put it on the boy's ankle, binding it with the cloth he'd used earlier. The boy winced, threw back his head. "So it hurts," the satyr said. "It's a bad sprain. You'll have to stay off it for a while. You're lucky it's not worse."

"Let me help," Vera said. "Just lie still." She sniffed Derin's ankle, took her tail and brushed it four times, rhythmically, over the boy's leg. She sniffed again, brushed her tail four more times, and then licked the ankle. "There," she said. "That should do it. How does it feel?"

"It doesn't," Derin said, amazed. "I don't feel a thing."

"Good," Vera said. "Then it worked. I deadened the pain to let the ankle heal. It's the least I can do." She looked at Matthew. "I led your friend on that wild chase. I thought I'd get the two of you through the swamp more quickly that way." She sighed. "Unfortunately, you can't always tell how things will turn out. Sometimes the best intentions. . . ."

"Well, thank you," Derin said.

"It was nothing. I'm a snow fox. I have the power of healing."

"And the power of transformation," Matthew said.

"Limited," the fox said. "Very limited."

"What about the real nymphs?" Matthew asked. "The ones who used to live in the meadowlands."

Vera smiled at him. "There were no real nymphs," she said.

"You're razzing me," Matthew said, laughing. "No wonder I never caught one. There *were* a lot of foxes, now that I think of it."

"Until the wind destroyed the clan," Vera said. "The wind the owl sent to bring the animals west. Many survived that night. But snow foxes are delicate creatures, sensitive and high-strung. The only ones who lived were those not taken by the wind. Every snow fox in the whirlwind perished. And soon after that the ones who remained left the meadowlands to live in the upper regions of the mountains to the west. I think I'm the last one."

"The last of your clan?" Derin asked.

"Those things most beautiful perish first," Vera said proudly. "There are no unicorns left."

"But how did you know about us?" Matthew asked.

"I knew about the owl," she said simply, "and about the moon. It seemed only a matter of time before someone headed west to try to rescue her. I am wiser than I may appear. Snow foxes — if I might brag for a moment — are not ordinary creatures."

Derin looked at Vera, and she sighed and complied with his silent request. Before him stood the nymph, so radiant she dispelled the green gloom of the swamp. It was as though the sun had reappeared. The boy groaned, amazed. The nymph disappeared and the fox was before them again. "I hope that did some good," she said. "It's a strain on me."

The fox gathered the knapsacks and gave them to the boy. Matthew bent down and Derin hobbled over and climbed on the satyr's back. It grew noticeably darker as they sloshed west, the fox cutting a single sliver in the water's skin, the satyr stumbling behind. "Slow down," he called. "I'm not as inspired as I was before."

Under Derin's hands, the satyr's shoulders rippled like the water below him. He was remembering the brief image of the nymph which had burned into his mind. He was lost in her radiance, in the memory of his fall, the frogs and their silent pulsing throats, aware now of a pull to the west toward the owl; it was as though he'd been hypnotized, and was being drawn more tightly into a net.

As they struggled through the swamp, night came, clamping down around them like the lid of a box. The satyr had to rest occasionally. During one of these stops, he untied the cloth around Derin's ankle and reapplied the poultice. The swelling had gone down, and Derin's foot had regained the color of living flesh, but an ugly bruise spread from the ankle and discolored the boy's instep.

The fox never spoke. She seemed intent on getting out of the swamp. She knew her way, even in the dark, as easily as Derin knew the way to Matthew's granite overhang, and they both agreed her presence was a rare stroke of luck.

Derin was beginning to nod when he heard a noise which brought him fully awake. It was like the roaring of a wind gathering far off. But there was no wind. The air was still and very cold. It was a rumbling undertone of sound, a solid sustained bass which never varied. The noise seemed to be coming from the swamp beneath him, filtering up into the highest branches of the cedars. It had strange gurglings and pauses in it, little sucks and moans.

He bent over and whispered in Matthew's ear, "What's that?"

"If my guess is right, we're near the Swollen River."

"Yes," the fox said. "That's the river. Don't let it worry you. We'll stop along its banks. Wouldn't think of trying to cross it tonight."

The swamp became more shallow, the ice gave way to solid ground, and as they came to a slow rise, the rumbling increased and Derin felt the earth tremble. When they were near the top, the satyr put him down. Derin held his right foot off the ground, stood on his left, and steadied himself by holding onto the satyr's arm.

"Careful now," Vera said. "It will still be tender."

The boy put his foot on the ground and applied some pressure. It held him. "It's not as fine as it seems," Vera reminded him, "but it looks like it's doing all right." And she was gone, up the rise overlooking the river. Matthew helped him hobble up after her. The fox looked out over the turbulence of river. Matthew stood by her side, his arms crossed on his chest.

The immensity of what lay before the boy took his breath away. True, it was difficult to see anything in so little light. The sky was a solid leaden sheet, and under it the river came rushing from his left and passed away to his right. Here, on its brink, the water made unearthly noises. It sounded like a storm coming out of the earth instead of the sky. Perhaps by daylight the boy would see the far shore, but as he stood there, he felt as he had when he'd made a trip with Matthew to the ocean. Its power humbled him. They were to cross this water? It seemed not like water at all, but like a stream of mud. It was thick and slippery, churning below him.

"I don't remember it like this," the satyr said uneasily.

The fox huddled between them in the dark. "The river is much wilder and broader since the owl took the moon. We should get some sleep. I'll gather wood for a fire." She set off down the rise they had recently climbed.

Derin stood close to Matthew. "There's something I have to tell you," he said. The satyr stiffened, ready for the rebukes he thought the boy had been hoarding all afternoon.

"I had the strangest vision back on that hummock," Derin said. Matthew looked at him and frowned. "I was racing after you, but you were so fast and I was falling behind. I got tired of having to run around things, so I tried to vault this cedar. That's when I fell and sprained my ankle. I was lying there and I opened my eyes and the frogs came. They just sat there in the water staring at me, and I started screaming, started talking to keep them away. They belong to the owl, don't they?"

"That's what Vera said."

"I don't remember anything else until you came back. I must have passed out. But I had this vision. I sank deeper and deeper into this hole and then I was a bird and I came flying up, into this clear sky. The sun was there and the moon, and I was the only bird around. I flew and flew. It must have been west because the sun was setting. And then I flew south. And I found this large thing that looked like a prison."

"Who knows what dreams mean?" Matthew said. "Not me. I've had them myself, but they never make sense." The boy stood silent at his side. "That's not much of an answer, is it?" he asked.

"If it's the best you can do," the boy said.

Matthew looked out over the river. "Years ago," he said, "fourteen years ago, I was awakened in the middle of the night and brought to this bank, to the edge of the river, the only other time I've been here. A creature wearing a dark cloak, I couldn't see the face, handed me a blanket. I know it may be hard to believe, but. . . ."

"Me?" Derin asked.

"Yes, of course," the satyr said. "So I brought you back to the meadowlands."

Derin stood, stunned by this information he'd waited so long for. "But where did I come from?" he wanted to know. "Who was the stranger?"

"He could have been your father. He could have been someone else. I don't know. And where he, or you, came from is a mystery to me. I'm sorry I can't tell you anything else."

Derin shivered in the damp air. He looked to his friend for reassurance, but Matthew was lost in thought. "Why didn't you tell me this before?"

The satyr looked at him and then reached out and touched the boy's shoulder. "What good would it have done? He said you'd be sent for. And you have been."

Derin said nothing. Below them, the river bubbled: a cauldron, a tempest. It's happening, Matthew thought, as the stranger said. It's happening, and I can't do a thing to change it.

"You're tired," he said, but the boy wasn't listening to him. He was off somewhere, thinking of the crazy twists his life had taken. "I don't have any more answers for you," the satyr said, almost harshly. "Leave me alone for a minute. Go warm yourself by the fire. And get off that ankle."

"Matthew," Derin said. "I'll be all right. I can take care of myself."

"I think you can," the satyr said. "You'll have to."

The boy limped down the slope. Matthew stood alone, watching the river pass below him. He shook his head in wonder. And how am I changing? he thought.

"Vera darted under him."

WEDNESDAY

The owl called the congregation of ravens for the early hours of the day, past midnight. As the darkness grew in intensity, the owl seemed to bloat. His golden eyes bulged and took on a reddish tinge, as though the beating of his heart had become so frantic that the blood moving through his veins had nowhere to go but into his eyes. He puffed in the clearing, his feathers bristling, until the bulk of his body was overpowering.

In small groups, the ravens arrived. Word had gone out that afternoon that the owl wished to speak with them, and the place and time were transmitted with a flick of wing, a blink of a red eye.

The meeting was held in another clearing, several miles from where the moon hung caged. Deirdre arrived late, but she was not the last. The owl sat dead-center, silent as an idol, and the glossy birds landed on trees and bushes around him, even in the edges of the clearing, all eyes intent upon the horned tyrant.

Deirdre was grateful she'd gotten there at all. When she returned from the swamp, she'd fallen asleep, in plain view, a silly mistake, but one she could do nothing about. She'd been awakened by a rustling in the limbs above her, and when she opened her eyes, she saw a small group of ravens perched there. It was already dark and their eyes shone down at her like live coals.

"Sleeping late," one of them said.

"Yes," she said, "I overslept," although she'd gotten barely six hours of rest.

They flew off, one after another, and when all had abandoned her tree, she flew after them. Now they sat, surrounding the owl, waiting for him to speak.

He was waiting as well, but Deirdre didn't know why. A few ravens straggled in late, and the owl fixed each one with his glassy bulbous stare, as if to question their right to remain alive. Deirdre began to get edgy; the encounter was eerie, like a showdown. When she thought she'd burst, two weasels came slinking through the underbrush and entered the clearing, remaining some distance from the owl. He looked down at them imperiously as they sank to earth, their eyes on him.

"You're late," he said, his voice conveying his displeasure. "You've kept us waiting."

One of the weasels spoke in a quavering voice. "We're sorry, my lord. We received your summons late, and we, as you know, cannot fly."

"I know you can't fly," the owl thundered. His gaze left the cowering weasels and slowly took in the ravens. He thought how they looked like a night sky, those blinking eyes like thousands of red stars. Not a raven moved as he surveyed them. Paranoid, Deirdre thought he stared too long at her, and did her best to appear inconspicuous.

"My friends here have something of interest to say," the owl said, nodding to the weasels.

"We are just poor weasels from the Outer Lands," the second weasel said. "We live on the plain to the east of the mountains."

"They can see what you are, you sniveling fool," the owl said. "Get to the point."

"Yes, my lord," the weasel said, shaking with fright.

"We've seen a raven fly out over the plain where we live, headed for the Swollen River," the second said. "And later we've seen him return."

"So you think it's a 'he'?" the owl asked, interested.

"We don't know for sure," the first weasel replied.

"Go on," the owl ordered.

"Twice in the last two days," the second hastened to add. "Since the moon was stolen."

"What else?" the owl asked.

"There's nothing else to say," the first weasel said. "That's all we know."

The owl was exasperated. "Look around you. Do you see the raven who flew east?"

The weasels were a model of concentration. Deirdre thought they were stalling, but still she tried to shrink into her feathers, to disguise herself. They took forever, looking closely from the clearing to the bushes to the tree limbs. Finally the second one spoke.

"It's no use, my lord. I can't tell the difference between them."

"May your bones rot in darkness," the owl said. "Get out of here." With great haste and equal relief, the weasels slunk from the clearing and disappeared.

"So," the owl said, frowning. "There seems to be a traitor in our midst. I have given strict orders that none of you should leave the Outer Lands. The Swollen River and the meadowlands beyond are alien territory. According to these weasels, someone has disobeyed me. Which one of you was it? I won't deal harshly with you if your explanation is fair and true."

None of the ravens moved for a minute or two, and then all heads began to turn, each bird glancing at his neighbors with suspicion. Deirdre looked right and left as well, trying to appear as unruffled, as critical as her fellows did. Ah, self-righteousness, she thought. Has there ever been such a heavy concentration of it?

She was alarmed by this turn of affairs, but not particularly frightened. She felt she'd done nothing to give herself away. True, she was an outcast of sorts, having no particular companions among the other members of her clan and thus she was vulnerable to suspicion. No other raven would defend her if she were called to account; none could say, "No, my lord, the raven Deirdre is your good and faithful servant. She was with me at the time in question." And since Deirdre could not offer this to any of them, she felt herself alone. But aside from the small group who had caught her sleeping earlier that evening, she was sure there were none who could accuse her.

Out of the darkness behind her and slightly to her right, the voice of a very young raven filtered past.

"My lord," the raven said, his voice shaking badly. "Perhaps it was I."

"Come here," the owl ordered, his voice as heavy as lead.

A flapping emerged from the night, and a small handsome raven flew past Deirdre. He landed some feet from the owl, doing his best to square his wings and face his master.

"What is your name?" the owl asked.

"Maxwell," the raven said bravely. In the deepness of the night, Deirdre thought she could see blue highlights flashing amid his feathers.

"Are your parents here?" the owl asked.

"No, my lord. They both perished in the ice storm of the winter."

"Have you any neighbors or companions who can vouch for you?" the owl said severely.

Maxwell looked behind him for assistance. "There are some I fly with," he said. "Bingor and Tera."

"Are you here?" the owl roared, his voice coming back at him, echoing off the tall dead trees.

There was no reply, only the deepest silence in which Deirdre could feel her blood pulsing in her throat.

The owl looked down at Maxwell, a strange gloat in his eyes. They seemed to have become more red, almost as red as the ravens' eyes. "No one will speak for you," he said. So, Deirdre thought, it has come to this.

"Bingor," the little raven implored, turning to look behind him at the hosts of his people.

"Silence!" the owl ordered. "You flew east?"

"Yes, my lord." The raven had lost his composure. He shivered in the darkness until Deirdre thought the earth picked up his fright and began trembling in empathy.

"Against my orders?"

"No, my lord, I did not disobey you. I was visiting the graves of the ancestors," he said bravely, "the ones who died in the great wind."

The owl's chest swelled. "You crossed the Swollen River?"

"No, my lord. I visited the graves on the Plain of Desiccation, the graves of those who dropped from the wind when it passed over the river. My mother and father often took me there, and since they died. . . ."

"An act of filial devotion, then?"

"Yes, my lord."

"I don't believe you," the owl said harshly. "Why was it never reported to me before?"

"I don't know," Maxwell said. "I didn't know I was doing anything wrong."

"You flew with this Bingor?"

"No, my lord, I went alone. I could find no one who would go with me."

"They were wiser than you, my son," the owl said. He called, and from the darkness behind him, three falcons swooped from the highest branches of a very tall oak. "Take him to the southern forest," the owl said. He paused for effect. None of the ravens knew of this place, except Deirdre. She shuddered on her branch, drawing herself tighter.

"And break his wings," the owl said.

Deirdre cried out in alarm.

"Who was that?" the owl shrieked.

"It was nothing, my lord," Deirdre said. "I have a cramp in my claw."

"Take him away," the owl said. "Take him from my sight."

Deirdre heard a soft noise in the distance, like weeping. Whoever grieved had not grieved enough to speak on Maxwell's behalf, but still Deirdre felt great pity. And she was beside herself with indecision. If she spoke up, if she offered herself in his place, she knew the owl would not spare the young bird. She would be killed, and he would still be banished and mutilated. And she would be abandoning the satyr and the boy.

The falcons bound the raven and took off, each of them holding a rope. They hovered above the clearing, displaying their captive, before heading south.

"Let that be a lesson to all of you," the owl said.

"But my lord, if I may humbly ask a question," a raven said from a branch to Deirdre's right.

"You may ask," the owl said.

"The young one did not cross the Swollen River, if what he said was true."

"But who would speak up for him?" the owl asked. "Not one of you. NOT A SINGLE ONE. You are a cowardly flea-infested lot, and it makes me sick to look at you."

There was total silence. The raven who had spoken did not speak again.

"Now leave me," the owl thundered. "All of you."

As Deirdre rose in the air, it was like the whirlwind which had carried her west. Thousands of ravens surrounded her, and she was buffeted by fierce currents. All was wing and beak and flashing eye. The sky reverberated with harsh breathing and cawing. Ravens collided in the air and fell away from each other, screaming. Feathers torn loose from their wings drifted below them. Bruised and battered, all left the clearing, Deirdre with them. She remembered the night she had been taken by the wind. Her parents lay below her on the ground, broken and bleeding, calling her name.

In the morning's dim light, Derin stood with Matthew and Vera, looking down at the Swollen River. By day, the water was molten rock, not mud. Blue-grey, like the hottest part of a fire, it laughed at them. A few boulders jutted from the water, their sleek black backs like seals. Around the rocks, the river churned, flinging spray high into the air. There were no islands, no sandbars, nothing but the deep channel.

Derin walked down the rise. His ankle was completely healed, good as it had ever been; even the bruise had disappeared. He knelt by the river's side and put a hand in the water. It felt like swiftly flowing ice. Down the bank, cedars gave way to tall firs which crowded to the river's edge. Across from him, Derin could make out the thin line of the opposite shore, marked by a rise of trees.

He climbed the bank again and pointed to what he'd seen.

"It's swamp at first," Vera said, "just like this side. But it's much more narrow. We'll have some wading to do when we get across. From here on there's nothing like the meadowlands again. You're in for a geography lesson."

"You said there were mountains," Derin said.

"That's right," the fox said. "That's where I live. They're at least two days away. After the swamp, we'll get to the Plain of Desiccation. Dry, dusty, hot and nasty. Not much lives there. I've seen a few weasels, and scorpions of course. Wild boars. They're all in league with the owl, so we'll have to be careful. And there are other pitfalls. Like getting lost in the sand. Just one hill after the next, nothing to even give you the sense you're moving."

"Sounds like fun," Matthew said. "I can't wait."

"After that, we'll get to the mountains, a more hospitable terrain, I promise. And I know them backwards and forwards. They're beautiful, but of course I'm prejudiced."

"And then?" Derin asked.

"Then you're on your own," Vera said. "I'll take you as far as the mountains, but I won't go into the Forest."

"The Deadwood Forest," Matthew said.

"That's right," the fox said. "A vast tangle of dead trees and bushes, the most desolate place you could imagine. Nothing grows there. It used to be full of oaks and maples, before the owl came to power. I wouldn't go near it."

"We'd better get started," Matthew said. "It's going to take time to build the raft." Long into the night, they had talked about how to cross the river, and Matthew had convinced them his was the best solution. They would need logs, and vines to lash the logs together, and a bit of luck.

The three of them left the overlook and descended to where they'd slept. The only logs they'd found were fallen cedars, big around as Matthew's armspan, heavier than he and the boy could even lift. "The firs will be better," Matthew said, rummaging in his pack for the ax head. "They'll float higher on the water. Derin, go south along the bank and look for vines we can use. They should be old and weathered, nothing too young or they'll snap. I'll find a handle for this and get to work on the logs." Derin stood and watched as Matthew honed the ax head with a whetstone, found a piece of cedar to use as a handle, and bound the head to it with rawhide. "Go on," Matthew said. "Get going."

Derin walked along the rise, the river on his left rushing much faster than he was walking. Firs rose around him. He looked for vines which matched Matthew's instructions, but there were none, nothing but the straight druidical presence of the trees, their needled branches drooping toward the ground. The light under the firs was like the swamp's, a mottled green.

As Derin walked, he peered across at the other side, trying to imagine it. From Vera's description, it was unlike anything he'd even dreamed about, a harsh and forbidding landscape over which the owl brooded like a malevolent cloud. Crossing the river seemed impossible. He thought of the three of them, huddled together on their flimsy raft, buffeted by those waves which even now rose and fell like the foaming backs of stallions, flinging spray sky-high. Behind him, he heard the first crack of a tree. The satyr's voice rang out, and then Derin listened to the slow crunch as it fell, breaking the branches of other firs, the slam it made as it hit the ground.

He shaded his eyes with his hands. There, above him, he saw what looked like a tangle of vines. It festooned the upper branches, hanging down toward him, taunting.

Derin shrugged and rubbed his hands together. He took a few steps back, approached the fir, and jumped. He wrapped his arms and legs around the trunk and inched his way up, raising his knees, hugging the fir, and grabbing above him with his arms. The rough bark scratched his legs, but he kept climbing until finally he could reach up and hold onto a branch. His legs let go, and he hung there by both arms. The branch creaked, bending downward, but it held. Kicking against the trunk to gain some leverage, he managed to swing a leg over the branch, and wrestled into a sitting position.

He stared upwards, breathing harshly. The vines still hung above him, up where the fir broke open and gave way to the sky. When he'd rested, he crouched on the branch, close to the trunk, holding on to other branches above him for balance. He climbed quickly, the fir providing an awkward ladder. Matthew would have to be satisfied with these. He wasn't going to climb another tree.

The closer he got to the vines, the odder they looked to him. They were smooth and shiny, grey and black. He was five feet from them when he realized they weren't vines at all. The entire tangle began to writhe above him, and the snakes' tapered heads appeared, waving in the air, their eyes red pinpricks of light. Derin pulled away, crouching on the branch he'd been straining to leave. He grabbed it with both hands and swung free, reaching with his toe for a safe hold below him. He found the branch, let go and tottered, lost his balance. He crashed against the trunk and fell, but he managed to grab a branch, and he hung there, almost wrenching his shoulders from their sockets when the tree ceased to give.

He looked above him. The snakes had made no move toward him, and he hurriedly let himself down from branch to branch, until he hung from the lowest one and let himself fall. He sprang to his feet, ready to run. Above him, the snakes were motionless, their heads hidden, looking again like a tangle of vine.

He caught his breath; for him, the owl was everywhere. Perhaps the snakes had not been threatening at all, simply a nest of tree vipers disturbed by his ascent. But he wasn't about to climb again to find out. The menace in their twisting heads had not been imagined, and whether they belonged to the owl or simply to themselves, they meant him only ill. He made his way back up the riverbank toward the place where the heave of Matthew's ax was again audible.

The river leapt to challenge him, and his face was wet with salt spray. "We're crossing you," he said. At his feet, the ground rustled. Sand grains and tiny stones rose from the earth and bounced off his legs. The river continued in its deep channel from north to south, ignoring his threat.

The ax fell through the air and bit deeply into the fallen fir. Matthew wrenched it loose, swung it back over his head, and down again. A wedge of wood bigger than the boy's foot jumped from the v-shaped cut. Derin scraped resin into the earthenware pot, added some water, and put it over the flames. The amber resin bubbled and boiled down into a darkened syrup. Off the fire, it thickened still more.

Together, the two carried the logs Matthew had cut until there were seven of them side by side near the riverbank in a small declivity level with the water. Vera watched as Matthew lashed the logs together with the leathery vines she had found lying on the ground while Derin was off on his own search to the south. "I didn't have to climb a tree," she said. "They were waiting for me." "Lucky for you," Derin said. The satyr wound the vines until the logs were as tight as he could make them, and then Derin caulked the spaces between them with the resiny tar.

At last, the tar hardened and, when Matthew splashed water between the logs, it stayed in glistening pools.

"Looks watertight to me," Vera said. "Let's go."

Matthew looked out over the river, and shrugged. "It's the best we can do," he said. He gathered together the belongings he'd flung from the pack, dismantled his makeshift ax and placed the head back in its sheath.

The river was even rougher than it had been that morning. As the day moved toward its zenith, the water rose in higher and higher waves which crested and broke as the river swept from north to south. "It's a tidal river," Vera said, "salty as the sea. It cuts across this whole land connecting the ocean's halves. But there aren't any tides since the moon's been gone. Why is it so rough?"

They maneuvered the heavy raft until a corner of it dipped into the water. The river met the obstacle and flew apart into spume, drenching the three. Matthew and the boy shouldered their packs, and the satyr told Derin and Vera to board the raft and stay together in the center. When they were ready, he heaved at it. It budged an inch and stuck fast.

"It's digging into the bank," Matthew yelled, trying to make himself heard above the river's noise. "Get off there. Help me push."

Even with the three of them, it was difficult. The harder they shoved, the deeper the firs sank in the mud at the river's edge. "We'll have to pick it up," Derin screamed.

"Be careful of your backs," Vera said.

Derin and Matthew braced themselves and pulled upwards on the raft. The mud didn't want to let go. "At least it's holding together," Matthew said.

"What?" Derin yelled, cupping a hand behind his ear. The satyr shook his head and waved a hand.

They pulled again, and the bank began to relinquish its grasp. From where Derin stood, he could hear the pops and sucks as the logs ripped loose from the mud. Suddenly, Derin felt the resistance lessen, and with an enormous slap, the raft came free and Matthew and the boy fell forward as the water tugged at the raft's corner, pulling it into the current. "Quick!" Matthew screamed. "We'll lose it." Derin was on his knees in the mud, the raft several feet in front of him, gaining ground. "Jump," Matthew said. "Both of you."

In a graceful arc, Vera leapt to the raft and hunkered down in the middle. Derin scrambled to his feet, thrashed through the water and threw himself onto the closest logs. His legs scissored, he pulled, and he crawled to the middle and turned to look back at Matthew.

With a groan which seemed to come from the timber's interior, the raft gave up its hold on the land. For a moment, Derin didn't know what was happening. He and Vera lay flat, trying to balance the logs, but they tipped landward in a precarious slant. Matthew clung to the far corner, his legs in the water, trying to climb the slippery logs to where the others were. Derin crawled away from the satyr to equalize the weight, and hung with his hands to the edge jutting over the water. "Grab my leg," he screamed and he felt his body being stretched as the satyr pulled himself toward the raft's center.

Spray flashed above them, drenching them with brine. The raft took off like a frightened animal. It reared and plunged, rising to the crest of a wave and plummeting to the trough beneath. Derin hung on; he grabbed the ropes which bound the raft together, wedged one foot under some vines at the other end. "Don't do that!" Matthew screamed. "If this thing turns over, you won't get loose." The boy jerked his leg free and began to slide. As the raft pitched forward, covered with icy water, there was little to hold him.

For the boy, the ride was exhilarating. The wild torrent required every ounce of his energy, and his concentration was taxed to the fullest. He felt equal to the river's demands as the raft was tossed into the air and thudded down again on the back of a cresting wave.

The boy looked behind him. Vera lay splayed on the logs, her eyes glazed. Her white fur was saturated with river water. The satyr had assumed the same position; all three of them clung to the raft, trying to burrow into the crevices between the logs as the land sped by in a dizzying rush. The river took the raft, spinning it so Derin alternately saw the water rushing at him and before him. He had lost all sense of direction.

They were enveloped in mist, the land dropped away, and the exhilaration the boy had felt changed to fear. He was swirling in a vortex whose only coordinates were noise and cold. Waves towered above them and crashed, trying to wrench them free. The roaring in his ears grew so loud he could no longer hear his own screams. A cold and brutal wind howled around him, attempting to rip the shirt from his back.

When the edge of the raft hit the rock, the log which took the blow splintered. For a moment, the whole raft stood almost on end, and then fell back with a mighty crash, sending a wall of water upstream. It met the oncoming waves, and the two waters thundered into the sky and splashed down, inundating the raft. Derin saw the splintered log tossed skyward where the wind hit and threw it like a matchstick. Something slapped his leg; he saw a vine unraveling, whipping through the air.

"Matthew!" he screamed. Matthew looked at him oddly, but the expression in his eyes was frozen there, as if he stared into a dead face. Then the boy noticed how far away Matthew was, and what he had feared had already happened. Matthew clung to a few logs which pitched forward, upended, and disappeared. He thought he heard a scream, but he couldn't tell if it was a voice or the commotion of the river. He looked behind him, but Vera was gone as well. Was that a paw he saw sticking from the water? It could be foam, or a skinned stick. It could be anything.

And then the small solidity beneath him disappeared. The logs tore apart, the vine washed away, and the pitch ripped from end to end. Derin was flung into the air like so much flotsam, his pack lopsided on his back, unbalancing him, and he fell ten feet from the crest of a wave into the valley of water which lay beneath him, beckoning with its furious icy arms.

Matthew clambered to shore, bone-tired, nearly frozen, his brain dulled by the cold. Twice he had been thrown by the water toward submerged rocks, but he had lunged to safety. Blindly, he let himself be taken by the current until he had a clear sense of its direction, and then he struck out toward the shore they had set off from not much earlier.

His pack felt unnaturally heavy on his back. He threw himself on the bank, panting, and attempted to calm himself, but waves of hysteria rose in him, threatening to engulf him as the river had the raft. Shaking, he stood up, shaded his eyes with his hand, and looked out over the turbulent water. He saw the rocks, the rearing waves, but not a trace of his friends. He stopped himself from yelling their names, knowing it would only be wasted breath.

How far downstream had he been taken? Here, too, firs rose from the riverbank so it seemed to the satyr he'd never left the land. But he knew he'd been swept further south. Still wobbly, he took off downriver. Maybe Vera and Derin had been washed ashore as well. He tried to be hopeful, but there was no reason for hope. Matthew knew how cold the water was, how it robbed him of breath, paralyzed his hands and feet. The river had two levels. A deadly calm, a slow suck downward, like gravity, lay under the furious rushing surface. In that lower stratum a body had no buoyancy, little hope of escape. The boy might be held in that calm now, or else he'd been dashed on the rocks. And where was Vera? Was her magic not enough in the face of this raging river?

He began to walk more slowly, as these thoughts sapped what little energy he had left. Across from him, the opposite shore appeared and disappeared through the mists the river flung into the air. Matthew stopped, shaded his eyes again, and looked. In the middle of the water, he thought he saw Derin's body rise and fall with the waves. Was it really the boy or only a log, a floating branch? He thought again of the temperature of the water, and realized that if it were Derin's body, it would be dead.

He stopped walking, he stopped looking, he stood on the riverbank, barely breathing. He knelt on the bank, raked his hands through the gravelly mud. Without thinking of the dirt, without thinking of anything but the boy, he put his face in his palms and howled.

Derin was taken by the water as though he were a leaf. He fought to the surface for air against the long tendrils of river wrapping themselves around his legs, pulling him under. The tendrils snaked after him, never let him go. He tumbled in the trough, a shell, a tiny pebble.

His body no longer felt the water's coldness. He felt no pain at all. As he relaxed, he felt a deep peace envelop him. He ceased fighting, let himself be taken by the current, and he drifted, weightless, just conscious enough to see the strange rock swim toward him. The water blurred his vision, but he made out the rock's elongated shape, tapering away at the end, covered with white weeds at the other. As it approached, the boy saw it wasn't a rock at all. Her hair streamed in the water, fanning out behind her, over her shoulders, and he followed the sleek curve of her body until, at the hips, she became a fish, covered with grey scales, honing down to the final finned flare as she dissolved into water.

Vera darted under him, her long arms stroking in front of her, and he tightened his legs around her as she swam between them. He felt her scales under his thighs. He reached down, held her shoulders with both hands, and she surged toward the surface.

The dark skin of water grew closer and broke around his head in a crown of spray. Together, they left the surface of river and rose into the air. Vera arched her back, and using her hands to scatter the surface, dove again into the river. Derin caught a glimpse of spray, of the shore toward which they headed, and he gasped, coughing deeply, before the silver-grey water closed around him. Again Vera broke the surface, allowing Derin time to breathe, and together they swam toward land.

The rush of wind and water on his face drew him awake. Under him, the nymph rolled and twisted around snags, rocks, dangerous stretches of current. He tightened his thighs, locked his ankles as she bucked beneath him. The water flashed from his back as though it could no longer harm him.

In the air, into the water they rocked. Tall firs loomed from the muddy banks, the sky hung low over the river. When they reached water shallow enough for Derin to stand in, Vera rolled, throwing the boy on his side. For a moment, Derin floundered, but then his foot hit bottom. Splashing, coughing, he staggered the few remaining feet to shore and fell on his knees in the mud. Behind him, he heard a rasp coarse as rock ground against sand, and when he turned he saw the fox drag herself from the water, gasping. She came and lay beside him, looked at him once with her large grey eyes before she closed them, and the boy reached out and ran his hand the length of her soiled sodden fur, in wonder, in disappointment. When Matthew found him, Derin was alone. The fox, after resting, had left him on the bank, but Derin was not thinking of the solid ground beneath him. He stared at the river's roiling surface, remembering the leaps from the water, the wild bucking of the nymph under him, the touch of her smooth scales against his skin. He was in an undiscovered country, trying to follow the course of a map which had not yet been drawn.

Vera battled her way upriver in search of fish. The water pulled at her, surging over her body as if she were a stone or a log blocking its natural course. She was exhausted. Her arms ached with the strain of swimming and her hips were bruised from carrying Derin to land. Her hair swirled in the currents, now hazing her sight, now swept backwards off her shoulders so she felt the rush of water fresh on her face. At times her struggle seemed useless, as though she were being inexorably swept downstream against all her best efforts. But she kept swimming, flexing her sinuous tail, flicking the great caudal fin in the icy water.

It was a crazy idea, but it just might work. They would take some convincing, for fish were stubborn and proud, inclined to silence, but they would not be frightened of the owl. Vera doubted they even knew of him. In the Deadwood Forest there was no water, and fish were the only animals who had no place in the owl's plans.

Ahead of her, in the shallows of a spot where the river bent and left in its wake a small pool of less turbulent water, she saw the torpedolike shapes of fish. They hung in the pool as if suspended by strings, barely moving their fins. Under them, on the sand of the river's bottom, were hundreds of shellfish, lobsters in their mottled green armor, the fluted shells of scallops, a colony of mussels, shiny and blue-black, studded with limpets and barnacles, attached to one another by golden byssus threads. They were silent under the dark canopy of swordfish and blues, sea bass, halibut, the square slatelike tail-whipped forms of skate.

Vera hurried toward them, wanting the quiet of their undisturbed water. If I can rest for a minute, she thought, I'll be fine again. But the sight of this strange half-fish swimming toward them threw the fish into confusion. They panicked. Swordfish swept to the water's surface and leapt, arching, flinging spray toward the clouds, slapping the water with their tails as they fell. Other fish swam upstream, fighting the current. The shellfish scattered across the bottom, mussels and scallops clattering like waterlogged castanets. The calm Vera had expected turned into a turbulent series of cross-currents, a slap in the face.

She called to them, worried she'd lost them all. She gasped for breath; her words were bubbles of sound only she could hear, for the fish were too far away, frantically trying to escape her.

She darted upstream but she couldn't catch them. This river was their home, and they were built for swimming, their sleek long forms adapted perfectly to the water. Vera let her arms drop, and felt the water take her. She twisted until she was headed downstream, then floated in the current, resting. When she was close to the shallows where the fish had been, she came alive again and swam there, letting herself sink almost to the bottom. She couldn't remember ever having been so tired.

Vera closed her eyes and opened them only after she felt the water push against her, crowding her. On the sand below, the shellfish had gathered, the lobsters' claws waving up at her like ominous underwater plants. She could see the scallops' twin rows of tiny blue eyes watching as they barely opened their shells. Above her, the bluefish and sword-fish, halibut and skate had returned, and for a minute she was the one who was frightened, surrounded. They stared at her, their cold round eyes unnervingly lidless. What were they thinking? The lobsters peered up from under their horned ridge of chiton, antennae quivering in the slightly moving water.

"I didn't mean to frighten you before," Vera said. "I'm sorry."

The fish said nothing. Streams of bubbles filtered from their mouths as they waited for her to speak again.

"I'm a sea nymph," Vera explained, and suddenly felt ridiculous, riding this water, trapped between skate and lobster. "Listen," she said. "I've come to help. I know why the river's so wild, why the current is stronger and the water colder."

She remembered seeing great schools of fish lying on the bottom of a pond, irradiated by the full moon's glow upon the water's skin, their scales shining like silver. She had seen fish surge to the surface and break through, throwing themselves toward the moon, splashing the silver drops of water into the air in homage, desperate longing. "The moon's been wrenched from the sky," she said. "Stolen. She's held captive on land, miles to the west."

A bluefish with cold dead eyes interrupted her. "In this river there are no directions but upstream and down."

"There are creatures whose lives are not so simple," she said. "A great horned owl who lives in a place called the Deadwood Forest has kidnapped the moon. Without her, the world's gone crazy. There aren't any tides. The river is running wild."

"You can say that again," a swordfish said. "It's worth your life to get caught in the current these days."

"I need your help," Vera said. "Or you'll never again have the moon's gold shadow cast upon this water. I have no idea what will happen to the river if she isn't rescued."

She was sure of it. A startled, frightened look shone from the fishes' eyes. They eddied in the water, looking at one another. Their tails twitched. Under them, all the scallops and mussels snapped open and shut. Vera saw a school of shrimp, translucent, almost impossible to find in the dimness, their pairs of legs jerking spastically.

The water around her began to churn and Vera was afraid they would all burst loose again, flying in different directions, upstream and down, the only life they knew.

"Please," she said. "Come with me. Help me."

The water calmed again, and Vera felt the force of all those eyes upon her, but now they were not so indifferent or cold. They pleaded with her in return, as she had pleaded with them.

"What would you have us do?" a swordfish asked.

"I have two friends who do not swim," Vera began.

"We have no friends who do not swim," the swordfish said, his eyes wild with confusion and distrust.

"Listen to me," Vera said, losing patience. "We're going to rescue the moon. There isn't time for quibbling."

"Why don't you swim them across?" a skate asked.

"Because the water's too cold," Vera said. "They'd freeze. They're warm-blooded creatures."

"And why don't you find someone else?"

"There is no one else," she said firmly.

* * *

As they stood on the bank looking out, the surface of water was troubled, a further turbulence not caused by the water roiling around rocks or submerged logs. To Derin, it looked as if the river's bottom had risen to the top. Fish began to surface, the glistening backs of dolphins, swordfish, the hard white shells of surf clams like stepping-stones. Holding parallel to the current, their sleek scaled and armored bodies shimmering in the grey light, they seemed like a rainbow rising from the water. Octopi wrapped their slithery suction-cupped tentacles around bluefish and halibut to keep them steady. Sponges the color of dried blood wedged between lobster and shark. Some of the fish brought seaweed in their mouths to use as anchors, to fasten them together. Derin watched in wonder as more and more creatures joined the rainbow, scallops and mussels mooring themselves to the sponges and eelgrass, spinning a web of byssus threads, barnacles anchoring themselves to mussels until a solid passage of fish appeared where there had been nothing but water.

The river splashed over the bridge, spume was thrown high in the air, but the fish held against the river's tug. "Are you ready?" Vera asked.

Without waiting for an answer, she waded into the water and deftly leapt up onto the backs of the fish. She slithered from cod to bluefish and they rolled their large round eyes upwards as if to wish her well. Under her, the bridge rocked and swayed as the current ripped at it. She was drenched by the flying spray which hit the fishes' tails and swirled above her.

Derin watched the fox, mesmerized, until Matthew gave him a shove, almost knocking him headfirst into the river. "Hurry!" Matthew said. "They can't hold forever."

The boy thrashed through the few feet of water to where the bridge began. He put his hands on the back of a shark, its skin rough as sandpaper, and lifted a foot out of the water. Balancing precariously, he stood, almost fell, crouched, and steadied himself. Beneath him, the bridge gave way a little, flexible, sinking into the water. He took a step and the fish held, another step, and another.

The river was as cold as he remembered. Ice formed in his hair and crusted his eyelashes. He twisted to look and saw Matthew clambering up on the first fish. "Just keep going," Matthew screamed. "Don't look back."

The fish were slippery, as though covered with slime, and his feet slid across their scaled surfaces. Ahead of him, he could dimly see the fox padding carefully across, shrouded by mist, and he tried to keep her in view. Below him, the surface of the bridge kept changing. He stepped from the soft bodies of fish to the harder rocklike shells of surf clams. Once he stepped on a skate and felt himself falling as its thin body refused to hold his weight, but he jumped to the back of a dolphin and continued.

Refusing to follow Matthew's command, he looked behind him to see where the satyr was. His hooves were giving him trouble. They hurt the fish who writhed under the sharp wedged horn. Matthew saw the boy watching him, and tried to scream something, but Derin couldn't hear him. He could barely see the satyr's arms flailing in the air. The only sound he heard was the roaring of the river. It came from upstream, sweeping down upon him, borne on the back of the wind. Water sucked and nibbled at his feet, whitecaps slapped over the backs of the fish before him, obscuring them in a wash of water. He couldn't see where he was stepping.

Suddenly he realized he had lost sight of Vera through the flying spray, and when he turned, Matthew, too, was obscured. Below him, the bridge buckled, nothing but a loose confederation of slippery fish. He saw the tentacle of an octopus writhe in the air and he thought of the vines coming loose, the raft disintegrating, being thrown into the air and falling. The fish seemed to be moving under him, and the waves, lashing his ankles, rocked him as he stumbled forward.

A wild fear seized him. He began to run, lunging ahead, wanting only the steadiness of ground beneath his feet. Out of the mist, he saw the opposite shore loom. Vera was safely there, looking back at him, anxiously awaiting his emergence from the river's fog.

Underneath him, the fish cringed at his heavy tread, and then began to fall away. He was scrambling, hardly able to hear his own screaming. He was about twenty feet from shore when the bridge disappeared altogether, and he was thrown into the water. It filled his ears, entered his mouth. The river slapped him down, under, but he struggled to the surface, his legs scissoring at the hip, his arms reaching out in broad strokes, not so much like swimming as like reaching for a lifeline. He saw the land in front of him begin to move; he was being swept downstream.

Vera ran up and down the bank yelling, but he couldn't make out the words. "Up!" she seemed to be screaming, and then he heard. "Stand up! Stand up!" He stopped swimming, bent at the hips, and his feet touched bottom. Under him was a thick ooze, but it was firmer than water, and though the ooze tried to swallow his feet, he pulled them loose and the water sunk beneath him, now at his chest, his waist, his knees.

He looked behind him for Matthew, and then he realized that as he'd run and scattered the fishes, he'd left nothing for Matthew to cross on. "No!" he screamed. "Matthew!" He stumbled upstream to where Vera was standing, looking out over the water.

There was the satyr, struggling against the raging river. He was holding his own against the current; it was not sweeping him away, but he was making no progress toward shore. He looked like a horse bucking a floodtide. He reared from the water, and then disappeared into a trough as a hand of wave came down upon him.

Wildly the boy looked around. Near the base of a fir near the water's edge, a vine hung. He ran to the tree, grasped its thick leathery bark in his hands. Above him, the branches swayed but refused to give up their hold on the vine. He jumped into the air, grabbing it, putting all his weight on the vine, and it began to slip. He hung there for a minute, and it ripped loose, throwing him on the ground, the vine rattling loose and falling over him.

He threw his sodden pack from his shoulders and staggered into the water. It churned around his knees, his waist. "Matthew!" he yelled, and this time when the satyr reared above the waves, he saw the boy.

Derin had wandered out so far the waves lapped at his elbow. He whirled the vine around his head and threw it toward the satyr. It fell short, was taken downriver. Hurriedly he hauled it in. This time, the boy threw upstream and the vine floated past Matthew as he grabbed out for it. The third time the throw was good. Whipped by the water, the vine raged into Matthew's outstretched hands and the boy flung himself backwards, holding on with all his strength. He almost lost his footing and went down, but moving slowly, he felt the water recede.

The satyr stopped struggling against the current as soon as he gripped the vine, so the river took him, playing with him like so much debris. Water crashed over his head. The boy finally reached the shore and began to pull him in.

Matthew was the biggest fish he had ever tried to land. Arm over arm, he grasped at the vine. His biceps ached, his breath came in short gasps, and just when he thought he could hold no longer against this weight, this river, this task, he saw Matthew touch bottom, unsteady as a tree limb in a storm, and plunge ashore.

The satyr collapsed on the bank and slowly rolled over onto his back. His chest heaved as he tried to fill his lungs with air. He pushed himself up on an elbow and retched, salt water spilling from him. Derin knelt beside him, pushed the satyr's muddy hair back from his forehead where the blood streaked his nose and cheek.

It was a superficial cut, but it bled crazily. Matthew lay back and pressed the heel of his hand against it to staunch the blood. He stared above him at the grey sky, the tops of the firs shaking in the wind.

"A lovely swim," he gasped. "But it's good to be ashore."

"Matthew," Derin said.

"I was hoping for a minute you'd save me," he said to Vera, who crouched on his other side. "I've always wanted to ride a nymph."

"Maybe some other time," the fox said, smiling.

"I'll look forward to it," Matthew said, and closed his eyes. "Derin has all the luck."

There was no longer any doubt about it, the sun thought. Something had happened to her sister. Another day had passed, and the clouds below her were, if anything, darker, more dense. Yesterday, as she'd traveled west, she kept looking for a break in the grey blanket beneath her, but not once did she get a glimpse of earth. It was time to take this matter upon herself.

The sun did not like to travel. She had a regular course, and the slow curve of her motion over the earth, fixed and familiar, pleased her. She disliked disruption in her routine, but she saw no way around this. If her fool sister had gone on another of her journeys and had gotten in trouble, the sun would have to be the one to rescue her.

So it was with a good deal of disgruntlement that she left her orbit and went to look for the moon. She knew the value of her light to the earth, that her trip would have to be quick.

Under the cloud cover, the earth turned dark. It was just past midday, but night descended like the blade of a hunting knife. Derin, Matthew, and Vera stood up in alarm. They huddled together, waiting for the world to end, sure their journey had come too late. In the Deadwood Forest, the moon hung caged in her oak and she cried out as the blackness settled over the trees. Around her for miles, she heard the ravens awaken from their daytime sleep and take to the sky. The noise of wings, of hoarse cawing tore at her. The owl, alone in a clearing to the moon's north, puffed his feathers in wonder. Had his plan come to fruition so quickly, days sooner than he had planned? The world was his! He gave a cry, a high shriek, which rang throughout the Forest.

And Deirdre, where was she? As the false night settled, she awoke with the other ravens, but as they went screaming into the sky, she stayed on her branch, folding her wings around her more tightly. It's only a nightmare, she thought. The sun does not disappear in the middle of the day. And she closed her eyes and tried to sleep again, but the ravens wheeling in the air above her, the shriek of the owl which curdled the air, deeply disturbed her.

So the world waited, breathless, while the sun disappeared. From the meadowlands, where the jay flew in circles screaming, "Hobnail! Milquetoast! Pigeonfeathers!" to the southern reaches of the Deadwood Forest where Maxwell, his wings broken, sat on a branch, terrified of the starfish who lunged through the blackness below him, everything was plunged into premature and unexpected darkness.

The sun's journey lasted only a short while. She soared above the earth until it was a darkened ball floating free in space. Ahead of her, the lights of other suns glowed and shimmered. She flew among them, looking everywhere for the moon, past great balls of molten lava, spinning frantically, trying to hold their centers. She saw other planets with moons and suns, they as barren as her planet had been years ago. Some moons were full and bright and others were odd shapes, lopsided ellipses, irregular blobs of light. And here and there, she saw the moons from which her sister had taken the vain idea of changing shape. She looked in the galaxies of fire and air, she hunted the confederations of stars and moons, but no matter where she looked, no matter who she asked, her sister was nowhere to be found, had not been seen.

The further the sun flew from earth, the more anxious she became, and the more convinced that somehow — but how? — her sister was not out here in the vast reaches of space, but under that cover of cloud, on the surface of the earth itself. And that was the one place the sun could not go. It would be dangerous enough to the earth if her sister were there.

She swung full circle and headed back. From around her, a brilliant nimbus shone. She illumined the bottom of black holes. She cowed the other suns and moons, still unsure of themselves and their power. And with the speed of light, she hurtled back to earth.

As she came closer, slowed down, jolted back into her orbit, the earth below the layer of clouds brightened. The terrified moon gave a sigh of relief. The ravens settled back to an uneasy sleep. And the owl rained curses around him. He cursed the moon and her sister; he cursed the fact that his plan had not yet reached a conclusion. For a moment, he had been ruler of the world. The darkness at midday had thrilled him with a sense of his strength. He swelled in the darkness: power, lust, pleasure were his. But the light had returned. He would have to wait.

Below her, the sun saw the clouds seethe. They were impenetrable. Are you there, little sister? she thought. Is it there you have come to rest? The moon felt a strange tugging at her heart, as though someone were speaking to her, but around her, the forest was silent as it had ever been. She was alone, she was bereft, but in the midst of her despair, she felt a slight warmth, a tinge of hope.

The three were resting when an eerie stillness crept upon them from the east. The river calmed as though pressed by a large and powerful hand; it swept past them more quickly, the current dizzying in its velocity, its surface no longer tongued by white water. It deepened past green to black, sucking all sound from the air. The wind died, the roaring of the river became a whisper, until they heard nothing but their own breathing and the solemn creak of firs and cedars shifting uncomfortably in the unearthly hush. They moved back from the river as darkness fell, seeking the harsh solidity of the trees' shelter.

"Night comes early in these parts," Matthew said. Derin laughed nervously and pressed his back against the trunk of a fir. The air was grainy, as though it had taken on the density of night, its muted weight. In that silence, each of them thought of the owl and the power of darkness. Derin looked up, expecting to see a vast black wingspread descend to them, talons tensed.

He felt a surge of fear, and on his wrist a blue vein pulsed. He closed his eyes and tried to calm the racing of his heart. Vera crouched low between the two of them, her ears flattened against her head. She growled deep in her throat and her tail bristled. Her breathing, like Matthew's, was quick and shallow. As the darkness had come, so the day returned to them, moving from the east. First the wind's sighing resumed in the upper branches of the trees, and waves reared upon the river's surface. And then the grey light surrounded them, casting ashes on their faces.

"What was it?" Derin asked.

"I don't know," Matthew said. "I've never seen anything like it." They looked at Vera, half-expecting her to understand what had happened, but she shrugged and stared at the sky. "I thought we'd come to the end," she said. "I never expected to be grateful for this thin light. It only goes to show how little time is left. We should push on."

As Vera had said, there was swamp on this side too. It stretched before them as they picked up their packs and headed west. Ice and water, moss-covered hillocks, the grooved trunks of cedars passed around them as in a dream. Derin had the feeling they'd gotten nowhere, but the river's thunder receded until its sound disappeared into the icy water. The fox, who was leading, turned, and Derin almost tripped over her. "It won't be long," she reassured them. "Don't worry."

Matthew whistled strange fragmentary pieces of a song Derin hadn't heard before. A few notes rose into the air and hung stranded, waiting for others which never came. He seemed preoccupied, half-dazed, and the boy wondered if the wound on the satyr's forehead were more serious than it looked. Derin kept up with the fox, who wasted no time threading a passage through the water, but the satyr lagged behind. He dragged his hooves, splashing water before him, and the constant noise began to wear on the boy's nerves.

He stopped and faced the satyr, waiting for him to catch up. "Are you all right, Matthew?" he asked, but Matthew didn't answer, splashed right past him, whistling.

Derin took two quick steps, caught the satyr by the shoulder, and spun him around. "I asked if you're all right," he said. Matthew shrugged free. "I'm fine," he said. "Just thinking."

Derin let him walk second, and he followed through the swamp, watching the rhythmic swing of the satyr's shoulders, listening to the occasional haunting notes without form or pattern. As he pulled his feet free of the mud, little whirlpools rushed to fill the emptiness. He thought of the day before, the declivity of silence he'd lain in. He glanced over his shoulder, suddenly afraid they were being followed, but he could see only the stately monotonous recession of cedars.

He heard the fox call back to him and Matthew, telling them they were almost out of the swamp, and he began to notice the change. The water lapped below his knees, the mud had given way to something more solid, and ahead, dimly, the boy could see the air brighten. It was like coming to the end of a long evening. In the swamp the light was stolen by the cedars and water, but where the water ended, the grey light they'd become accustomed to resumed.

Derin was beginning to breathe more easily, anxious to escape the walled-in closeness of the swamp, when he saw the eyes. They peered at him from a thicket of pepperbush some distance to the left. He grunted, as though he'd been struck in the stomach, and stopped short. They disappeared. He stood where he was, scarcely breathing, his arms arrested in midswing, and stared at the thicket, sure he'd imagined them. But they blinked at him once more, what seemed to him hundreds of gleaming eyes, red as coral, as amanitas, and then he heard a soft swishing, water rippling, as the frogs swam away.

He yelled to Vera and Matthew, now climbing the steady slope out of the swamp, and began to run, thrashing through the water, drenching himself again.

He fled from the water, past the two who stood waiting, and Matthew reached out and grabbed him, almost wrenching him off the ground.

"Wait," the satyr said. "Hold on."

"They're back there," Derin gasped, his eyes wide. "Let go of me." He pulled his arm loose, but the look on the satyr's face kept him from running again.

"What did you see?" Matthew asked.

"The frogs. There were hundreds of them. Let's get out of here."

"Calm down," Matthew said. "Your mind's playing tricks on you."

"I'm not so sure," Vera said. "We're in the Outer Lands, remember. I expect we'll be reported. You didn't think we'd sneak up on the owl without his knowing, did you?"

"I didn't know what to expect," Matthew said.

"You saw hundreds of frogs?" Vera asked. "What did they do?"

"They were in a bush. I saw their eyes."

"They didn't follow you?"

"No," Derin said, calmer. "They swam off. To the south."

"There's nothing to do but keep going," the fox said. "We'll have to be careful."

The land beyond the swamp was low and marshy. Cattails, reeds, tall knife-edged grass grew from the ground. Derin walked between the others, and his eyes searched the reeds for the red eyes he was sure were watching them. They traveled more quickly now; even Vera was unnerved by the thought of animals out there recording their passage, unseen presences they could do nothing about. Matthew tried to whistle to break the tension, but he soon stopped. Low shrublike bushes, waist-high pines, manzanita, dotted the terrain. There were places for things to hide.

"What else lives here?" Derin asked, and Vera answered without breaking stride, speaking into the hollow air before her. "I told you before," she said. "Snakes and scorpions. Some weasels. I've seen a wild boar or two, though not in years. Up ahead, when the ground becomes desert, there are fewer aninals. Sand squirrels mostly and a few other clans who have learned to get along without much water."

"Desert?" Matthew asked.

"The Plain of Desiccation," Vera said. "We'll be there all too soon."

The weasels saw them coming and ducked out of sight. They slithered through the underbrush, bellies flat to the ground. They'd seen foxes before, but the other two creatures were unfamiliar to them. Through the network of reeds and rushes, the weasels watched the three pass, the strange white fox, the slim hairless one, the last with the hindquarters of a goat. They looked at one another, uncertain what to do, and crept toward the swamp.

On its bank, they stopped and stared across the watery waste, searching the thickets for a glimpse of red eyes, the surface for a ripple. One of them crouched low and snarled, a rough invasion of the stillness, like wood cracking.

They saw them before they could hear them. The swamp was disturbed by a low wave and then the eyes shone, reflected in the opaque water, doubling their number. The frogs looked like slowly moving scraps of log worn down by the ravages of weather, bulbous, dark, water streaming from their backs. They stopped several feet from the bank, but the wave continued until it lapped at the weasels' feet and washed back again.

Silently they contemplated the shore, their underbellies pulsing like little hearts. "Have you seen them? The intruders?" one of the weasels whispered and the frogs shut their eyes once, together, so they glared out of the water with a fierce affirmation when they opened again.

"What should we do?" the weasel whined. The frogs stared at them and the weasels shivered deep inside their coats. They knew the frogs would not harm them, but the vision of these specters filled even them with dread. The frogs felt nothing, no fear, no hurry, no anger. They glided undisturbed through the water of the swamp.

"Should we tell the owl?"

As before, the frogs blinked their eyes, once, red as freshly drawn blood. The weasels got out of there. They had tracks to make.

It was a formidable sight. The sand stretched before them, level as calm water. In the distance, a slight undulation was visible, rolling sand hills broken only by an occasional tuft of sharp grass. Behind them, the cattails and reeds, the low shrubs fell away until there was nothing but desert. It slithered up over Derin's feet, around Matthew's hooves as Vera padded along on top of it.

"Was it always like this?" Matthew wanted to know.

"No," Vera said. "At one time the river spilled over the marsh and onto these plains in spring, and there were lakes and ponds like the ones in the meadowlands. But that was many years ago, before the owl. The animals who lived here have been taken west. It's desert almost all the way to the mountains."

"And how far is that?" Derin asked.

"We'll reach them tomorrow."

Matthew groaned. "I hate the sand," he said. "I can hardly walk." He struggled along behind the others, stopping to dislodge the grains which wedged in the cleft of his hooves.

For Derin, the walking was not much easier. The sand dragged him down. With each step, his feet disappeared, sinking into the desert, and his calves soon ached with the effort. "Can we stop soon?" he asked. "I've had it."

"At least we can see who's watching us," Vera said. "There's nowhere to hide."

"How much further are we going?" Derin asked again.

"Just a little," Vera said. "I have something to show you."

Matthew said nothing, but he silently agreed with the boy. He, too, was exhausted, and his head throbbed from the blow he'd taken in the river.

Just when Derin thought he couldn't go any further, he heard the fox say, "Up ahead. Can you see it?"

In the dim light of the failing day, the boy thought he could pick out something rising off the plain before him. It looked like a grove of trees, maybe a pond? Derin imagined fresh fruit bursting from the trees, a place to swim, a clear sky, the moon and stars hanging in equilibrium in the dark field of night. But as they drew closer, none of them speaking, he saw that what stood before them were rocks, not trees, irregular boulders arranged in an awkward circle. They looked like the bodies of large animals hunkered down on the plain, sleeping.

After trudging through the flat, dimensionless sand, the boulders were a shock. Something mysterious about the place stopped Derin from asking questions. The stones had been placed there, that was clear, but by whom and for what reason? The tension between their monstrous shapes and their careful placement awed him.

"It's the grave of the ancestors," Vera said. "When the wind took the animals from the meadowlands, it whirled them up in a large black funnel. But over the river it lost its center, and as it crossed the plain, animals rained from the sky, thousands of them. From the river to here and beyond, the ground was choked with bodies."

"How do you know this?" Derin asked, in wonder.

"All the animals west of the river know of the grave," Vera said. "Every snow fox who was taken by the whirlwind died. My children are buried here."

"I'm sorry," the boy said. "I didn't know."

"It can't be helped," the fox said. "It was years ago." She paused and looked west across the sand as if she could see over the mountains and into the Forest. "I hate him," she said. "I lost a brother and sister as well."

What could they say after that? Matthew and Derin stood silent, waiting for Vera to speak again.

"The owl did not take our sorrow into account," she said. "The animals who survived were of no use to him. The Deadwood Forest was filled with their keening. Not an animal was taken who did not lose some of her family. There was nothing he could do. And so he allowed those who wished to return to this place to bury the dead. None crossed the river; that was forbidden. They came, mourning, to this spot, and gathered the bones of our families and buried them here."

"Deirdre told me of the wind," the boy said, "but nothing about this place."

"The raven," Vera said absently, her mind elsewhere.

"Yes," Matthew said. For the first time that day he thought of their frantic friend. He hoped she was getting some rest.

"What I don't understand," the satyr said, "is why the owl was not destroyed long ago. If there was such sorrow, such anger, why do the animals follow him?"

"An interesting question," Vera said. "One I wondered about for years." She looked older suddenly, as though this place aged and saddened her. "He's very powerful, you must never forget that. He caused the wind to bring them west. And they were so broken down. They had no families to retreat to. Most had no friends. Each was isolated from the others of his kind.

"And the owl promised a new world where all would live peacefully together. They believed him. Perhaps they had no choice. There were confrontations, but the instigators disappeared and were never heard of again. Over the years, most of the animals taken by the wind died, of old age, disease, or grief. And the children seem to have forgotten. The owl and the Deadwood Forest are all they've ever known."

Derin cleared his throat, and Vera and Matthew looked at him. He stared at his feet, and he kicked the sand so it sprayed in front of him.

"I wondered. . . ." he said, and cleared his throat again.

"What, Derin?" Matthew asked.

"Are any of my family buried here?"

The fox looked away from them toward the west. Matthew's eyes suddenly burned. "No," he said.

"I just wondered," Derin said.

The three of them were silent, and the night came on. It was different on the Plain, sudden and swift, like the advent of a storm. There was no intermediary between earth and sky, no trees or rocks or water. And so it seemed to Derin, as he stood in the deepening chill, that one minute there had been light and the next minute none.

"Are we sleeping here tonight?" he asked.

"Tomorrow night," Matthew said. "Tonight we're sleeping with the frogs in the swamp."

"Very funny."

"I can hear them croaking," the satyr said. "They're calling your name."

Vera crouched by one of the largest rocks. She was silent and motionless, like a stone herself. The boy shrugged, took off his pack, and sat down. The air was cold, but still, and the silence was immense. The earth rose up to the sky, and the sky reached down so that Derin felt enfolded by enormous arms. Around him, in the dark, he thought he saw thousands of animals gather. In this magic circle of friends, they would be safe.

The weasels, out of breath and frantic from their travel, returned to the owl that night and told him what they'd seen. He was still in the clearing he'd awakened in earlier, still in a foul mood at the disappointment he'd felt when the sun's light returned to the earth.

They crept from the underbrush, staying as close to the ground as possible so they seemed to the owl, who had been aware of their proximity long before they thought he was, like two furry snakes whose bellies dragged leaves and twigs behind them. "You're back," the owl said, his voice as close to a growl as was possible for him. "You bring good news. No more ravens flying east, I trust."

"Sire," one weasel said in a quaking voice. "It is worse than that." The owl's eyes opened more widely. "Three strangers approach the western reach."

For a moment, the owl ceased to breathe. His eyelids drooped, and then they flew open, and their red fire blazed out at the weasels. He spread huge wings and beat them so that a cloud of dust rose from the ground, blinding the two frightened animals.

"You come to tell me this?" the owl thundered. "Better it had been news of a reigning darkness. Better for you to have discovered where the sun spends her nights!"

"We are sorry, my lord. We can only tell you what we know to be true." The weasel's voice was almost a whisper. "Today a fox, white as snow, and two strange creatures who walk upright, like bears, have reached the grave of the ancestors. One is slim and young, and practically hairless, a male. The other is older, with the hindquarters of a goat. Above the hips, he most resembles the other creature. They are very strange."

"That's impossible," the owl said. "You're lying." He gave a cry and a volley of wings stained the air of the clearing. The falcons descended, thudding into the dirt around him.

"They lie to me," the owl said to the falcon's leader. "They're perverse. It displeases me. Take them away."

"My liege," one of the weasels said desperately. "Three creatures have arrived at the grave of the ancestors. I swear to you." The other weasel scuffled in the dirt, wildly looked around, and made a break for the forest. He thrashed in the underbrush, but the falcons were too quick for him, and his screams for mercy grew weaker.

"Your friend seemed eager to depart," the owl said. "What did he have to fear, if you do not lie?"

"You, my lord."

"And are you frightened of me as well?" the owl asked.

"T-t-t-terrified," the weasel stammered. "My lord, if I might say one thing. . . ." He stopped, asking permission, but the owl didn't say a word, just fixed him with his gaze. "I know this news angers you. And there is nothing I would not do to avoid your anger. Why then, if this were a lie, would I put my life in danger?"

"What do you think?" the owl asked the assembled falcons, but as usual, none said anything. He turned to the weasel. "Perhaps you are telling the truth. Your logic is persuasive. Get out of here." The weasel disappeared, taking it as reward enough that he had escaped with his life.

"Gather the ravens," the owl ordered. "Now. Be quick about it."

As one, the falcons ascended and dispersed. They flew east and west, north and south, spreading the word of the owl's command.

The owl remained where he was. His solitude did nothing for his mood. He seethed there on the forest floor, his breathing harsh and rapid, almost convulsive, wild thoughts racing through his brain. "A boy," he thought. "A BOY. It's impossible. No one has escaped the Keep." He would wait until the ravens were gathered. And then he would find out what they knew. His breathing grew harsher and deeper until he thought he would burst.

"It's true," Deirdre said. "I couldn't agree with you more. I didn't like the way he talked to us one bit."

She'd grown considerably more outspoken since the sun had disappeared that afternoon, had begun to talk to the other ravens, edging around them cautiously to find out what they thought. She wasn't taking too large a chance in this, having overheard some conversations which gave her a great deal of hope.

Many of the clan were upset by the owl's punishment of Maxwell, peremptory and vicious as it had been. For years, they had managed to maintain an image of the owl as just and fair, but his coldness, his insults of the nights before made some begin to question him. Camps formed among those who were angry with the owl and those who blindly followed him. It was with a group teetering between these choices that Deirdre settled. She masked her voice, her ardent feelings, and tried to appear dispassionate.

"Of course he has a right to say anything to us he wants," she said. "And to do anything he wants. He could torture each of us, one at a time. We're his, aren't we?"

"It's not fair," a young raven named Condor said. "Not fair at all."

"But what in this world *is* fair, young one?" a withered crone asked from a branch some distance below Deirdre. "The idea of justice creates false hopes. There is only strength."

"Wait a minute, wait a minute," another raven said. "What's this talk about torture?"

"I asked whether you'd submit to torture," Deirdre asked.

"Red herring, red herring!" the old crone cawed, hopping on her branch.

"Are you hungry?" Condor asked solicitously, but the crone stared at him disdainfully.

Deirdre was flustered and she backfeathered for a minute. The crone had a subtle mind and would bear watching. Deirdre had not expected to be called on her illogical leap. "I mean only this," she said. "Until now, we've been content with our part in the owl's general plan. He wants to rule the world, am I correct?" They nodded. "But would we still owe him our allegiance if we had reason to believe that in so doing we would contribute to our own demise?"

"What?" Condor asked, baffled.

"She means would we follow him if we knew we'd die."

"I hope not," Condor said. "I don't want to die."

"Yes," the crone said, her voice deadly, deep, serious. "He is our lord and we must follow him, regardless of the cost. We bow before his power. He is stronger than we."

"But strength on the part of another does not diminish the power of personal choice, even in those who are weak," Deirdre said. "And I believe—due to no fault of his—that the owl, from the beginning, was doomed to fail."

"Would you say that again?" another raven asked, and Deirdre took a deep breath, and calmed herself. Nothing would be served by her impatience.

"Let me put it another way. The world is changing," Deirdre said, and waited for a moment to see if she'd be contradicted, but nothing was said, and she continued. "Its laws are not set. But we know one thing for certain. There is a balance to our lives. Now tell me if I'm wrong."

Around her, the ravens turned to one another and argued. What, she thought, is this all about? She hadn't said anything the faintest bit controversial.When they quieted, the crone said, "Of course there's a balance. Of power."

"What do you mean?" Condor asked. Deirdre was afraid she'd lose the attention of the group, which swung between her and the old witch, if she didn't move quickly.

"We are ravens," she said.

"Go on, go on," the crone said crossly.

"And we are not alone in the world. There are other animals besides our clan."

"Of course, you stupid cluck," the crone said.

"My dear," Deirdre said harshly, letting her anger show for the first time. "Keep a leash on your runaway tongue. I listened to you when you delivered up your apothegms. Kindly do the same for me. Or I will take umbrage at your rudeness."

"*What?*" Condor asked.

"She'll get mad, you fool."

Deirdre looked at them imperiously. "As I was saying. There is a balance. On one side there is sleep, and on the other, wakefulness. We fly and we sit. We eat and we void. These activities *balance* each other. Can you imagine a life of ceaseless flying?"

"We'd get pretty tired," Condor ventured.

"Shut your crooked beak," the crone screamed, and she hopped on the branch and flapped her wings.

"Likewise," Deirdre continued, "other things balance each other. We have friends and we have enemies. The jay is our friend, the hawk our enemy. And though many of you may be too young to remember life anywhere but here in the Forest, I am not. When we lived in the meadowlands, many years ago, there were things called seasons. Spring was a time when the earth came alive, flowers bloomed, trees put out new leaves, we raised our broods."

"What are flowers?" Condor asked, for he had never seen one.

"Please, Condor," Deirdre said. "Let me finish. And later came a season called fall when the leaves fell from the trees, the flowers withered, and the earth came to rest. These seasons oppose each other."

"Like life and death," Condor said.

"Exactly," Deirdre said. "It is the way things are. East has its west, and north its south; everything is defined by its opposite. And finally, if you will allow me to finish, there is night, and there is. . . ."

"Day," Condor blurted, as if it were the most important thing he'd ever said. Deirdre was pleased. She'd gotten through to the dumbest raven in the group, and if he understood, surely the others did as well.

"There are those who rule and those who follow," the crone said. "Do not mistake your station."

There was general unrest for a minute, and then the group quieted down. They seemed not to have heard what the old crone said.

From the air above them all, a great whoosh was heard, and like a thunderbolt a falcon fell and landed with a slap against a thick branch. His hood was black as the night, and his eyes shone, beady and evil. "The owl orders you to the clearing of last night's meeting," he said, his voice steady as rock. "What were you talking about?"

No one said a word, and Deirdre felt fear seep from the group like a rank odor. "We were speaking of the sun today," she said, "and how it dimmed. We were saying how soon it would be that the sun was gone completely."

"She's telling the truth?" the falcon asked.

"Yes," said Condor. "We umbrage the sun's demise."

Everyone hushed, and the falcon looked at Condor keenly. "What is your name, young one?" he asked.

Condor quaked on his branch. "He means nothing," Deirdre said. "He doesn't even know the import of those words. He heard them in our conversation this evening and he lacks the ability to use them correctly."

"That's right," the crone said. "He doesn't know what he's talking about. He's stupid as a stone. All of them are."

"Old one," the falcon said. "May your wizened heart fail if you lie to me."

"In that case, I have nothing to fear," answered the crone, and she flew in a huff into the sky.

"Be off, all of you," the falcon said, and he rose and headed east, looking for other ravens.

"Thank you," Condor said to Deirdre when the falcon had gone. "You saved my life."

"It's nothing," Deirdre said. "It is I who should thank you. Your felicitous questions aided the successful conclusion of my argument."

"What?" Condor said.

It was like the night before, but the owl was meaner, clearly more angry. Deirdre looked around her slowly, trying to see if the conversations of the past day had had a visible effect upon the other ravens. If there were a change, she couldn't see one. All were silent, obedient, careful to show the owl complete attention and respect. He wasted no time.

"It has been suggested to me that perhaps the punishment meted out last night was too severe," he said. Deirdre was instantly cautious: had he a plan to win back those who were turning against him? Did he even know of the dissenters? "But first, a more important matter. It seems there may be a further traitor in our midst, one who knows far more than that puny little imp. Which of you flew south beyond the boundaries given by me? Who passed into the southern reach?"

Deirdre stayed quiet. She had flown there completely by accident and had told no one. She was safe. But still, this line of questioning piqued her interest. Why was the owl protective of the southern reach? There must be some secret, something none of the ravens knew. Since Maxwell's mutilation, they understood the south as a place of exile, although they hadn't an idea of the starfish or ferns.

No one spoke. The owl's last words had been completely absorbed by the ravens' feathers, and a quiet like softly falling snow lay over the clearing.

The owl was beside himself. He fumed below them. His great chest heaved. Since the weasels had come with their information, he'd been obsessed with the thought of betrayal. Which of them was it?

"Listen," he said. "Tonight I was given information that strangers have entered the Outer Lands, are even now at the grave of the ancestors. Does one of you know something about this?"

Deirdre's heart leapt in her throat. They had crossed the river! They were on the Plain of Desiccation. She could hardly contain herself; she felt like cawing jubilantly, like dancing on her branch. They had made it!

"I WANT TO KNOW!" the owl thundered. "WHO ARE THESE THREE?"

Three! Deirdre jumped. *Who had they picked up?*

"Begging your pardon, sire," a sycophant murmured from a branch directly over the owl. "But if your worship doesn't know, how would we have the slightest guess?"

"Shut your mouth, you imbecile. I don't want sugary words. I WANT SOME INFORMATION."

The raven all but disappeared. Deirdre looked around, but it was clear that no one had a thing to say, out of fear, out of perversity, out of disdain.

"It doesn't matter to me who they are," the owl said, making every effort to regain his composure. "I know what they look like, and how far they've come. I will keep careful watch over their progress. I will look forward to their arrival in the forest. I will prepare a welcome they won't forget. Do they think I can be beaten at my own game, and in my own territory?" Deirdre shivered. She'd hoped this news would frighten the owl, but fear seemed the farthest thing from his mind.

"I await them with great anticipation," he said.

"Now. In the interest of a free and open discussion, let me offer a trade. If whoever flew south without my permission will reveal himself, I will answer questions concerning the justice of my punishment of last night. I am not above reproach. I depend on your good will."

As before, the ravens stirred on their branches, distrustful. None seemed willing to try him again. Maxwell's example wasn't easily forgotten.

"None of you knows a thing about this," the owl said, his body beginning to shake with the tension of keeping his anger throttled. "All are completely innocent. No one flew south; no one knows about the strangers to the east." His breathing became harsher, and his talons dug more deeply into the ground.

"I DON'T BELIEVE IT!" shrieked the owl. "NOT ONE WORD."

The ravens began murmuring to one another. Never before had the owl appeared like this. Always icily cool, always under control, he had made decrees, handed down orders with total aplomb.

"SILENCE!" he screamed. He shivered in his feathers. His eyes, blood-red, matched the crimson of his bib. Apoplexy, Deirdre thought with glee. *Angina pectoris.* But she was wrong. He was not about to die.

"All right," he said, more under control. "Let's pretend your naïveté is real. But let this be known. I will not stop this inquisition, whether you be here or elsewhere. I will search until I find the traitor. And I *will* find him. If it means pulling your tongues out one by one, if it entails torturing you in view of the clan, I will discover who stands against me. Nothing can stand against me. You should have realized that years ago.

"I want the moon moved to the southern reach," he said. "Tonight." The groan that arose from the ravens was unmistakable. "I want her taken from her tree and carried south. My falcons will show you where to put her. She can keep that broken-winged toadstool company. Are there any who question my command?"

Yes, thought Deirdre, but she made no sound.

Whatever hope the moon had felt at the disappearance and reemergence of her sister that afternoon was gone. The warmth she'd felt had long since dissipated. She was wretched, underfed, losing her silver sheen. She was trying to keep in shape, but there was nowhere to exercise. And she was very lonely. It seemed she hadn't spoken to a soul since Deirdre had left her the day before. Was that how long ago it was? In the forest, time was endless.

From the distance, she heard a faint thunder which grew louder the more intently she listened. She'd heard that noise before. She'd been floating serenely in the sky, bothering no one, when that roar had crept up behind her. There was no mistaking it; the ravens were coming.

They swooped at her from all directions. The wind made by their wings buffetted her, threw her against the branches of her cage, forced tears from her eyes. They settled around her, on the trees of the forest, on her own oak. And then, like the other day, the owl fell to earth and sat in the clearing below her. He was not friendly; he was not sarcastic. He was enraged.

"You're being moved," he said unceremoniously. "Now. Tonight. And I don't want to hear a word from you." The ravens moved toward her. "No," he said. "Wait." His voice became more mellifluous. "Before they go to unnecessary trouble, I want to know if you've thought about my proposition."

"Your proposition," the moon echoed dully.

"I want to know where your sister sleeps," the owl said. "It is of great interest to me."

Deirdre thought it very bold of him to ask this in front of the assemblage of ravens, for the owl had been at pains to let them know there was nothing he needed toward the completion of his quest except the moon, safely in his grasp. She was not even sure why he wanted to know where the sun slept, or what he would do with this information.

The moon wavered in her cage, and Deirdre wondered if she'd been sufficiently worn down to give in, give up, tell the owl what he wanted to know. His tone became more wheedling. "You are beautiful," he said. "I have always admired you. But you grow weak and wan in your cage. Tell me what I want to know, and you will be freed. Together we will rule the night."

"I cannot tell you," the moon said.

"She has always been brighter than you, always has thought herself better than you. I give you the opportunity to rule over her, and you turn it down?"

"She is not brighter than I, and I am far more beautiful."

"Not any more, my lovely," the owl said cruelly. "You are tarnished and tame. You are like a beautifully groomed animal lost in a briar patch."

"May you bite off your foul tongue at the root," the moon said. "Your breath infects the air."

"I don't mean to insult you," the owl said. "I mean only to remind you of all you would give up. And for what? A sister who despises you, uses you, who all along has thought herself superior to you."

"You miserable bloated bag of feathers," she said. "She may be many things, but she is still my sister."

"You will suffer far worse where you are going than you have here," the owl said coldly. "Take her away from my sight."

The falcons held back the branches, and a host of ravens entered the cage with their net. It was the same gauze, and it wrapped around the moon as though it had longed to return. She struggled against it, doing all she could to make herself more difficult to manage, but it was no use. She was lifted from the cage by the ravens, who now flocked through an opening made by the falcons. They struggled with their burden, for the moon was indeed heavy, and several times she felt herself being lowered, as though they couldn't garner the strength to get her free. But more and more ravens flew to the oak's top, tangled their talons in the net, and slowly she was lifted.

She swung loose above the trees in a hammock of gauze, and the rolling motion as the ravens ascended and headed south sickened her. But she was free of her cage. She took deep breaths, shedding her pale light around her. It illumined the tops of the Deadwood Forest, those broken branches which now, instead of holding her, seemed to be reaching up in farewell. It reflected off the ravens' underbellies, a sea of feathers.

The journey lasted some time. She was quiet, listening to the harsh rasp of wind in the ravens' throats. They were struggling, tiring. Perhaps they'd drop her and she would float free, up through the clouds, away from all this. But she knew there were too many of them for that to happen, and replacements who flew behind, should any of those carrying her tire too much.

They lowered her carefully at the appointed time, their wings outspread and floating on the wind. She felt herself dropping, and another tree surrounded her. The falcons strained against the branches, holding them, and finally the last raven released the gauze. It was whipped from under her, and she was alone again, listening to the faint flapping as the ravens headed north.

She closed her eyes and listened to her heart. She was breathing shallowly now and her light was dim. Above the sound of her breathing, above the beating of her heart, she heard another noise like the ocean, a faint rising and falling of breath, waves beating themselves against a foreign shore.

Miles to the north, the owl sat in the clearing, alone but for one raven who had left the entourage to return early. It was the withered crone, her black feathers rumpled and dusty. She was breathless, and she thought her old heart would give out on her before she could say what she'd come to say.

"My lord," she ventured.

The owl looked up at her as she hovered in the air inches from his beak. One snap would cut her in half. "Ancient one," he said. "I have never trusted the very old or the very young."

"I would speak with you," she said. "I have some information you will want."

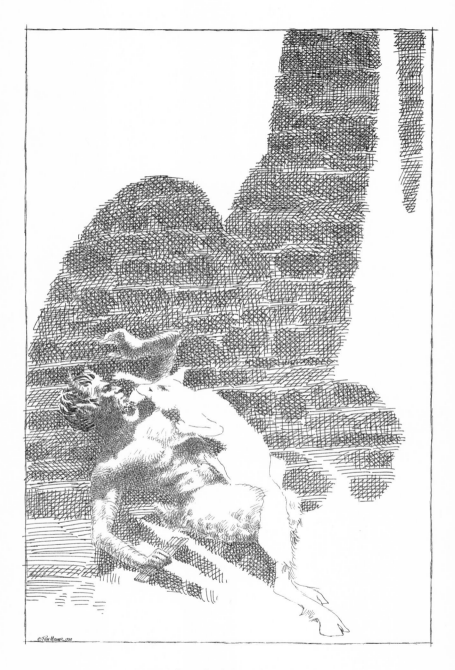

"Matthew had found his pipe."

THURSDAY

Vera didn't sleep much that night. The boy and satyr rested on the sand, surrounded by the large boulders. They lay huddled in their blankets, for night on the Plain was very cold. The fox sat and watched them a long time, not thinking much of anything. The boy appeared dreamless, almost dead, as he lay on his back, the blanket tucked around his chin, his face turned upwards to the blank sky. The satyr rested on his side, his hindquarters bent at the hips and knees, his back to Derin.

And then the fox's eyes clouded over, she ceased to look at her companions, and she was very far away. She was remembering, sifting through the past as one might walk along the beach, vacantly, stopping now and then to examine something which lies on the sand—a bright washed pebble, a piece of shell, each story distinct from all others, but connected by the great sea which has given it up.

The longest hours of the night stretched before her. In the shifting winds which swept the plain, small pillars of sand rose up in a whirlwind and disappeared. If the bones of her children beneath her could understand, they would want her to rest. And so she lay beside the satyr and the boy and closed her eyes.

"What do you have to say to me?" the owl asked, his eyes bright with interest. The ancient raven dropped to earth. The owl towered in front of her, but she didn't seem frightened.

"I don't know much at this time," the crone said. "Members of the clan are beginning to talk against you, several in particular. I have heard it said your plan is doomed to fail."

The owl's eyelids lowered as they did when he was thinking. The crone was unaware of the fury behind that thought.

"There are more than one who question me," he said, his voice muffled, as if it were of no concern to him.

"Yes, my lord. I've listened to many conversations since last night, and ravens who do not know each other are saying the same things."

"It will not matter," he said. "I will clamp down so swiftly upon whomever questions me the others will understand they have no choice. And in a few short days nothing anyone could do will make a difference."

There was silence in the clearing. The ancient raven and the owl stared at each other across the distance between them. "The old are either very foolish or very wise," the owl said. "Which are you?"

"I am not foolish enough to think myself wise," the crone said, and the owl was pleased with her response.

"You speak well," he said. "What did you have in mind?"

"I ask only that you allow me privately to serve you," she said. "I would act as a spy on your behalf."

"Go then," the owl said, almost gently. "Bring me the names of those who speak or act against me. And if you should discover a connection between the three strangers I spoke of earlier and a member of the clan, it would be of special interest to me."

"What will you do about them?" the crone asked.

"I will deal with them, if they get this far," the owl said fiercely. "But before they arrive, I have ways to make their journey more difficult."

"If I may be so bold as to ask. . . ."

"You may not."

In the darkness behind them, the sound of the ravens returning from the southern reach began to build in intensity.

"They are coming," the crone said. "I have to go." She hesitated. "My lord, when the new kingdom is established, if there should be a post for me, I would humbly accept it, were you to offer."

"Surely," the owl said, for he had nothing to lose in this. "In the meantime, keep your eyes open. I will await your report."

The crone lowered her head. "My lord," she said, and flew away.

The wind carried the sound of beating wings closer and closer to the owl. "It is done," he said. "The moon is in the southern reach." He tried to experience his pleasure, but every time he began to gloat, the knowledge of his betrayal stuck in his throat. Unbeknownst to him, a raven had been working—slowly, carefully, with great foresight— against him.

The moon slept that night more deeply than she'd slept in days. Her exhaustion was coupled with depression and when she felt depressed, the only response was unconsciousness. The rhythmic suck and moan of the forest floor beneath her accompanied her dreams.

Maxwell did not sleep that night, nor had he slept since his wings had been broken and he'd been brought to this place. He still ached, a now familiar pain which made him nauseous and dizzy. He watched the moon sleeping, her dim light waxing and waning as she breathed, and her presence gave him comfort. Below him, in the light the moon cast around her, he saw again the creatures he had watched all day.

Starfish crept up the trunk of the tree on which he sat, and as they lurched toward him, he realized the true desperation of his condition. There would be nothing for him to do but submit to them when they reached him. For now, they stayed on the trunk, refusing to venture out on the branch he inhabited.

He watched them approach the moon. A host of them slithered toward her, so many they covered the trunk of the tree in which she was caged. They crawled over one another, their groping points reaching out for anything they could fasten to, until they hunched at the place where the tree broke open into branches and surrounded the moon.

They stayed there all night, and so Maxwell felt no need to interrupt the rhythms of her sleep. Instead, he watched her breathing and her dim illumination, rising and falling with the noise the reddish slime made as it quaked.

As the first dim light of day filtered into the southern reach, chasing away the shreds of night still clinging to the treetops, the moon awoke. For a minute, she looked around her wildly, unaccustomed to this new place, and then she calmed. She had been moved. She was still all right.

The calmness dissolved when she looked below. The ferns' black fronds waved in the wind, worms and toads and scorpions visible beneath them. At the tree's heart, a mass of starfish clung like a malignant growth, waving its free points, curling them up at her vaguely before withdrawing. Violently, she hit her side against the cage to wake herself. But it was no dream, this was where the owl had sent her, and she grunted in horror.

At the first notice that the moon was awake, the starfish came alive. They began rolling towards her, separating from one another, taking different routes on the tree's branches. As she huddled in the center of her cage, she watched them come.

"Ignore them," Maxwell called to her across the stand of trees. "Don't pay attention."

The moon whirled around as though she'd been stung. "Who's that?" she asked in panic. "Who speaks from this place?"

"I'm over here, said Maxwell. "Don't be afraid."

"Don't be afraid?" the moon screamed.

"I can't come closer," Maxwell said. "But listen to me carefully. Close your eyes. Pretend to be asleep."

The moon did as she was told. She feigned unconsciousness, although she hardly needed to pretend. She swooned, the thoughts in her head racing through without stopping to be understood.

The starfish hesitated. They wrapped themselves around the branches and waited. Maxwell watched them, disappointed. His plan hadn't worked. They were simply holding fast until the moon awoke again, and she couldn't maintain the façade of sleep forever.

"Breathe deeply," Maxwell advised. "Shine with all the light you have." And the moon, her eyes closed, listening to a voice she'd never heard before, took deep draughts of the fetid air. She glowed, and then became dark. She glowed more fiercely with each breath she took. She became dizzy, thought she might faint, but the voice encouraged her, told her to breathe more deeply still.

As the light in the cage increased, the starfish cowered. With each incremental brightness, they flinched, as if the glow the moon gave off were dangerous to them. Maxwell watched as the light surged, and the starfish, one by one, moved back down the branches of the tree.

"It's working," he cawed. "Don't stop. They hate the light."

So the moon, her eyes still closed, glowed and glowed and glowed until she thought she could do it no more. "It's all right," Maxwell called. "They're gone." She opened her eyes. She saw the last of them slither down the trunk beneath her and disappear among the waving black fronds.

"Thank you," the moon said. "Whoever you are."

"I'm over here," Maxwell called, and the moon tried to see through the forest's branches. She thought she saw something, but it looked like a part of a tree. Beyond her, a small lump sat, darker than the branch.

"Is that you?" the moon asked. "*What* are you?"

"My name is Maxwell," the raven said. "Can't you see me? I'm a raven."

"Come over here, then," the moon said. "Let me get a better look at you."

"If only I could," Maxwell said, his voice mournful. "I can't move. The owl had his falcons break my wings."

"Oh, no," the moon cried, horrified. "Oh, my heavenly body."

And so Maxwell told the story of his mutilation. The moon wondered at the young bird's calm, amazed at the lack of bitterness in his voice.

"I don't think it was you the owl wanted, but another raven named Deirdre. She came to tell me she had flown back to the meadowlands to get help."

"I don't know anything about that," the young bird said.

"Don't despair," the moon said, trying to be cheerful. "If the owl had the ravens move me here, I expect it's because he's feeling threatened." Yes, she thought. Deirdre! A feeling of great affection passed over her. Maxwell was thinking of other things.

"Is there any way for you to help me?" he asked piteously. "I have no way to feed myself."

"I don't see what I can do," she said. "I'm caged in this tree."

"I'm afraid I'm going to die," the raven said.

"There, there," the moon said kindly. "There, there."

In front of Derin, in the distance, so far away they looked like heat distortions on the horizon, the mountains shimmered. "How far?" he asked, pointing.

"A good day's march," the fox said.

"Then we should be marching," Matthew said. "And hoping for a good day."

It was hot on the Plain. They'd awakened, bathed in sweat, throwing off the blankets which had barely kept them warm during the night. The temperature rose as they walked; the sand sifted under their feet. It seemed the heat ascended to the clouds and was reflected back, intensified.

The boy thought of the mountains ahead, the ascent from this plain. There, his feet would touch rock and solid earth, something permanent. He hated this waste; the heat made him dizzy. It was one step after another, with no sense of forward motion, no landmarks to judge distance against. They might be walking in place, for all he knew.

He stripped to a thin cloth around his waist, and still the sweat streaked his chest and back. The salt stung his eyes. A haze of fine sand hung in the air, and as he walked through it, it dissolved and ran in rivulets down his thighs and calves.

Matthew reached in his pack and pulled out his panpipe. He began to play, falling into step behind Derin, and his music picked up the cadence of their walking. It floated up to the vault of sky and hung there, a bright cloud of its own making. Against his will, Derin felt his bad temper begin to evaporate. The music was sly, infectious; it nagged at his mood, refusing to allow it room to grow. The melody Matthew played reminded the boy of the meadowlands, provided a tie to all he'd left behind.

He thought of how Matthew would sit in the clearing's edge as day waned and play until animals came from the woodlands and the meadow, birds flitted across the fading colors of the sky, mesmerized by the music. At moments like that, Matthew was hypnotic. His eyes would gleam in the gathering dusk. He would stand as if possessed, his hips would pick up the rhythm, and then his hooves began to move. As Derin watched him, feeling the music enter through a portal in the head more mystical than the ears, Matthew's horns would glint and seem to grow, the fleece on his hips become shaggier, until he was more animal than man. The music would throb in the clearing, sensual and cool, like the touch of a hand on burning skin. Derin had seen him change that mood with a few haunting bars, each breathy phrase poised on the edge of attainment before it trembled and faded off. Then he would change keys again, alter his rhythm, and the dirge would become wry, insouciant, building in speed until the clearing was full of animals who shuddered and twitched, possessed as well.

Vera's ears pointed, and she sniffed the air. It was as though she were remembering something from long ago. She tried to shake it off, but couldn't, and finally she turned to Matthew and glared at him. Without missing a note, the melody changed abruptly to a quicksilver tune Derin hadn't heard in years. It was a song the satyr had taught him when he was a boy, and the old words came back to him and he sang.

> There was a tortoise and a chub
> Who swam all day in a wooden tub
> Their life was simple as could be
> The tub was theirs and the air was free
>
> The tortoise had a magic shell
> The chub had scales and a silver bell
> Their cymbal was a lily pad
> And they sang all day of the luck they had
>
> And this is how the world is made
> With fire and laughter, stone and wind
> And this is how the music's played
> We will sing this song till our throats give in
>
> And when the turtle's stomach growled
> The sun burned down or the water howled
> The chub would bring him icy snow
> A fly to eat or a boat to row
>
> By day the sun, by night the moon
> Though storms rain down, they'll leave us soon
> And winter's cold will fade away
> The deepest night will turn to day
>
> And this is how the world is made
> With fire and laughter, stone and wind
> And this is how the music's played
> We will sing this song till our throats give in

By the time the song had ended, Derin was out of breath. They were moving more quickly. The music changed again, recalling the melody Matthew had played earlier, and this time Vera trembled from the tip of her nose to her tail. The boy felt light-headed, as though he were made of air. Around him, the sand took on subtle colorations, the yellow grains streaming into runs of red and blue. He was no longer tired, or dizzy from the heat. He thought he was floating above the surface of desert; the sand buoyed him up. Under him, so far away they seemed someone else's, his feet were dancing.

He saw a smear of silver hair, the startling image of white skin, the flash of a collarbone. And he was running, Matthew behind him, whooping, both of them flying, throwing sand behind them like a smokescreen.

Deirdre woke alone, as usual. It was full noon, grey and dim. Around her, the walls of trees rose as before. For a moment she found that difficult to accept. So much had happened during the past day; the forest should have changed, begun to bud or flower, or fall away entirely. But the dense pattern of treebranch and leafless shrub repeated itself into the distance. She stretched her wings and folded them again, trying to relieve the ache that had developed during the flight the night before. Deirdre thought of the moon then, and how she had swung helplessly beneath the ravens as they'd carried her south. She'd tried to capture the moon's attention, to let her know the fight continued, but the moon had closed her eyes and let herself be taken, and Deirdre hadn't had the nerve to make herself known.

Above her, a branch creaked, and when she looked up, she realized she wasn't alone. Condor sat there, staring down at her intently. His head was cocked to one side, and his beak was slightly open, like an idiot's. "Hi," he said jauntily. "I didn't wake you, did I?"

"What are you doing?" Deirdre asked, flustered. "How long have you been here?"

"Since it began to get light. I want to talk to you. I want to be with you."

"Your candor is unnerving," Deirdre said.

"My what?" Condor asked.

"You don't understand a thing I say." Deirdre wasn't ready for Condor's blend of innocence and stupidity so early in the morning. "Why don't you go find someone to fly with? I haven't the time to take on an abecedarian . . . er . . . beginner."

"But I understood what you said last night about the owl," Condor objected. "Besides, I don't want lessons. I just want to be near you."

Deirdre shuddered on her branch. How was she going to get rid of him?

"I have something you'll want to hear," Condor said quickly, afraid he'd be ordered to leave if he didn't speak fast. "The whole clan is arguing. There's only one thing being talked about."

Deirdre looked at him with sudden interest. Her anger subsided a bit. "What do you mean?" she asked.

"I followed you last night after you saved my life. . . ."

"Do me the favor of eschewing the melodrama," she said, and brushed right past Condor's puzzlement. "I only offered a word on your behalf. The falcon did nothing more than ask your name."

"But he would have reported it to the owl," Condor said. "Anyway, I followed you after we carried the moon down there, and then when you slept, I went off to see what was going on. Everywhere I flew I found another group talking about him. Some say he's crazy. Lots are beginning to think his plan won't work. And now those three strangers are coming. Who are they?"

"Never mind, Condor."

"But do you know them? Are they friends of yours?"

Deirdre's vanity got the better of her. "Of course they're friends of mine," she snapped. "Why do you think they're on their way?"

"To visit you?" Condor asked. "But I'd think that now was hardly the time. . . ."

"Shut your beak!" Deirdre screamed.

"I'm sorry," Condor said. "I'll be quiet."

Deirdre sat for a minute until her heart resumed its natural rhythm. She looked at Condor, so good-natured yet so dull-witted she wasn't sure she could endure his company another minute. Her forbearance won over her anger. "Come with me," she said, and rose into the air.

The younger bird flew after her. As she dipped and spun in the subtle currents, he followed at a respectful distance. She hovered over the treetops, and then headed east, her eyes trained on the forest below. She hadn't flown far when she saw a cluster of ravens, and she tucked her wings and dived. She and Condor settled quietly on a remote limb and listened to the conversation.

It was like nothing she had heard before among the members of the clan. Most were given to small talk, idle chatter. But she was riveted now, galvanized by the intensity she heard in their voices. A dozen birds were engaged in an argument about the owl, just as Condor had said. Those inclined to follow him held the edge, but the few dissenters clung to their views with a tenacity which impressed her and gave her hope. She kept her beak closed and tried not to look too pleased.

When she'd heard enough, she flew off again, and Condor, who had remained silently beside her, keeping his promise, flew off as well. They circled above the forest's top and headed west. They passed over a clearing, and when Deirdre looked down, she saw another group of ravens. Though she could not hear what was being said, the voices rose to her, angry and discordant.

Everywhere the two of them flew, the same drama unfolded. It's happening, she thought. The owl has overplayed his hand.

She settled on a tree limb. Condor was right behind her. "See?" he said. "Isn't it just as I said?"

"Yes," Deirdre replied. "Now I must be off. So be a good bird and keep watch. Let me know what's happened when I return."

"But I want to stay with you," Condor said. "I won't be any trouble, I promise. I'll keep out of your way, and I'll be there if you need anything. And I'll be quiet."

"You can be of more help to all of us by remaining here and finding out as much as you can."

The younger bird looked at her mournfully. "Please don't send me away," he said.

Deirdre became exasperated. "There are things you are too young to understand," she said. "There are things I have to do alone."

"Please," he said. "Please let me come. I think I'm in love with you."

As they raced across the sand, the spell of Matthew's music wore off, and before they could reach the nymph, she was a fox again. Derin collapsed on the sand, still light-headed, this time from the heat and his exhaustion. If he had been bathed in sweat before, now he nearly drowned in it. His face was a brilliant red, and when Matthew wheeled to a stop beside him, spraying sand, the satyr's first thought was that he'd killed the boy. But Derin threw back his head and laughed, drawing in the desert heat in burning draughts.

Vera hadn't found the episode so amusing. She scowled at the satyr as she lay on the sand, panting. "I'm sorry," Matthew said. "I couldn't help myself."

"You're cynical and perverse," Vera said. "I didn't know you could do that."

"I'm afraid so," Matthew said. "Trouble is, it never works. I can't run and play at the same time." Vera looked away disdainfully, as though she hadn't heard him. Her pretense didn't stop him. "If I'd caught you before you changed back into a fox," he said, "could you change after I'd caught you?"

"No," she said. "Not until after you let me go."

"Damn," he said. He slapped his thigh with his open palm and laughed. He was so good-humored about it, so like a small boy who finds he can do something clever, that Vera couldn't hold onto her temper for long.

"Next time I'll have to run faster," Matthew said.

"There won't be a next time," Vera said. "I'm warning you."

Over them the sky grew darker. All three looked up at the clouds, now more ominous, beginning to ripple. Without saying another word, they rose from the sand and started toward the mountains, more quickly than before, trying to outrace whatever it was that threatened them from above.

The rain came at them vertically, like knives. Soon they could see nothing but the grey walls enveloping them. The water stung them as though it were more than water, something almost animate with a mind of its own. Vera's fur became sodden and matted, smudged and yellow with sand. The water streamed down Derin's neck, into his eyes and mouth, so that he spluttered, shielded his mouth with his hand when he tried to breathe.

Its velocity increased; it came at them so fiercely, Derin felt himself being pounded into the sand. But where was the sand? He was up to his ankles in water. It no longer seeped into the desert, but sat on its surface like a small lake.

They sloshed through this sudden swamp more slowly, the water now above their ankles, dragging them down. A tiredness came over Derin which made him stumble. He thought he could no longer pick up his legs. Vera and Matthew were also dazed, their bodies numbed by the driving rain, their senses lulled into a state approaching sleep. They were all too lethargic to be worried.

Derin stopped walking; his legs buckled and he sank to his knees in the water. He cupped some rain in his hands and brought it to his lips, but it was warm and brackish, like the water in the stream in the meadowlands. Matthew, throwing water before him with each step, reached the boy and walked past, catching Derin by the elbow and dragging him to his feet. The gesture was unconscious, concerned only with survival, as though a dream had overcome the satyr and he had lost his power of thought. He was moving to rhythms he would not have been able to explain, but forceful enough to draw Derin out of himself. He watched the satyr and the fox, lost to him now, responding to their animal natures, and he knew he would have to follow them, to do as they did, without talking, without even thinking, if he hoped to outlive this onslaught, this plague of rain.

And then it lessened. First, Derin began to see further and further ahead, as though grey curtains were being lifted in front of him. The stinging drops became less heavy, and the storm front moved over them, headed north. One minute it was raining, and then the wall of water was to their right, receding rapidly. They watched it go, like the retreat of fever, and the boy became dizzy, as though he'd been returned to himself after a long absence. He dared not speak to his companions who seemed still dazed; the sickness which had lifted from him still had them in its grip.

It was steam the rain left behind. As the sky brightened from dark to light grey, the heat increased and the water evaporated from their clothes, from Vera's fur, from the sand under their feet, sinking into the desert and lifting from the Plain in shimmering waves.

Only when the water under their feet was gone did Matthew and Vera seem to awaken. Matthew rubbed his eyes, as after a long and turbulent sleep, and Vera hung her head and shook it from side to side. They looked at one another in wonder, having shared something they didn't understand, and Derin, for a moment, felt an almost unbearable wave of loneliness.

As they walked, the Mountains of No Return became more and more visible. They rose vertically from the line of sand, their peaks jagged and white with snow. The mountains gained in altitude with each passing minute, and they filled the boy with wonder, the last stronghold before he would encounter the owl.

"You live up there?" he asked Vera, and she nodded, not yet ready to speak. "How high are they?" he continued, and this time received a response.

"At the summit," she said, "there's perpetual snow, and the air is so thin you'll have trouble breathing. But it shouldn't be too bad. I know the way, including a shortcut or two."

As if to help them, the ground beneath their feet became more firm. The sand had something hard under it, a layer of rock or dirt, and the three of them had less trouble walking. The mountains loomed before them, and a sparse vegetation returned, wisps of dried grass, an occasional shrublike bush, its bark the color of sandstone, its leaves a faded green on one side and silver on the other. Rocks appeared, as though the sand had begun to coagulate.

It was nearing twilight when they saw the dust cloud. Forming at the base of the mountains, the cloud moved toward them, swirling over the Plain. In the hot wind which swept down the mountains, the cloud looked larger than it was. Spouts of reddish dust spun off its top and dissipated in the warm air. As they watched, the cloud grew higher and wider until it seemed not made of dust at all. It deepened in color, past red to a darker hue, like a bruise, and continued darkening until it was almost black. It rose above them, towering, and the silence of the desert grew even more still. All they could hear was the low moaning of the wind as it turned around on itself and it came toward them, the moan rising until it was a shriek. Bits of rock and stray pieces of vegetation lifted off the desert and struck at their legs and chests. Vera glanced at Matthew again, the look Derin had seen pass between them before.

The cloud was a funnel now, snaking toward them, weaving over the Plain. There was no need to ask where this wind had come from. Derin looked for cover, anything, a large rock, a tree he could hold onto, but there was nothing except those small bushes. When Matthew tried to scream at him, the boy could hear only the whining of the whirlwind, a circular roar which had entered his head, displacing everything but fear.

They ran, their exhaustion forgotten, but the cloud seemed to know their movements in advance, and wherever they darted over the open surface of the Plain, the cloud moved to meet them.

Above him, the sky darkened perceptibly, and when he looked up, Derin saw a squadron of peregrine falcons, hooded, swooping toward him. He threw himself upon the sand and covered the back of his neck with his hands. He could hear the thud of their wings as they passed above him, and when he raised his head, he saw Matthew, ten feet away, his mouth wide open, waving at him. He ran in a crouch, staying as close to the ground as possible, found Matthew and Vera splayed on the sand. Matthew had wedged himself between two bushes, their leaves already stripped by the wind, and was holding on with both hands. He lay across Vera, pinning her there, and as the boy crouched beside the satyr, he felt himself gathered in as well. He reached out and grabbed onto the bush, feeling the heaviness of the satyr's haunches on his legs, the strength in the arm as it crossed his torso, and with his other arm, Derin encircled Matthew's waist. They lay entwined, holding on to one another and to the earth, as the cloud came on.

Above him, Derin heard the thudding of the falcon's wings again. And then he closed his eyes. The wind had kicked up such a cloud of dust there was nothing to see.

The force of wind increased until it flew under him as well as over him, attempting to loosen his grip. It seemed to have fingers, hands, arms, wedges, iron chains. His body stretched, dragged four directions at once. He let go of the bush and felt himself lifting, but Matthew's body clamped down even harder than it had before, squeezing all the breath out of him.

Derin's mouth and ears were full of dirt, his eyes were clamped shut, but even so, the sand threatened to blind him. The wind shrieked and screamed, an almost human sound, until he wasn't sure if it was Matthew's voice he was hearing or the wind's.

It passed, finally. After what seemed hours of being buffetted and torn, pummelled and beaten, the wind moved over them to the east, the ground they'd covered earlier. He was afraid to open his eyes until he heard Matthew's coarse breathing and knew he was safe. He was bruised and his arm felt as though it had been torn from its socket, but when he looked, there was the satyr, and under him the fox. Behind them, the cloud meandered more crazily now, its power diminishing until it was the dust storm they had seen at first and then nothing at all.

"Get off me," Vera groaned. "You're smothering me."

"You ungrateful little snot," Matthew said. "I saved your life."

"Your horns and hooves, you did," Vera said. "I escaped the first time the owl sent the wind. I could have made it a second."

"But I've got you right where I want you," Matthew said. "Now where's my pipe?"

Vera flashed him such a look the satyr laughed and let her wriggle out from under him. He got to his knees and groaned, carefully examining his arms and legs for injury. Then he said, "Come on. Let's get to those mountains. I've developed a strong hatred for this desert."

"Thank you," Vera said, her voice even, her eyes on the mountains.

"What?"

"I said, 'Thank you,' " she said simply.

"You're welcome," Matthew said. "I'll cover you any time you like."

Condor sat forlornly on the tree limb where Deirdre had left him. He'd agreed, finally, to remain behind and see what he could discover about the ravens' mounting resentment, but his heart wasn't in it. He'd never felt like this before, his stomach fluttery, his wings heavy. He didn't want to fly, or eat, or talk, or sleep. Deirdre had been kind to him, he knew, but he still felt the sting of her rejection when she refused to allow him to accompany her.

He was staring mournfully at the ground when the old crone found him.

Condor looked at her for a moment before he remembered who she was. "Hello," he said, his voice hollow as a gourd in late fall.

"Young one," she said. "Are you sick?"

"I don't think so," he said. "Do I look sick?"

"You certainly do," the crone said. "What's the matter?"

"All I feel is sad," Condor said. "It's like I have something growing inside me that wants to get out but can't."

"Indigestion," the crone said. "You're not chewing your food properly."

Condor shot her a disappointed glance. "I don't think this is something for you to joke about."

"But I'm not joking. If you have. . . ."

"I think I'm in love," Condor said meekly.

"Ahh," the crone said. "I understand. It's *sort* of like indigestion."

"That's not what I thought," Condor said. "I thought love made you happy and light-headed and carefree."

"Years ago, when I was your age, I knew the feeling you have. I'm afraid it's wasted on the young. You're too inexperienced to understand the bittersweet side. And who is this love of yours, if I might ask?"

"I met her yesterday," Condor said.

"But then you hardly know her," the crone said. "And does she love you?"

"I don't think so," Condor said. "At least, she didn't say she did. That's what makes me sad."

"Unrequited love," the crone said, and sighed.

"What?"

"Never mind, little one. Never mind."

"I wanted to thank you for helping me last night," he said, remembering his manners. "She said that nothing would have happened to me, but I'm not so sure."

"I only said what I knew to be true. And I should apologize for the harsh things I said. I'm sorry I told you to shut your crooked beak." Her red eyes gleamed at him, overwhelming in their sincerity.

"That's all right," Condor assured her. "I talk too much."

"Yes," she said. "Even that raven I argued with last night said so."

"Then you remember her," Condor said, a hint of cheer creeping into his voice for the first time.

"Indeed I do," the crone said. "Indeed I do. I was much impressed with her vocabulary."

"She's gone now," he said. "She wouldn't let me go with her."

"Where did she go?" the crone asked, almost diffidently.

Condor's eyes narrowed. "Wait a minute," he said. "Are you for or against the owl?"

"How do *you* feel?" the crone asked solicitously.

"I hate him," Condor said

"Then so do I," the crone said. "And so does your friend, I suppose."

"Yes," Condor said. "I hadn't considered it until I heard her talking last night. She's right, don't you think?"

"She has a nimble mind and a persuasive tongue, yes, indeed."

"And she's beautiful," Condor said.

"That may be so. My eyes have long since clouded to such things. But you didn't answer my question."

"What?"

"Where did she go?"

Condor was crestfallen. "I don't know," he said. "She wouldn't tell me. I guess she was afraid I'd follow her." He puffed out his chest then, and he stretched his wings. "But you can bet she's doing something important. She flies around a lot. She even knows those three who are coming, those strangers from the east. What do you think of that?" he asked proudly.

"Very impressive," the crone said.

"Yes," Condor said. "She hates the owl. She wants to see him dead."

"And what is her name?" the old crone asked.

"Deirdre," he said with fervor. "Her name is Deirdre."

She reached the southern forest by late afternoon. The moon hung in the new cage, anxiously talking to Maxwell, who tottered on his branch, holding on with all his strength, by this point so tired and weak the moon had almost given up all hope for him. "Deirdre!" the moon said. "You've come back."

"I would have come sooner. I've discovered, much to my chagrin, the truth about only being able to be in one place at a time."

She settled near the moon and gave her all her attention, until she realized the moon's gaze was directed away from her to another tree limb. It was then she saw Maxwell, his body huddled like an outcropping of bark. She flew to him in one swift burst of wings, and he looked at her, barely able to swivel his head.

"It is I who should be in your place," Deirdre said, deeply moved. "It is I the owl wanted to punish."

"Can you help me?" Maxwell asked. "I haven't had a thing to eat since I was brought here." His breath was raspy and shallow, and Deirdre thought she could hear his heart pulsing within his sunken throat. His eyes were glazed with pain, and she left immediately to find food for him.

But where to go? Under her, as she hovered in the air, lay the ferns and starfish. There were worms down there; she had seen them, long and slithery, but she shuddered to think of diving for one. She could fly north, where the forest floor was familiar, but it was clear that Maxwell needed food soon.

So she steeled herself and dove. She came within inches of the ferns' tops and arrested her flight, and then she entered. The thin black fronds closed over her, blocking out most light, and she blinked in the darkness and tried to see. The ferns were far taller than she'd thought.

The forest floor lay several feet beneath her, and as she'd feared, starfish humped there, limpid and white. Among them, over them, the other creatures lay. Scorpions with their spined curved tails looked up at her, and a mottled black toad with red eyes hopped toward the spot directly under her. To her left, she saw the dull pink shine, the elongated pencil-thin form of a worm, and she darted at it. She caught it in her beak and swooped toward the sky. The toad tensed his legs and lunged, but he missed her, snapping in the air as if she were a fly. The commotion was terrible, starfish waving their sickly arms, slathering, and the undulating tails of the scorpions.

But she was free, and as she broke through the canopy of fern it was as though she'd come back to a world in which the sun shone. The worm, longer than her entire body from beak to tailfeathers, writhed in her beak, but disgusted as she was, she did not drop it. She flew to Maxwell's branch and his beak tilted upward as though he were her child, and accepted her offering. The worm took some time to eat and Maxwell never said a word, just snapped off segments of its ugly pink body, jerked his head back, throwing them into his throat, and swallowed.

"Thank you," he said, when he was done. And he began to cry.

It was the first time, since she'd awakened that morning and become aware of him, that the moon had seen Maxwell give in to his fear.

"I feel so humiliated," he said. "It would be better if the owl had simply had me killed."

"Are you still hungry?" Deirdre asked gently.

"Yes," Maxwell said. "I am."

And so Deirdre dove again, this time breaking through the ferns and heading straight for the ground. If the starfish and their cohorts were waiting for her, she'd surprise them and be gone before they knew it.

But it was not so easy. In a panic, she looked around for another worm and couldn't find one. She flew upwards in a burst of fear and reentered the sky, and then dove again further off. There in the dimness another worm glinted. She grabbed it in her beak and flew upwards, but was pulled back as though she were on the end of a tether. The worm did not let loose, and she pulled again, but it did no good. She dropped it, turned, and lunged down to see what was holding it. Then she settled on the ground for a moment, grabbed it again, and twisted it in her beak. It released its grip, but at the same time, Deirdre felt her left claw surrounded by the rasping mouth of a starfish.

Her stomach knotted, she dropped the worm and broke for the sky, but the starfish held tight, and her flight was labored and lopsided, as though an enormous weight were pulling her back to earth. She struggled through the air, trying to shake the thing loose, but it held, even seemed to be gaining. She felt its leathery underside groping past her claw and up her leg.

She whirled in the air, circling, afraid to land. "Over here!" the moon screamed. "Fly over here! Inside the cage." Deirdre did as she was told, blindly, without thinking. In her terror, she misjudged the distance between branches and bruised her wing entering the space where the moon hung. The moon meanwhile was drawing in enormous gulps of air and she shone so brightly that Deirdre had to close her eyes. In that glare, the starfish flinched, slithered down Deirdre's claw, and released, falling point over point until it was swallowed by the ferns.

Deirdre landed on a branch above the moon and sat there shivering, gasping for breath, unable to talk. The nightmare of that floor spun in her head. She opened her eyes, but the tree limbs were the points of starfish and she saw, as if they hung in the air in front of her, the scorpions and toads. She closed her eyes hurriedly, but they were all there, scurrying in her brain.

"Deirdre," the moon said. "Deirdre! Talk to me!"

"Her name is Deirdre," the old crone said. The owl looked at her thoughtfully, wondering if she were to be trusted.

"Are you sure?" he asked. It was clear to him that Maxwell's punishment had belonged to another and he couldn't afford to make that mistake again.

"As sure as I can be," the crone said. "I heard her talk last night before you called the second congregation."

"What did she say?"

"She spoke of balance and opposites. Really, a very ingenious argument. She convinced the other ravens listening that you were disrupting the natural order."

"She's wrong, of course," the owl said. "I am establishing the natural order if she could only see that. All things lead to darkness. All things die. You would understand that, old one."

"I have no intention of dying," the crone said mildly, cocking her head to the left.

"Be that as it may," the owl said. "I want you to find her. Bring her to me."

"Begging your pardon," the crone said. "I don't think that's possible. I have no idea where she is. She seems to have left the forest."

"And this is the raven I'm after? The one who knows of these three travelers?"

"Yes, my lord, I spoke to a stupid little raven who is in love with her. He claims they are friends of hers."

"Perhaps they'll make it," the owl said. "I didn't believe it possible. I sent a rain, a wind to trouble them, but they haven't turned back."

"They'll never survive the snow and cold in the mountains," the crone said.

"Perhaps they will," the owl said. "I almost hope they do. I'd like to see them."

"What will you do with them?" the crone asked.

"You ask too many questions, old one. I will play with them in my own time, in my own way. My falcons tell me one of them is a boy. Does that interest you?"

"That clan hasn't been seen in the Forest for years. I would have thought them all dead."

"It may be so," the owl said.

"How odd," the crone said. "It makes me think. . . ."

"Of what, old one?"

"Nothing, my lord. My brain is old and feeble, as you know."

"Don't condescend to me," the owl said. "Never do that." He glared at the crone. She'd been useful to him, but she was getting on his nerves. She was too familiar, and he disliked her wheedling insinuation.

"One question more, and then you should leave me," he said. "How would I know this raven, this traitor?"

"She is of medium size," the crone said. "She has a small white lump on her left claw."

"Deirdre, you said her name was?"

"Yes, my lord," the old crone said wearily. "Her name is Deirdre."

She shivered for a long time, huddled into herself, unable to escape the slithering nightmare. She was rattled down to her claws which gripped the branch as if they would never let go. The white knob of calcified ooze was a constant reminder of their grasping mouths. "I can't go back down there," Deirdre said. "Don't make me." She was alarmed at the whine in her voice.

"No one is making you do anything," the moon said. "Just rest. You're overtired. You're distraught."

"I can't rest. I've so much to do. Maxwell needs more food." Deirdre looked across to the limb where the broken bird sagged, his feathers greying.

"You won't do anyone any good in this condition," the moon said.

Deirdre shook herself, willing her strength to return. "Excuse me," she said, and flew over to Maxwell. "I'm sorry," she told him. "I tried."

"I know," Maxwell said. "You were very brave. I don't blame you for any of this. I'm just so cold."

"I'll get food elsewhere. I'll fly back north, if I have to."

"It's no use," Maxwell said mournfully. "I'm going to die."

"Nonsense," Deirdre snapped. In his whine, she heard her own. "Now, none of that. What's happened to you is terrible, I know, but you can't give up."

"I hear such noises when I'm quiet," Maxwell said. "Such moans and wails. I'm afraid they're coming from me, but I can't tell."

"You're in so much pain," Deirdre said. "You're imagining it."

"No, he's not," the moon said from her cage. "I hear it too. It comes from the south, I'm quite sure of that. Howling. Moaning. Long and drawn out, like a faint wind. Perhaps it *is* the wind. But then it stops for hours."

Deirdre perked up immediately. "Let me fly there and see what I can find," she said. "I'll get some food for Maxwell and bring it back. Everything will be all right."

Deirdre flew south, glad to leave that part of the Forest behind her. She wondered what was making that noise, and she didn't have long to wait. From the ground beneath her, a low wail, a single voice, rose. The noise was like none she had heard before, certainly not made by any animal she knew. As she flew, her wings flapping smoothly in the still air, the sound ascended again, almost palpable in its keenness. She saw ahead of her what looked like a mound of dirt. It grew from the forest floor, an enormous contusion on the earth's surface. As she hovered over it, afraid to let herself drop, she could see it was made of tree trunks, rock and mud. The low wail rose again, so loud and so hopeless the feathers on her chest and neck tingled.

Against her better judgment, she let herself drop like a stone, and she landed on a tree trunk jutting from one side. The hardened mud walls, fortressed by the wood and stone, were thick, and the roof sloped gently above them. From where she sat surveying the mound, Deirdre could imagine the effort that had gone into its construction. But who had built it?

Another voice rose to join the first and the two eerie sounds mingled in the air, wavering like a lament. Deirdre searched for a chink in the armor of the fortress to look inside, but the walls were impregnable. She flew across an area the size of a large pond. Its massiveness, its mystery stunned her. She, usually so quick, could come up with no satisfactory explanation.

There weren't animals inside this mound. But what were they, then, and who had put them there? The keening rose and fell on the air with the regularity of breathing, and each time Deirdre felt she was hearing it anew. The edge of pain in those voices overwhelmed her. She took a deep breath, cawed loudly, and instantly the wailing ceased. In the silence which swept over the place, Deirdre nearly lost her balance. "Hello," she said, as loudly as she could. "Who are you?" Her voice echoed back from the hardened walls. She was talking to herself.

"Answer me," she said. "Talk to me."

With one sharp intake of breath, a host of voices began to moan. The sound was immense. Waves of grief washed over her, cresting and breaking, all of them tumbling in despair. What could she do? She hadn't expected this response. Perhaps the inhabitants of the fortress could not speak, or spoke by means of this unearthly howling. She would never understand who they were.

The noise seemed to come from deep in the throat and it rose in a spiral, gathering force until it reached a shriek and fell away, but as one voice descended, another took its place and the Forest reverberated with the high-pitched apex of the cry. It was like the sound a coyote makes baying at the moon, or the strange painful cries of animals who knew no words which fit. Still, this was different, intelligent, carrying on the wind of its howl an entire vocabulary of suffering. There was history in that noise, a sense of an ancient wrong which had not been avenged, might never be, yet for all the knowledge that history gave to the howling, there was no understanding.

It died away as quickly as it had grown, and Deirdre sat there shivering in her feathers, the silence as deafening as the keening had been. She drew in her breath, deciding to try again.

"I'm sorry if I alarmed you," she said. "I don't mean to. I just flew down from the north. There's nothing to be frightened of."

One voice, old and crumpled as fallen leaves, answered her. It was harsh, untrusting, unwavering in its suspicion. "What are you?" the voice asked.

The sudden use of words surprised her. "A raven," Deirdre said, "in search of food."

"Have you come from the owl?" the voice asked. Deirdre heard something familiar in the voice, some note of difference. It sounded somehow like Derin's and for an instant she was totally confused.

"Derin?" she called. "Is it you?"

A voice began to howl but the old one cut it off short. "Answer me," it said. "Have you come from the owl?"

"No," Deirdre said. "I come on my own. The owl is my enemy, the enemy of everything which breathes."

"Then he's been fought?" the voice asked, shedding its cruelness for a moment.

"No," Deirdre said, "but we're trying. If you will pardon my asking, to whom am I speaking?"

There was silence for a moment, and the old voice resumed. "We are the remnants of those who lived in this Forest before the owl," it said. "We have lived in his darkness for years. We are the last of the People."

Deirdre was dumbfounded. She had heard stories as a young raven, after the wind had brought her west, but they were just stories the old ones told, wild-eyed myths she'd never believed. "People?" she asked. *Like Derin?* "You walk upright? Are you half-goat?"

"We used to walk upright before the darkness crippled us. For all we know, we could be half-snakes, half-pigs."

"How many of you are there?"

"I couldn't say. So many of us have died."

She remembered her surprise at first seeing Derin, and now she'd stumbled upon a group of others like him. "I know a People," she said. "A young one, a boy. He's on his way to the Deadwood Forest now."

"What?" the voice cried. "You say a young boy is coming? Coming here?"

"Yes," Deirdre said, "but I don't see. . . ."

The old voice broke in, cautious and in tight control. "He's coming," he said, almost breathless. "The raven says he's on his way."

From the fortress arose the wildest outburst of noise Deirdre had ever heard. There were screams such as she imagined the dying made when their lives were snuffed short, and shouts of exultation. Voices wailed and moaned and changed to cries of joy. Amid them all were voices clamoring for quiet, for peace, older voices, and slowly the screams ceased. "I'm sorry," the voice said, shaking. "We've been waiting for him for years."

"What?" Deirdre said sharply. "For whom, if you please?"

"For the boy you tell me is coming. Before we were forced here long ago, one of our people rescued a child, a newly born boy, and carried him east away from the Forest. We did not know if he lived or died. The one who rescued him never returned. But the child, it is written in our history, *would* return. And now you say he's coming?"

She could make no sense of it. The creatures inside this place knew of Derin? "How did you come to be here?" she asked.

"The owl," the voice said. "He came with his animals — hordes of them. We fought as best we could, but we were outnumbered and we didn't know how to fight. This forest was once a garden of such beauty I can hardly describe it to you."

"And you've been here ever since."

"Yes, in this stink and filth. Among the bodies of our friends and family."

"I don't know what to say," Deirdre said, which was not often true. "The owl has captured the moon."

The people began wailing again at this harsh news, but their elder quieted them, asking Deirdre to continue.

"The moon is caged in a tree not far north of here, and the days are getting dimmer and dimmer. The owl plans for darkness to be total, and that time isn't far off. But many of the animals are beginning to turn against him. I'm afraid the outcome will not be pleasant, or even forseeable. We are doing what we can. If the owl isn't stopped. . . ."

"I understand," the old man said.

"What is this place?" Deirdre wanted to know.

"It's called the Keep."

"I'm off," Deirdre said, resolved. "I'm going to the boy to tell him of this. He has no idea."

"Good-bye, then," the voice said. "What is your name?"

"Deirdre," she said.

"And how do you know of this boy and his journey?"

"I'm the one who told him of the moon," she said. "I knew his friend Matthew, a satyr, years ago, and when I went to Matthew, the boy was there."

"Then Deirdre is our savior as much as he," the voice said.

"I'm sorry to say it was out of no conscious motivation," Deirdre said. "I'm not easily surprised."

A chorus of voices rose in gratitude and Deirdre took to the air. She saw herself almost objectively, as in a dream. All she had done had been ordained, a most disturbing feeling, her flight east to tell the satyr of the moon, her flight south to the Keep. But there was such accident involved in it. The pieces didn't fit together.

These people once lived in the Forest. But they had not been there when the wind brought her and the other animals west. So they'd been imprisoned in the Keep before that night. And a garden? Ever since she'd lived in the forest, its trees had been skeletons. The owl was responsible for all of that.

Ahead of her, the line of trees stopped and the mountains began. She would fly along the easternmost edge of the Forest until she was sufficiently north to cross and look for the boy. The mountains' craggy snow-covered summit jutted into the air on her left and the dense tangle of forest continued in front of her. She felt she was flying down a dark tunnel which had to have light at the end of it. But then she chided herself. Such clichés, after all, were beneath her.

For most of the afternoon, the moon chattered madly at Maxwell, trying to keep him thinking of things other than the food Deirdre would bring. She talked about her sister. She told him of the trip she had taken through the universe and all she had seen. But she might have been talking to one of the trees for all the interest she aroused in him.

The moon understood Maxwell's slow sink inward. She had felt inklings of it over the past days as no help came, and no one spoke to her, and her world, previously boundless, was restricted to an oak and its surrounding branches. He hunched deeper and deeper into himself, his eyes glassy, more red than those of any other raven she had seen. When she called his name, he would pick up his head which lay tilted to the side and look in her direction, but she couldn't be sure he saw her. After a while, his eyes closed, and then, even when she called his name, time after time, her voice growing louder and sharper, he didn't pick up his head or open his eyes.

Where was Deirdre? The moon stopped her chatter to catch her breath and anxiously scanned the sky for a black shadow. From the south, the eerie moaning and wailing she had heard all day rose and fell, stopping and then beginning again, riding on the still air, a creature unto itself.

At the trunk of Maxwell's tree a starfish humped as though it could smell his despair. Soon another joined the first, and then the moon watched as a trail of them ascended the tree. "Maxwell!" she screamed. "Wake up! Listen to me!" If he heard the terror in her voice, if he heard her voice at all, he gave no indication.

They climbed, a small army of them, one glistening white point after another, leaving a trail of slime behind. The moon was beside herself. She writhed against the tree branches. There was no way to stop them, and they reached the juncture of trunk and limb and started slowly down the branch on which the crippled raven sat. "The starfish!" the moon yelled. "Maxwell!"

Was he unconscious? Neither her anguished cries nor the proximity of those creatures affected him. He sat, asleep, his head almost hidden from view, his broken wings tight against his shrunken body.

The moon began taking deep breaths, pulling as much air as she could into her. She pulled so hard she thought she might create a vacuum and the whole forest would let go and come at her, headed for her mouth. With each breath she took, she glowed more strongly, sending as much light as possible in Maxwell's direction. But it was no use. She was too far away and the solid glow she sent into the forest did not penetrate as far as Maxwell's tree.

"Deirdre!" she yelled. In the ensuing silence, the only sounds she heard were that faint wailing which came from the south, and the rasping scratch of the animals' underbellies as they grabbed the tree limb and pulled themselves along, closing in on Maxwell. She stopped screaming; she stopped looking. She shut her eyes tightly and tried to block everything out.

When they reached the base of the mountains, they stopped for a moment to rest. Vera was anxious to move on. She was close to home, and her excitement was evident. Her tail twitched, her eyes were bright, their pale depths obscured. Derin saw that the mountains didn't rise vertically from the Plain; the change in elevation was more gradual and the way was clotted with boulders and brush. Dried grass the color of straw stirred in the slight wind which swept down the mountains.

The beginning of the ascent was not difficult. The ground rolled before them toward the place where the rock face rose, solid and black. Manzanita, chokecherry, and brambles broke the monotony of grass with thorns, silver leaves, the dried blood of the berries. The grass hissed as they walked through it, and Derin wondered if anything lived under this cover, something dangerous or poisonous, in hiding, waiting for them.

Vera led the way. No one spoke. The boy was glad to have left the soft sand behind. The dirt was solid under his feet, and the grass and brush were a relief after the aridity of the Plain. Matthew was delighted. He bolted ahead of Vera, scrambled up on the boulders, and leapt back to the ground, disappearing beneath the grasses until they came upon him. Vera seemed not to see him, intent only on the climb.

A new rapport had developed between the satyr and the fox since the owl's wind swept down upon them. The banter between them had changed in coloration, was warmer, more intimate. Was it because he'd saved her life, as he was so bold to claim, or had it been more subtle — the heat of his haunches as he pinned her to the ground, the memory of the music he had played? Perhaps the sheer inexhaustibility of his energy stirred her, the strong curve of his back.

Matthew had walked beside her during the last stretch on the Plain, and Derin walked behind, watching the satyr's hand sweep the air and land, almost unconsciously, upon the fox's head. He stroked her, scratched behind her ears. From what Derin could see, she didn't seem to mind.

Now, though, she ignored Matthew and the satyr couldn't keep himself from teasing her about it. "Hot and cold," he said. "That's what you are. Can't be trusted." She didn't answer, acted as though she hadn't heard. "You're killing me with your indifference," he said. "You're breaking my heart." When she didn't respond, he ran ahead, climbed a boulder, clutched both hands to his chest as if he'd been stabbed, staggered, and fell, disappearing once again into the tall dry grass.

Vera found a stream bed, its water long since gone, and began to follow it. The stream wound through the hills, fairly level, clear of debris and undergrowth, and the satyr and boy followed the fox. Where the stream bed disappeared, the climbing became more difficult as the slope of mountain increased. With Vera still leading, they began to switchback. Neither of them thought to question her.

Before them, the rock face rose. The underbrush became more dense and they threaded their way through bushes and vines. The brambles' thorns tore at Derin's legs, and the manzanita, spiny and sharp, jabbed him. From time to time, Matthew scrambled up on a boulder, his back to the mountain, staring out over the Plain which now lay below them, its undulations constant, so far they couldn't see where the sand ended. Hands on his hips, his head thrown back, he took deep draughts of the mountain air.

The underbrush became more sparse and the incline gave way to the speckled grandeur of granite. The mountains had the authority of great age, their broken precipices and overlooks worn down by weather. Derin knew nothing of their geology and he wondered what had created this great rocky upheaval. They were so much *bigger* than he was, as the river had been. He seemed puny, insubstantial, hardly worth the small claim he had upon the earth. As he climbed he thought what little impact he could ever have upon them. Though they might change from year to year, a rock slipping and tumbling to the Plain below, taking other rocks with it, rearranging the side he now scrambled up, it seemed to Derin they would remain inviolate.

As they threaded their way along the path Vera summoned out of rock and air, the mountain peaks began to surround them, solid, silent, threatening the darkening clouds. Night was falling, but in the shadow of these peaks, it had already come. Soon Derin was pulling himself along, placing his foot on a level spot and heaving his way up. Matthew leapt from rock to rock, his cleft hooves giving him an advantage in the most unlikely spots.

Vera grew more excited the higher they climbed. She joked with the satyr, but as she and Matthew increased their lead the boy could no longer hear what she said. He thought he saw the satyr point a finger at her, saw her lower herself to the ground, could only imagine their banter. Ahead of him now, so far he could no longer see them, Matthew and Vera climbed. Their ascent was a faint scratch, rock upon rock, in the overwhelming stillness. The only immediate sound was his own breathing, the noise of his feet among the stones.

Above him, the sky descended, the tense dark blanket of clouds which had hung in the air the past four days. Small swirls of mist clung to the mountain's surfaces, issuing through fissures as from its interior. He came to an overhang of rock blocking his passage, stretching so far to either side he couldn't see above it. In lagging behind, he had lost the way; his friends had found an easier route. He descended a bit, holding fast to the rock, slowly lowering a foot at a time until he gained a solid purchase. Darkness had come quickly, the mountain above him shrouded in fog and the cold mask of night. He inched to the right along the ledge and started up again.

"Matthew," he yelled. "Vera."

There was no sound, neither their voices answering him, nor the crackle of rocks under their feet. He called again, and this time Matthew's voice floated down to him, filtering through the increasing mist. A fine rain, its tiny drops like the softest goose down, tickled his cheeks and forehead as he strained to see where the voice came from.

"Up here!" Matthew's voice said. "Derin, we're up here."

The boy clenched his teeth and began to climb again. His legs were beginning to feel like water. The pack weighed him down, seemed intent on tumbling him to the Plain below. But he reached up, grabbed a piece of rock, placed his left foot on a small obtrusion of granite, and together, his leg and arm lifted him up.

When he found them, they stood together at the foot of what seemed an unclimbable cliff. The rock was sheer, without footholds or handholds, at least until it disappeared into the darkness above them. Derin felt a knot forming in his stomach. All this time he'd believed she knew the way, and now she'd led them to this impasse. Before him, the mountain rose, only to be replaced, he knew, by other mountains. They were stranded in the middle of a maze.

"Where were you?" Matthew asked. "We were beginning to think we'd lost you."

"Then you should have waited," Derin said.

"Watch it," the satyr replied. "I had just started to believe your disposition had permanently improved."

"It hasn't," Derin said. "At least, not permanently." He turned to the fox. "What are we supposed to do now?" he asked. "We can't stay here for the night."

"No," Vera said. "We can't. I thought we'd just keep climbing. Follow me." She padded along the base of the rock face, disappeared behind a boulder, and didn't reemerge. Both Matthew and Derin stood there, waiting for her. "Come on," she said, her voice muffled by the huge rock. The boy looked at the satyr, and Matthew bent low at the waist, sweeping his hand along the ground.

Derin slipped behind the boulder and there, in front of Vera, a fissure in the rock, almost like a staircase, rose above their heads. The wall wasn't unclimbable after all. Vera scrambled up and disappeared. Derin entered the fissure, his shoulders scraping the rough stone, his arms and legs splayed against the rock's surface. He climbed steadily, inching his way along. Where was Vera, and how had she gotten so far above him? He couldn't believe a climb like this was easy for her. He reached up, found a handhold, placed his left toe in a crack, and rose.

When he was almost to the top, his legs began to shake. Below him he could hear Matthew breathing hoarsely. He reached above, and when he pulled, the rock gave way and a piece the size of his fist tumbled into the blackness. He heard Matthew's startled yell and a stream of obscenities. His legs trembled so violently he couldn't move; he could hardly hold on.

The boy shifted his weight to his left leg and his right momentarily stopped shaking, although his left now took up the trembling for both of them. His body rebelled. He made the mistake of looking down. There, between his legs, was an enormous darkness, for the night had swept up off the Plain and was approaching him from below as well as above. He was no more than a fly about to be swatted dead by the encroaching blackness.

He reached up again, and this time his hand closed around an out-cropping of granite which held when he tested his weight against it. In the darkness below him, he heard Matthew's coarse breathing, the scrabble of his climb. And then the satyr's head appeared, the tight curls of his hair, the two horns. The face strained upwards at him, staring at the legs, still shaking so violently the boy was afraid the whole rock face might give way beneath him, up past the waist until Matthew's eyes met his.

"Derin," Matthew said, his voice low. The obscenities were gone, the bright tonalities missing. "Are you all right?"

"Yes," he answered, as calmly as he could. "I'm just catching my breath."

"Catch it as quick as you can," the satyr said. "I can't hold out much longer."

The boy closed his eyes. The shaking in his legs slowly subsided, and when he looked down again, he realized Matthew had grabbed his right ankle and held on, an anchor, a ground. It was as though the trembling had drained from him, into Matthew's arm, into the rock itself.

He began to wriggle up the last section of the fissure. Painfully, moving one foot, one hand at a time, rotating his shoulders so they rubbed against the rock, wedging him there, he approached the top. He reached upwards, felt his hand close over the granite. His legs began pumping. He shot up the last few feet, heaved himself over the edge, and lay on the rock, gasping for breath.

Derin watched as Matthew slowly, tortuously emerged from the fissure. Together, they lay in the dark. The satyr rolled onto his back and laughed. "Look at the sky," he said. Derin sat up and stared above him. Nothing but blackness greeted him, no pinpricks of light. "Only kidding," Matthew said. "Wanted to see if you were still on your toes." He picked himself up off the rock and stood squarely on his hindquarters, his arms stretched toward the clouds. He groaned, an exaggeration. "I've had it," he said. "This trip has done me in."

Derin stood beside him. The mist had soaked his hair. He could only imagine that Matthew was as wet. He looked at his friend, but the darkness was so intense he could hardly make out the other's features. Derin reached out to touch Matthew's shoulder, to reassure them both.

The satyr moved closer, and without warning, hugged him so tightly he could feel Matthew's heart beating. He didn't resist, let himself be crushed, up in the mountains, in the darkness. They stood a while, neither speaking, the boy thinking of this trip and beyond that to the years in the meadowlands. He had no idea what Matthew was thinking.

The last part of the climb was easy. Ahead of them, they saw the fire the fox had kindled, glimmering like a constant star, and they headed for it.

"Good of you to drop by," Vera said. "Welcome to my home."

The fox had gathered enough dry wood to last the evening. They ate their small supper by the fire's light and talked about the day's adventures. The rain, the owl's wind, the hooded falcons thundering over them were distant images from a bad dream which had lost its private hallucinatory power. What was left was their camaraderie, the peace they had established with one another.

"We've made it this far," Matthew was saying. "I think we've done pretty well." The satyr, sitting by the fire, looked fierce in its glow. His chest was ruddy; his face glistened; his eyes were brilliant, almost demonic.

"Tomorrow we get to the top," Vera said. "Not far from here the snow begins. I'll take you over the summit and point you on your way."

Matthew's expression didn't change. He looked into the fire intently, as though Vera had made an idle comment about how cold the air was.

"You should go with us," Derin said. "You should finish what you've started."

"No," Vera said. "I told you from the beginning. I stay here."

The moon still lay ahead, over the mountains, down into the Forest. Derin had surrendered so totally to the owl's spell he had forgotten the moon, her rescue, the sense he had that his own mystery might be unraveled by this journey. He looked up into a blackness so profound he thought it would never be light again. The moon should be hanging there, a pale gold disk, but she was caught in a tree instead, a prisoner.

Before he could say another word, the music began. Matthew had found his panpipe and the notes flashed like sparks from the fire. The satyr rocked to his knees and then was standing, swaying, his shoulders, hips moving in time to the music. The melody was low, breathy; to Derin it sounded like leaves rustling. And then the string of notes ascended, bird calls, several at once, answering one another. Vera's eyes glazed over, and she crouched low, her head resting between her paws. Her hindquarters rose in the air and then hunkered down.

Though he tried to fight it, the music made Derin light-headed, almost queasy. He felt himself falling, as from a great height. Blood pounded in his ears; he tried to catch his breath. The fox rolled on her back in the dirt, arched, scratching. Derin saw her as she'd appeared earlier that day, her silver hair streaming behind her.

The satyr began to dance, circling the fire. He kicked up his hooves, his black curls writhed, his horns caught the orange light as if they burned. The boy and fox stared as he crouched, leapt, dancing to a rhythm all his own, moving faster and faster, the harsh rasp of his breathing breaking the music as he gasped for air. The music reached a crescendo, Matthew spinning so rapidly now he was only a blur to the boy, until he stopped as suddenly as he'd begun and collapsed in the dirt between them.

Derin scrambled to his feet, confused, breathless himself, dizzy from watching Matthew whirling in the dark. He swayed where he stood, closed his eyes, tried to regain his balance. He staggered away from the fire, wanting to be alone. He found an outcropping of rock and sat upon it, his knees bent, his arms wrapped around them, hugging them to his chest. Behind him, he heard a voice beginning, a low growl. The hair on the back of his neck bristled.

Surrounded by darkness, he tried to clear his head, taking deep breaths of the cold air. Below him the Plain, above him the mountains. He was caught in limbo, stranded between where he'd come from and where he was going. The meadowlands lay miles behind them. The world as he'd known it was only a fraction of the world as it truly existed, the truth was more complicated than he'd ever expected.

Matthew was also in limbo, half-animal, half-man, caught between those poles, belonging wholly in neither. It was this animal side which drew him to the fox. But Vera was part human herself, at least during those rare moments of transformation. Which half of Matthew responded?

Shrieks of laughter sounded behind him. He whirled and saw Matthew, up off the ground, chasing a nymph. For an instant, he was totally taken by the sight of Vera, her long hair glinting in the firelight. He ran back toward them, but well before he'd gotten there, Vera had changed herself into a fox. She crouched, breathless, her white fur gleaming in the orange glow of the flames.

From the black sky, a black shadow fell. Deirdre perched by the fire and looked at the three of them. "What's going on here?" she demanded. "Who's this?"

The darkness was velvet, the air as soft, as fragrant as the owl could ever remember. It smelled of decay, leaf mold and tree rot, and he was deeply happy.

His victory seemed so close he could almost touch it. He had the name of this traitor—this Deirdre—and soon she would trouble him no longer. Although the wind had not destroyed his unexpected guests, it had undoubtedly delayed them. Once the sun lost her power, no one—

not all the creatures in the world — could raise a feather or claw against him. And from what he had been told by the falcons, these three were more like wraiths than real adversaries.

He could imagine them now, clinging like spiders to the rock face in the dark, ripped by that cold wind which swept from the mountains' summit to the east, caught in cross-currents as other air rose from the Plain, if they had even gotten that far. He shivered with pleasure. Soon they would freeze to death, soon they, too, would become part of the natural decline.

Or if by some miracle they survived the onslaught of the mountains, if by luck or magic they descended into the Forest, he would be ready for them. At this moment, he had outposts settling along the eastern perimeter. No one could enter his domain without his knowledge.

So he would face them if they came; he would be the first one they met. He felt the pride and power of a hunter who has laid his trap well, who need only sit back and await the arrival of his prey. He could turn his attention to other matters. In the morning he would find this raven with the white knob on her claw. He would make an example of her before the clan.

And then he would discover where the sun spent her nights. His eyes gleamed; unconsciously he tensed his talons. So little stood between him and the everlasting dark.

"It's happening," Deirdre said. "Just as I hoped it would. Ravens are beginning to rise against the owl. He's become increasingly vindictive, stooping to torture and intimidation. He's moved the moon to the southern part of the Forest. I've just come from there.

"My, my," she gasped. "I'm still out of breath. I'm so excited I can barely enunciate. And you know how rare that is for me." As she spoke, she watched the changing emotions on their faces, wondering how they would take the revelation of the Keep.

"He's heard about the three of you, although I *must* say when I learned there were three, I didn't know what to make of it. I thought at first — correctly, of course — that the two of you . . ." (nodding to Matthew and Derin) "had met with a third, but *then* . . . then I wondered if three others, three entirely unknown to me, had started west, and I thought. . . ."

"Deirdre," Matthew said.

"Yes, yes, of course," she said. "I'm sorry. Anyway, he doesn't know who you are, although he knows *what* you are, and he hasn't figured out how you know about him. He doesn't think you'll survive these mountains. His plan isn't exactly clicking as he hoped it would. He thought he'd just sit back and wait for the sun to burn herself out, but it's more complicated than that.

"The moon is doing well, not pleased of course, can't stand the confinement, but she's alive, I'm happy to say. And the biggest news is. . . ." Here she paused for emphasis. The fox, the satyr, and the boy all looked annoyed, although they were listening to every word. Had she gone on too long?

"The biggest news is so big I can hardly believe it myself. It's something none of us ever dreamed of. It's almost impossible. If I hadn't seen it with my own eyes, if one of you were to tell me, I don't know if I'd. . . ."

"Deirdre," Matthew said, angry. "Get to the point."

The raven stopped and looked at the satyr haughtily. "You always were a fussbudget, a fly in the ointment. I must say, I'm not delighted with your interruption."

"*Deirdre,*" Derin said, standing up.

"And you're right to be impatient," the raven said to the boy. "For it involves you more than the others." She puffed herself up, preened under a wing. "I have discovered a prison in the southern reach of the Deadwood Forest," she said, "a large structure built of mud and stone. It was constructed by the owl years ago, before the wind took us from the meadowlands. And it isn't empty."

"What's in it?" Derin asked.

"People," the raven said, spitting out her prize as if it were the pit of a ripe fruit.

"Who?" Derin asked. "What are people?"

"My dear boy," Deirdre said. "*You.* You are People."

Matthew watched all the color drain from Derin's face. He looked as though the air in his lungs had been punched out of him. His legs trembled and he sat back down.

"Me?" he whispered. "Others like me?" He had never head the word *people* before. The idea that there were enough of them to have a name of their own stunned him.

"This is cause for the greatest excitement!" Deirdre said. "There should be peals of thunder, lightning flashes."

But Derin didn't hear the raven. He sat staring into the fire, watching the small blue flames at its center.

"The messenger returns," Matthew murmured, and he moved in the darkness to where the boy sat and touched his shoulder.

Derin looked up at him. In the paleness of his face, his eyes shone blue as the fire. "Did you know?" he asked the satyr. "Have you known all these years?"

"No," the satyr said. "I swear, I didn't."

"But listen to the rest," Deirdre said. "I haven't finished. Years ago, before you were conceived, before I was a meteor in my father's *eye* for that matter, the People lived in the Deadwood Forest. But it wasn't dead then. It was transcendent, from what they said, verdant and lush, much like the meadowlands. It only commenced to die when the owl seized power. Who knows where he came from? One day he marched on the People— the Keep had already been built—and the ones he didn't kill, he jailed in that prison where they've stayed until this day."

"Derin, listen to me," the satyr said. "I didn't know. I told you almost everything. I told you at the river how the stranger—a man in a hooded cloak—gave you to me when you were a baby. I didn't know about the People, or even the owl. All he said was there was terrible trouble in the west. That I was to keep you and care for you until you would be sent for. He left before I could ask any questions. I don't know anything about him, how he crossed the Swollen River, how he disappeared after. And then you grew, and I almost forgot about what he said. Until Deirdre came."

"Have *you* known?" Derin asked the raven.

"I wish I had," Deirdre said. "It would have been less harmful to my pride. I'm the unwitting accomplice in a scenario I had no knowledge of."

"I'm the one who knew," Vera said. "It just wasn't my place to tell you." The boy, who'd been ignoring the fox, swung to meet her gaze. "I'm older than you think," she said. "I heard of the owl's march on the People. The slaughter was worse than you can imagine."

"Why didn't you tell me?" Derin asked angrily.

"Are you satisfied with these words from the raven?" she asked. "Could anything we say answer all your questions? Your past is your own secret, perhaps the only thing in the world which belongs solely to you. No one else can know it as you can. And if some part of the mystery is hidden from you, only you can discover it. Our history — the myth by which we each continue — is our greatest treasure. It would mean nothing to you if it were handed down, like a curious rock, a memento."

"Tell me everything," Derin said. "I want to know."

"What good would it do?" the fox asked wearily. "You think you'll gain from hearing the tale in its entirety? Everyone's past is bloody, filled with tragedy. You know all you need to know: that somehow you were spared the destruction of your people, that someone carried you to safety in the east, that Matthew raised you from a baby, and now you've been called back. So you didn't know your parents. Which of us does? It's an old story: it's happened before, and it will, I dare say, happen again."

"We've got to rescue them," Derin said fiercely.

"Derin," the raven said. "You're forgetting the owl. You're forgetting the moon. First things first."

"But isn't my past the most important thing?" he asked. "Isn't that just what Vera was saying?"

"To you, Derin," Matthew said. "Only to you."

"We've got to keep the larger view," the raven said.

"I don't think I can," the boy said, "right now. I just want to sit here awhile." He was silent for a moment. "I don't understand," he said finally, "why this is happening to me."

"Don't worry about it," Deirdre said. "You're not so special after all. It could be anyone."

They left him by the fire. He built it up with a few branches remaining from the pile Vera had gathered. Deirdre flew to a point of rock, faced out over the Plain, folded her wings, and was soon asleep. The satyr and the fox retreated from the fire, but it was too dark to venture far from the campsite and they stayed within range of the light. Matthew threw the blanket over himself, turned on his side, and closed his eyes. Against his back he felt the slight pressure of the fox as she huddled close to him for warmth. He thought of two things — the image he'd always pursued of the nymph, and the small child he'd held in his arms fourteen years ago. Both seemed illusory, imaginary. He sighed deeply and slept.

Derin sat for a long time, staring into the flames. They rose and fell, casting shadows around him, illuminating for a moment the grotesque outlines of rock, the wall of mountain which rose in the west. As before, the hottest part of the fire burned blue, and under it, the orange bed of coals pulsed. The flames died away as the wood was consumed, and he found himself looking at a landscape of shifting heat, the cracks in the embers like fissures in the earth, as small breezes flew over the fire, creating visionary patterns among the glowing coals.

His mind wandered as he stared at that landscape, until he wasn't sure where he was. If one of his companions had been watching him, they might have thought he'd fallen into a trance, so fierce was his concentration.

In the fire's embers, he thought he saw a cloaked and hooded man. The stranger was tall and gaunt. His hair was white, his skin leathery, his eyes hidden by the rough black folds of cloth draped over the head and shoulders.

The man stood on a riverbank; below him rushing water, black as obsidian, leapt into view when the sky was cracked by lightning. The roar filling the air could have been the river or thunder. One shoulder grown into the bark, the stranger leaned heavily against a tree, and a jagged network of branches, wet and dark in the fierce illuminations, struck upwards above him into the sky.

The stranger cradled something under the cloak, something which squirmed and cried until the man bent his head down and whispered, and the crying stopped. Out of the darkness, the elegant shape of a heron became visible, its beak rocking forward with each step. It was followed by a wild-eyed figure, half-man, half-goat, stumbling through the swamp, his chest gleaming with water in the flashes of lightning.

The satyr stood perplexed, staring out over the river. He looked behind him, but the heron had disappeared. When the cloaked apparition appeared from behind the tree, the satyr grunted, threw his hands in front of his face and stepped backwards, almost pitching himself over the lip of bank and into the water.

"Don't be afraid," the stranger said. "I mean you no harm. I've come a long way and you mustn't leave me now." From the cowl, the stranger's eyes shone. "There's been terrible trouble in the west. These storms the week past are but a poor mirror of the catastrophe."

He reached out, delivered into the satyr's arms the small bundle he had cradled beneath the cloak. "Here," he said. "You must take him.

Keep him safe. In time to come, he will be sent for. His name is Derin, delivered from death."

Derin looked into a face at once astonished and frightened. Blue eyes, pointed ears; two small horns poked from a wet mess of tangled hair. He was held roughly, awkwardly.

"But I can't take care of him," Matthew said. "I don't know how."

"You must," the stranger said. "You have no choice."

"What are you?" Matthew asked, but the stranger had disappeared. The satyr looked around him in a panic. There was no trace of the hooded man.

"What will I do with a *baby*?" Matthew wailed. Derin was lowered by two strong arms, he felt the wet coldness of mud, and he watched the satyr's back as he darted off in the darkness away from the river. He lay there, quietly listening to the roaring of the water. And then he was picked up again, hugged tightly, and he felt the wind rushing around him as he was carried by the satyr back through the woods to the meadowlands.

"She opened her beak and screamed."

FRIDAY

Matthew awoke in the dark, craggy as the mountains over him. His head hurt slightly; his tongue was thick with sleep. He sat up and rubbed his eyes and shivered in the cold air. As he tried to clear his head, the darkness cracked, and in the distance, a squall line of light moved across the Plain below him as the dawn came on.

He wondered what it would have been like a week earlier, to be hunched there while the light, invisible but for a brightening of air, hurtled from the horizon and turned the snow of the summit a pale yellow, to see the sun break over the world's rim, a bloodstone, its brilliant flood engulfing the still flatness of the Plain until the bands met, bathing him and his friends in first light, first heat.

It was hard to imagine, for what he saw was a wavering phantom, grey as granite, as morning made its way over the vast preponderance of land. It lapped at the mountains' foundation and crept up the rock, revealing the visible evidence of the hard climbing that lay ahead.

The light was too wan to warm him. He thought, almost wistfully, of the heat they had left below them. When had that been? The previous evening and its revelations seemed years ago, as though he knew what he'd always known, but more clearly, as though it was information he'd grown up with but understood for the first time.

Derin lay still, huddled by the fire's blackened pit where he'd fallen asleep. The boy's face was blank as the sky, grey as ashes. All his life he'd had questions the satyr couldn't answer. Now that the boy knew he wasn't alone, that there were others like him, Matthew couldn't fathom how it would affect him.

Boy? He was a young man. This last piece of knowledge had clinched that fact. Derin now understood his personal investment in the journey's outcome. As Matthew stared, a shadow passed over Derin's face. Lying there, he looked older than the satyr, as old as the mountains. Derin had outgrown him, had reached down or been plunged down into a wellspring of responsibility which Matthew found alien, frightening. What Derin saw now, behind those closed lids, Matthew would never see.

The light grew stronger and the raven's profile materialized from the darkness. She slept perched on a rock, looking like a darker piece of stone, carved from the softness around her by wind and rain. Derin flung an arm up and covered his eyes with the crook of an elbow. Deirdre's head bobbed, she spread her wings, stretched them until they shuddered, and folded them. And the fox rose from the dirt, shook herself, and settled back again.

They began the ascent after a simple breakfast. The four of them spoke little, content to inhabit for a while longer the separate countries of their sleep. In the morning light, the mountains looked less forbidding than they had in the gathering darkness of the previous evening. Pale as the light was, it revealed the full stature of the summit and made clear the fact of a pass. Between the peaks, like a vast white tongue, a glacier loomed in the distance. Above it, on either side, granite walls, shrouded with snow, thundered toward the dark grey clouds.

Deirdre flew ahead of them, scouting, swooping up the incline and hanging there, her wings fluttering in the wind which rose from the Plain and soared up to trouble the snow. Like the pillars of sand, the wind had raised from the Plain, white funnels spiraled up and fell away, dancing over the glacier's face.

Derin passed the fox who had again that day begun the march, swept by her without a word. She watched him go, not surprised, and then waited for Matthew. The boy climbed quickly, almost unconsciously, finding a solid footing among the brittle shards of shale and slate. He was sure of himself, urged upward by a new desire to reach the crest of mountain and descend into the Forest.

Derin's neck soon ached from the strain of always looking up, for as he climbed, he continued to stare at the snow-covered peaks. Even in the grey light, they gleamed like diamonds, their harsh edges immaculate beneath the canopy of cloud. He would pass between those teeth, on the glacier which separated them.

The rise they began to ascend was covered with scree, rocks little larger than gravel which had fallen into the valley from the mountains' crest. The stones rolling and tumbling under their feet made climbing difficult. Matthew's hooves, such an advantage the day before, were now a handicap. He found the scree treacherous. The sharp outer rim of horn couldn't edge the rock. He walked cautiously, aware of the danger of his legs slipping among the scree and wedging there.

They were above the tree line, had left behind the stunted pines sticking from the rock. All was a vastness of granite and the blinding surge of glacier ahead. Beyond the scree, the rock rose in ledges, like steps, stained with water, snow melt and glacier melt.

Derin's hands became numb. As he wound his way, sometimes edging along a thin lip of rock until he found a hold large enough to pull himself up by, the water dripped down his arms and onto his chest until the front of his shirt was soaked. He began to feel the height. A slight tingling in his legs spread up his torso and into his arms. The sensation ended at his wrists, his hands too cold to feel anything. Breathing was more difficult. As hard as he tried, he couldn't fill his lungs with air. He looked below him, and was dizzied by the fall. He was living in a vertical world, nothing solid but the rock under his hands and feet.

They hadn't talked in quite a while, each intent on the hard climbing, and even Deirdre, returning to them from time to time before flying further off in search of the easiest route, was uncustomarily silent. To keep them closer together, Matthew picked up the fox and draped her over his shoulders as a shepherd might carry a lamb. At first Vera protested.

"Put me down," she said. "I should be leading now; I know this mountain."

"Let him go," the satyr said. "He needs to learn. He needs to take this trip into his own hands."

Vera rested on Matthew's shoulders, and the satyr followed the boy's twisting path. The tongue of glacier was temporarily lost from view, but as Derin and Matthew pulled themselves over the final ledge, it loomed above them, thirty feet at its most imposing height. The ice sloped steeply down to meet the rock. Deirdre perched on the snow above them and urged them up, but Derin was wary of the glacier.

"I think we should climb above it," he said, "on the rock around it. I'm afraid the cold might slow us down."

Vera tried to say something, but Matthew clamped a hand over her mouth. He shaded his eyes from the ice's glare, and looked at the route Derin had suggested. "I'm not sure," he said. "The snow looks easier."

"I don't like it," Derin said. "It's hard to walk in that stuff." Vera, on the ground again, said nothing.

"Get up here," Deirdre urged. "I'm appalled by your pusillanimity."

"Stop the chatter," Derin said. "I'll feel safer on the rock."

"It's up to you," the satyr said, and so Derin took off again, climbing to the left of the thick white ribbon spilling down from the heights above them. The landscape they found themselves in was rough, outsized, wintery. Pockets of snow dazzled the crevasses between the boulders. The sky overhead was grey with storm clouds, torn by the imposing peaks.

They hadn't counted on rain, and as they circumvented the glacier, it began to fall in a fine mist as it had the night before. It froze on the rocks, forming a coating of verglas, making their climb extremely dangerous.

"We *have* to get down to the glacier," Vera said, her tone strong enough that Derin asked no questions. His own feet slipped beneath him at every step, and more than once his hands clawed at rock which no longer offered a handhold. His breath came in short gasps and his heart raced. Could they lower themselves down now without breaking their necks?

"Over here," Deirdre shrieked below them. "You can get down here." She sat still on the snow, a small dark spot in the middle of that endless white field.

"Where?" Derin called impatiently, for Deirdre hadn't moved, so she flew to where he hovered on the rock and told him to follow her. The descent was steep, but it wasn't far to the glacier's top. Derin moved slowly, aware that the smallest misstep would send him crashing to the ice below. Matthew was even more thorough. He cracked through the verglas with his hooves, scattering the pieces which fell with the faint sound of breaking glass.

When he was ten feet above the snow, Derin jumped. For a moment, he was afraid he hadn't thrown himself far enough out. Cold air whipped around him. He lost his balance, and landed on his back in soft thick powder. It was like hitting a crusted pillow. He struggled to his feet, his hands sheathed in white gloves, wiping away the dusting from his face, and turned to watch the other two descend.

Matthew wouldn't jump. He cautiously lowered himself the last few feet to the glacier's surface. And Vera was having a difficult time. No longer on Matthew's shoulders, she was pointed nose down as at the top of a slide, her back legs attempting to grip the rock. She slipped, and as she fell, she stretched her body into a long thin plain and cascaded down the ice-covered rock, burying herself in the drift at the bottom.

Matthew dug her out, laughing. She was covered with snow, her white fur bristling with ice crystals. When Matthew attempted to brush her off, she moved haughtily away and shook herself.

"I told you," she said. "You should have let me lead." Deirdre watched them intermittently, intent on keeping the rain from freezing on her feathers. She was afraid her wings would be weighed down with the thin coating of ice, and she would be no use to anyone if she couldn't fly.

The three finished brushing themselves off. In front of them, a solid hill of snow rose slowly until it met the blue-black crease of sky at the pass. Matthew struggled in the deep powder. His hooves sank in; it exhausted him to pull his legs loose for each new step. Derin thought he felt the ground tremble. "Come on," he said urgently. "Let's get out of here."

"And where will we go?" Deirdre asked mildly. "A more temperate clime?"

"I'm all for it," Matthew said. "Why don't you fly ahead and see how far it is to the summit?"

"What purpose would that accomplish?" the raven wanted to know.

"It'll get you out of here for a minute or two."

"I'll ignore that," she said.

Nevertheless, she did as Matthew asked. The pass was not too distant, although Deirdre knew it would take the three on the ground a considerable time. Where would they spend the night? They weren't equipped for this. There was no wood. They had no really warm clothes. A prickling sense of dread spread through her.

When she came to the pass, her heart sank. What looked like miles of snow lay on the other side. The bleakness of the descent was interrupted by fierce thrusts of rock which broke through the whiteness, but as she hovered there at the top, she couldn't see the place where the snow gave way to mountain, or where the mountain dissolved in plain. They'd never make it. The owl was right.

Behind her, she could barely make out the three tiny figures struggling up through the snow field. What would they do? The mist obscured everything; the rain was beginning to fall more heavily.

And then it turned to snow. From the sky, like the fall of leaves, thick white flakes descended. She cawed loudly in dismay, but the three below her couldn't hear. It was as though the snow absorbed every sound in the world. Before, as they'd made their way up the mountain, they'd had the sweep of wind for company. Now the snow swallowed even that.

She flew down to them again, wishing she might pick them up and carry them, to hurry them, anything to get them over this mountain and down the other side. They became larger as she flew, but they were no longer dark. Each was heavily coated with snow. The satyr looked bearded, ancient. All three shivered miserably. They had spread out some, Derin still in the lead, followed by the fox and the satyr, and each looked dismally alone, forgotten by the others.

Derin plunged on as best he could. He tried to kick out footholes in the snow to make it easier for Matthew to follow, but he could no longer feel his legs, and his arms were like dead weights only vaguely connected by his shoulders to the rest of his body. Matthew's hooves were ice, the soft inner soles packed tight with snow. Vera floundered up behind. She swam through the thick powder, trying to keep her head above the surface.

"I've never seen the weather like this," she gasped. "I should have realized."

"What?" Matthew asked, stopping to wait for her.

"The mountains are more fearful since the moon was stolen," she said. "Like the river, like the Plain. Worse than it was before. Headed downhill. Catastrophe."

Derin turned and saw the fox scramble up on the satyr's shoulders again. The sky brightened visibly, even through the snow. The boy heard a monstrous thunderclap, the sound of ice cracking in the middle of a pond, but much more enormous. At the edge where Vera and Matthew stood, a deep black fissure opened. Clouds of snow were thrown high in the air over their heads, like a waterspout. The air filled with a roar such as a tidal wave might make. It came from far off and bore relentlessly down on them. Matthew froze. Derin screamed and started to plunge toward them, but Deirdre flapped around his head and yelled at him to run in the other direction, up the mountain, away from the avalanche. He stopped in his tracks, unable to move. The fissure grew. It was like watching the petals of a dark rose open all at once. The satyr, with the fox wrapped around his shoulders, stood and watched the earth fall away below him, a massive wall of snow and ice tumbling down the mountain, gathering force as it went. From the darkness, white plumes reached up to grab him. And then there was nothing beneath his feet but air and he tried to run, threw himself forward, clawing at the crumbling face of snow which separated him from a blizzard of chaos.

When the ravens received word the owl would speak to them again, many wondered at the extraordinary command. Never before had he called them together in daylight. Even those inclined to disobey were awed. They flew from all directions, the air thick with suspicion and distrust.

For in the Deadwood Forest, the fight had begun. Reasoning and patience had given way to screaming disagreements, and in a few instances, to confrontation. Bitter words were hurled by those opposing the owl against others who supported him, friends with whom they'd spent their whole lives flying.

Condor was alternately elated and confused. Where was Deirdre? If she would only return, she could explain all this to him. He was too embarrassed to ask any of the ravens he had just met what was going on. By the time they reached the clearing, the trees were already clotted with dark hunched forms, the air above them black with hurrying wings. Condor settled himself and was quiet.

The owl appeared to be sleeping. His great hooded eyes were closed. Not a raven said a word. The only noises to be heard were the flapping wings, the creaking of branches when birds landed, the occasional far away *crauk* as one of them called to another.

Condor looked around him furtively. He became frightened, but he didn't know why. And then he noticed something he'd never seen among the clan. At other times, they had scattered themselves evenly on the trees and bushes, but today they huddled in small distinct groups. Red eyes darted from side to side, sizing up the others, and the glances were murderous.

The young bird looked again at the owl and saw the lids slide upwards like the rising of twin moons. The great yellow eyes stared, unblinking, at the ravens. If the owl was aware of unrest among the branches, he gave no sign of it. Then Condor saw the old crone from the previous day. She sat on a branch directly over the owl. Unlike the other ravens, she appeared unruffled, and she gazed keenly out at them with the same immutable stare which shone from the owl's eyes.

Little by little, the birds realized the owl was preparing to speak, and they stopped their brutal glances at one another. All looked expectantly at him, but he didn't say a word. Condor began to squirm on his branch. He didn't understand what was happening, and the tension was making him crazy. The owl continued to look calmly out over the assemblage, his eyes appeasing, almost friendly.

Through the bare branches of the Deadwood Forest, a rustling arose, like a faint wind coming through thick grass, the vast uncomfortable bustle of the ravens engaged in losing this war of nerves. The owl's eyes brightened. His enormous head swung from side to side, taking in all of them, one after another.

"I hear some of you have turned against me," he said in a voice so mild it belied the content of his speech. "But here in my presence not one of you dares to challenge me. Isn't that so?"

No one contradicted him. He paused, and Condor shivered on his branch. He looked to his left but every eye was riveted upon the owl. Enormous confidence and power surged from the center of the clearing, and the birds, for the moment, were in that sway.

"I have received information that another raven was seen flying east," the owl said. "This raven was not visiting the graves of the ancestors. This raven was bent on my downfall. Her name is Deirdre. Where is she?"

Condor started. He looked at the crone, and she was staring straight back at him, a wicked smile creasing her face. "WHERE IS SHE?" the owl thundered. "I want her now."

The branches were filled with a tumultuous uproar. Condor looked around him frantically, searching for Deirdre, but he didn't see her anywhere. "Who gave her away?" a raven shrieked, and in the aftermath of that question, Condor couldn't hear himself think. Through all this, the owl sat placidly, waiting for the noise to end. As it did, he calmly spoke again, clearly not in any hurry.

"If she is among you, she will come forward," he said. "If she is here and tries to escape, she will be apprehended. And if she is not here, she will be hunted down. She will be found. Now where is she?"

"I don't see her, my lord," the crone said from over the owl's head.

He looked upwards blankly. "But your eyes are not the best," he said. "Where is the one who told you about her?"

The crone nodded her head toward the tree in which Condor sat. "Over there, my lord," she said. "The little one with the stupid face."

For the first time in his life, Condor felt the force of the owl's stare fall squarely on him. It was as though he'd been pinioned by thick steel bands. "Come here," the owl said.

Around him, the air hissed with the whispered word *Traitor!* The other ravens he had flown with that day looked at him with surprise, contempt, hatred. "You snit!" one of them said. "You creeping snitch!"

Condor was dumbfounded. What had he done? "Come here, I said," the owl repeated, and the young bird obeyed. He stretched his wings, flew from the branch, and sailed across the clearing. Through every inch of air, the taunts were thrown at him — *Traitor! Miscreant! Canary! Quisling!* — and he flinched as though they were rocks.

He landed in front of the owl and looked up. Condor had never seen him from this perspective before, and the young raven quaked with fear. Above him, the huge yellow eyes stared down, the curved beak hooked over him like a rock ledge. In the soft wind blowing through the forest, the barred feathers fluttered and the curved talons, like tree roots, grew from the ground.

Behind him, the ravens were silent again. "Where is she?" the owl asked.

"I don't know," Condor said.

" . . . my lord," the owl murmured. Condor looked at him, baffled.

"I do not know, *my lord*," the owl said impatiently. Condor meekly repeated the sentence. "Why don't you know?" the owl asked.

"I don't know, my lord." Above the owl, the old crone cackled.

"You are a stupid little bird, aren't you?" the owl asked menacingly.

Condor stared at the ground. "Yes, my lord," he whispered.

"Answer this, if you can. When did you see her last?"

"Yesterday," Condor said.

"Yesterday when?"

"Yesterday morning."

"And where was she going?"

Condor twitched on the ground. Great spasms of remorse throbbed in his chest. He had told the crone about Deirdre and she had told the owl. He had betrayed her. It did him no good at all to remember that he hadn't meant to, that he had done nothing to be ashamed of.

"I don't know, my lord," he said, and looked bravely up at the owl, this time meeting those great yellow eyes without flinching.

"You're lying," the owl said.

"She flew off," Condor said. "She didn't tell me where she was going."

"In what direction?"

Condor continued to look at the owl, realizing there was no safe answer. "South," he said. "My lord."

"Of course," the owl said. "I should have known." He stared out over Condor's head at the other ravens. "What do the rest of you know?"

"She's gone," one of them said. "She's flown over the mountains."

"Shut your beak," another said.

And the air around Condor swirled with insults and threats from both sides. The owl remained calm, as though he knew without question that his force would prevail, that no matter how many of these birds turned against him, it would be nothing more than a minor irritation.

The insults died away. And from the center of that silence, a clarion voice rang out. It came from the far reaches of the Forest, back where a few stragglers had gathered. "If you harm her," it said, "you will have more to answer for than you even know."

For the first time that day, the owl became angry. His eyes tinged with blood and his chest swelled. "Who is it that dares to threaten me?" he thundered.

"I am just a voice speaking for many," it said. "It could be any of us."

"Your name!" the owl said. "I want your name."

"You won't be given it," the voice said. "Unless by another traitor."

Condor whirled around, deeply stung by the remark. "I didn't know," he said. "I didn't. . . ."

"Silence!" the owl said. But Condor wasn't finished addressing the distant voice. "I had no idea I was talking to a spy," he said. "It wasn't my fault."

"Stupid one," the owl said, but Condor paid no attention. Already facing away from the owl, he rose into the air and flew. Below him, the owl's voice boomed, but it was soon muffled by the hoarse screaming, the disintegration of peace, which had broken the meeting before. No one flew after him. Before him, the daylight crossed its short bridge toward nightfall.

He had never been so alone.

Derin stood and watched the bottom half of the world disappear, Matthew with it. The fox, hardly visible through the sheets of flying powder, leapt from the satyr's shoulders, arced in the air, and came down on the bucking glacier. Swimming through the snow, she escaped the breaking edge and made her way toward Derin. Deirdre cawed madly in the air by Derin's ears but he hardly heard her. The roaring continued, wave upon wave of noise, bounding up at him from the lip of snow where Matthew had been standing, rolling past him, and reverberating off the snowbound peaks. The boy was deafened by the thunder. He made a move toward the edge, but Deirdre screamed, "Don't!" and he stayed where he was. "You'll only make it worse," the raven said. "You'll knock more loose."

The fissure crept toward the boy, coming closer. He would stand there and watch it come, and if it overtook him and threw him down into the darkness beside his friend, so much the better. But the crumbling stopped, the roaring fell away below him, pealing down the valley with the snow. He stood there in the growing silence until he could hear the panting of the fox beside him, the frantic flapping of Deirdre's wings in the air above.

It was then he started down the glacier, alone. The fox huddled where she was, in shock, indistinguishable from the growing piles of white feather. Deirdre hung in the air like a tiny black dot but finally settled down on the fox's back and stonily watched Derin's descent.

The boy came to the jagged edge, a hard crust of ice. Cautiously he knelt and splayed his body on the surface, inching forward until his head hung over the break. Below him, he saw nothing but snow. A fierce wind, white with crystals, slapped his face, whipping up the valley from where the avalanche continued. From this vantage point, the roaring was still faintly audible, and then it stopped and there was a hollow thud as the snow finally ceased its downward spiral and settled. The noise landed in Derin's stomach and then there was nothing but the whisper of flakes as they fell past his face, down to join the rest.

Derin scanned what lay beneath him. About fifteen feet of white air separated him from the next layer of snow, and the slope slanted steeply from there. But he saw no trace of Matthew. Had the earth really opened up and swallowed him? Derin felt two claws on his back where Deirdre settled and looked out over his head to the whiteness below.

"Can the heart ever rebound?" Deirdre asked the air. "How many years have I known him? I'm afraid he's gone. He's buried."

"Hush," Derin said. "Don't say that." He stared down at the snow until his eyes hurt, half-expecting the satyr to rise from the depths of powder, brush himself off and make a joke. Nothing moved below him but the shifting face of glacier, rippled by wind. "He can't be gone," the boy said. "He can't be."

"What can we do?" Dierdre asked. She was trying to remain calm, but she felt the thin wire twisting in her gut, hysteria, robbing her of breath. The boy stood up, shaking the raven loose. She rose in the air above him, cawing angrily. Derin cupped his snow-caked hands around his mouth and shouted the satyr's name out over the abyss. It came back to him on the wind, softer but unmistakable. He shouted again, and only his voice answered. He threw himself down on the lip of ice again, so hard he knocked a piece loose. It fell straight and was lost in the soft snow. The wind flew at him and forced tears from the corners of his eyes.

He squinted. Below him, the wind picked up some snow, and in that instant, the boy thought he glimpsed something black jutting from the incessant whiteness. "Dierdre," he said. "Do you see it?"

"What?" the bird asked, settling on his back again.

"That," Derin said, pointing. "That black spot down there. Fly down and tell me what it is."

Deirdre swooped off the boy's back and into the chasm the avalanche had made. She beat her wings hard in the face of that rising wind, ripping up to where the boy lay. Several times she felt herself blown backwards, but she kept her eye on that speck of black and battled through the air toward it.

It was a single cloven hoof, stabbing through the snow like a broken stick. She landed on it, pecked at some of the powder around it, called up to Derin, *"It's Matthew,"* and watched in astonishment as the boy dropped his pack, stood, swung his arms out and leapt. She watched him fall, his arms flailing, knocked off balance by the wind.

Derin hit with a shock which surprised him, and he sunk in the snow to his waist. He clawed at the tight belt of white, falling forward in his frenzy. His face was frosted with it, and slowly he waded over to where Deirdre perched.

It was Matthew's hoof all right, but where was the other one? He tried to pack some powder down to give himself a purchase but still he sunk to his knees. Frantically, taking large armsful of snow, he began to dig the satyr out. Deirdre flew into the air and hovered there watching him. Vera had crept back down the slope and was peering at them from the lip of ice above.

Derin found Matthew's other leg under the first one. The satyr was on his side, his head tilted downhill as the avalanche had taken him, buried under feet of snow. The boy ripped it from around the satyr, digging to his waist. He grabbed both legs and tried to pull Matthew loose, but the body didn't budge. He uncovered the torso, the arms and finally the head. Matthew's eyes were invisible, his eye sockets packed with snow. Snow crowded his pointed ears, frosted the thick black curls. Carefully the boy wiped the eyes clear, unplugged the ears, and called the satyr's name. Matthew didn't respond. His face was blue and he was barely breathing. His skin felt like ice.

Derin slapped the satyr's face, trying to bring some color back. And then he grabbed him by the shoulders and shook him. Matthew's head lolled on his thick shoulders, no life in it.

"The flask!" Vera called from the air above him, and Derin turned Matthew over, opened his pack, and rummaging through it, found what he was looking for. It was almost empty, but a few rich drops still swirled in the bottom. With the snow falling around him, Derin uncapped the flask, turned Matthew over and waved it under the satyr's nose. He didn't respond. He tilted the satyr's head back, pried open the mouth and poured a small amount under the satyr's tongue. Matthew coughed once, twice, and then was still again.

He poured the rest of the flask into Matthew's mouth. The satyr gagged, but his eyes didn't open, and his breathing remained shallow. "Matthew," Derin said, "it's me." He slapped the satyr's face again, and a faint pink blush rose in the cheek, the shape of his hand. The boy put his ear near Matthew's lips, hoping to hear the long suck of wind as the satyr's lungs filled. But all he heard was the sweep of snow as it filtered past them, the crystals covering Matthew's forehead again, shrouding him.

After the ravens left, the owl remained in the center of the clearing, brooding. He was surprised at the number siding with this wretched traitor—he hadn't thought they'd have the character to resist—but he wasn't particularly worried. He would quench their fire. He would make an example of her, one the others wouldn't forget.

Around him lay the wreckage of the forest floor. Rotting tree limbs crumbled over the moldering leaves. Here and there, the ground was dotted with a black feather, evidence of the fights which had broken out among the ravens upon their departure.

From the east, a rumble broke the stillness; the earth beneath him trembled perceptibly. The sky turned darker by several shades, and he waited for the light to return as it had before. He expected it, was steeled for it, but when it didn't, he glowed with pleasure. Let this be a lesson to them, he thought. I cannot be stopped.

He opened his beak and thundered out an order. The falcons, always within hearing distance, hurtled across the dark sky and into the clearing. Behind their leather hoods, their eyes regarded him blankly. As he stared back at them, he tried to discern a flicker of emotion but could find none. Coming so soon after the outbursts of anger and hatred which had shattered the clearing, their cold efficiency struck him very deeply.

"I have a task I wish done," he said. "But before I tell you what it is, I want to know something." He cleared his throat. "Why do you always regard me blindly? Why are you so silent?"

"That's how you wanted it," Hazzard, the leader of the falcons said, his voice absolutely without inflection.

"And if I wanted it differently now?" the owl asked. The falcon said nothing. "I want to know if you love me," the owl continued. "As I have commanded all my subjects to love me."

Hazzard's eyes left the owl's and looked to the right and left, searching out the other falcons. When he met the owl's gaze again, his eyes were as blank as before. "We obey your orders, my lord."

"And do you pity me?" the owl asked, amused.

"We have no pity," Hazzard said.

"Good," said the owl. "There is a raven I want killed. The one who has betrayed me. The one I was speaking of earlier. I've heard reports she has flown to visit the moon in the southern reach. I've heard she's flown east over the Mountains of No Return."

"Do we search for her?" Hazzard asked.

"No," the owl said. "I don't think that will be necessary. She'll return, sooner or later. I want you to be ready for her when she does."

"How will we know her?"

"Her name is Deirdre. I've heard her eyes have a most peculiar glint. Uncommon intelligence. And she has a small white knob on her left claw."

"Is there anything else, my lord?" Hazzard asked.

The owl was silent for a moment. He thought of Deirdre, wondered if he had even seen her. What would it be like to speak to a raven who had worked so diligently and for so long as his adversary? He imagined her flying east, flying west, attempting to knit together the slowly forming threads of disillusionment and resistance, and he felt secret admiration. Perhaps he should have her captured and not killed. He would enjoy sparring with her.

But then his anger boiled in his throat, and when he looked at the falcons, still blank beneath their leather hoods, his eyes blazed. Who was he but the most powerful animal in the world? And these trained machines of death were his, as well.

"Yes, there is something else," he said. "I want you to think carefully about this bird. I want you to be ingenious. I want her death to be as meaningful as possible. Do you understand?"

"Yes, my lord," Hazzard said, and for the first time the owl caught a glimpse of something in those opaque eyes.

"Good," he said. "That's all."

With a great whoosh, the falcons spread their wings and ascended the dark sky, smudged as if by charcoal or the blackened embers of a fire.

"They may not love me," he said. "But they obey."

* * *

"What should I do?" Derin cried, to the raven, the fox, the wind, whatever would listen. "He's still alive, but he's so cold."

"Can you get him up here?" Vera called.

"How?" Derin asked. "How would I do that?"

"Carry him," the fox said. "Unless you can think of something better."

Derin tried to lift Matthew's body, amazed at how heavy it was. The satyr's head and arms hung like weights, his legs like roots anchoring him to the snow. He had never carried the satyr before, had not even known he had the strength, but now, in these extremities, he wrenched Matthew free from the ground and staggered toward the ice cliff. It didn't take long for him to realize he couldn't do it. Trying to wade through the snow was hard enough; carrying the satyr made it impossible. Matthew's head hung limply backwards, exposing the full vulnerability of his neck, and the boy placed him carefully on the snow as if he were sleeping.

"I can't," he said. "He's too heavy."

He trudged to the base of the cliff and looked up at the fox's mournful face, peering down at him. The sheer verticality of the cliff depressed him. Even in the dark air, the ice shone blue.

Deirdre had abandoned all pretense of calm. "What will become of us?" she asked. "What will become of the moon? Poor Matthew, oh, it doesn't matter, we'll all die sooner or later. This is just such an ignominious ending, so sordid, really. . . ." She chattered madly, but Derin didn't hear her. She chattered while the fox stood up, shook herself, and leapt out into the empty air.

Vera disappeared beneath the snow at the cliff's base and struggled to dig herself out. Only her head was visible, her pale eyes burning as she forced her way through the heavy powder toward Matthew.

"Vera," Derin called. "What are you doing?"

The fox ignored him, intent on reaching the satyr. He lay on his back, his arms at his sides. "Derin," she said. "Pack some snow down, will you?" The boy thrashed over to her, and with his hands and knees, he hardened a space for her.

"How will you get up the cliff?" Deirdre asked. "Now all three of you are down there. Oh my freezing feathers! What will become of us?"

The fox began to lick Matthew's face, long soft strokes which melted the snow obscuring his features. She licked his cheeks, his chin; she nuzzled his ears. "Matthew," she whispered. "Matthew, wake up."

"That's right," Deirdre cried. "Good idea, don't stop!"

"Shut *up*, you feathered bagpipe," Vera called. "Aren't you good for anything but noise?"

That sobered the raven. She was ashamed of herself, hysterical in the midst of a crisis. Usually she was so calm, so composed, but this unseen disaster had shaken her faith. She settled on Derin's right shoulder as he knelt by the fox, afraid for a moment he might shake her loose, disgusted with her. Instead, to her eternal gratification, he reached up with his left hand and soothed her ruffled feathers.

Vera continued to lick the satyr. She cleaned his chest, his arms with her tongue. "It's no use," Derin wailed. "He's not coming around."

"Don't *you* start," Vera said. She moved back from Matthew's body, twitched her tail, and disappeared. In her place was a nymph, her long hair streaming over her shoulders. She stood there, unembarrassed, defiant. Derin had seen her three times—in the swamp for an instant, more an image than a real creature, on the Plain when Matthew's music had entranced her, and on the previous night, from a distance. The creature who stood before him was covered with skin, very different from the sea nymph who had rescued him. Now she faced him, reached a hand out to calm his amazement. He forgot where he was, knee-deep in snow, completely under her spell.

Deirdre was so astonished she flew into the air. When she tried to speak, no words left her throat. The nymph said nothing, either. She knelt beside the satyr and touched his cheek. She smoothed his forehead with her fingers, gently massaged his closed eyes. Derin watched as the nymph stroked Matthew's face and then lay down beside him, shielding him from the snow, warming him.

Deirdre was embarrassed, didn't know what to do. She looked to the west, and as she glanced upwards at the pass, the sky brightened. The edge of the storm moved slowly over them and the raven watched the swirling mists of snow drift down the mountain toward its lower reaches.

"Well, that's something," she said, glad to have words at least. "Look! The snow's stopped." But to whom was she speaking? The satyr lay on his back; beside him, the nymph huddled as close as she could. Derin stared at the two of them, stunned, moved, stirred, dreaming of other places, or maybe not dreaming at all.

* * *

The sun slept in a cave below the eastern horizon, and for almost a week now, she'd been troubled by nightmares. For years, her life had been orderly, quiet, full of repose. At day's end, she would slip below the edges of the Deadwood Forest, pass back across the solid bottom of the world and into the cave. Its walls were iridescent, mother-of-pearl, and as she entered, her radiance shone back at her so blindingly she never failed to be thrilled. The light would wake her sister who hovered in the back, dim in her sleep, and with a grumpy word or two, the moon would pass her in the high-walled corridors of the cave and ascend the sky. The sun would hang in the cave's mouth and watch her sister, pale, luminous, a trembling edge of light. Then, content that all was in order, she would move to the back of the cave, gather the darkness around her, and sleep.

But for the past five nights, all this had been disturbed. No longer was she awakened in the morning by her sister's return. Her rising was erratic, early one day and late the next. She had awakened early that morning, unsure if it were time to mount the sky, but too anxious to wait. She left the cave and broke over the rim of the world. Below her, the clouds rumbled and tossed their gloved fists at her again, another day. She sighed, breathed deeply, tried to gather her strength. How much longer could she continue like this?

Each day she dimmed a little, and each night when she entered the cave, she was alarmed. The brightness the shining walls flung back at her had shrunk, until she no longer blinked in the glare but faced it straight on. She waited for the day when the walls reflected nothing at all and she would curl in the back of the cave, alone, without her sister, and sleep, and sleep, and sleep.

She hung in the sky watching the clouds. They were ribbed today and grey as dirty wool. They looked impenetrable, packed tight by the accumulation of almost a week, and still a mist troubled the surface, wisps of a more ethereal grey reaching toward her.

What was the use? If she couldn't find her sister, she would be lost, and with her the world. She knew now — for it was the only explanation which made any sense — that her sister lay below her, under that curtain of cloud. The day, like the ones preceding it, was endless. She knew by instinct when she crossed the meadowlands, when the Swollen River rushed through the cleft which split the land. Then the Plain of Desiccation stretched beneath her. Where the mountains rose, the clouds rose also, and so they lay closer than at any other point in her orbit.

She couldn't tell how thick the cloud layer was, but below it, not too far, lay the earth. She decided to descend, and though she tried to weigh the possibilities again, her mind had been made up: she might as well take matters into her own hands as waste away slowly, withering until her light was gone.

At the sun's approach, the surface of the clouds churned, the ribs rolled back and up at her. Cold mist wreathed her, and she shuddered, never having been touched like that before. Involuntarily, she retreated a little, and then steeled herself for a further descent. She let herself down and the clouds became more turbulent, boiling as though they were water.

Although she could not see it, the earth trembled. Far to the east, the placid surface of ocean, untroubled by waves for days, contracted, curled back still further from the lip of sand, revealing nearly a week's decay, and then rose as a single sheet and hurled itself against the stone cliffs on which Deirdre had been born. The Swollen River fell and rose, tossing fish high into the air. They arced in the silver dimness, threw their heads and tails backwards until they resembled perfect scaled circles, and fell again into the racing water.

Directly below her, the sun heard an enormous crack, and then the roaring began. It catapulted through the clouds, borne on the back of a furious wind. The clouds swirled up at her, enveloping her, carried the pounding of the avalanche in their mist. The noise seemed to issue from the earth's core, rumbling through the layers of rock and dirt, until it broke free through the crack and flew into the air, throwing snow in front of it, up into the highest reaches, through the clouds, until it reached the sun.

She was horrified, couldn't continue. She surged upwards, away from the clouds, leaving them frothing, below her. She reached her orbit and still retreated, hoping by moving further away she could restore the balance she'd so clearly upset. Beneath her, she heard one solid sigh as the pieces of earth settled. Only then did she return to her path, the slowly curving arc she should never have left. There would be no further rescue attempts. The outcome of that was clear.

She shone as brightly as she could, and the tongues of cloud stretching up at her cast wavering shadows on the ribs. They mocked her, everything did. In the face of that mute laughter, she felt herself growing weaker. The shadows disappeared. She had overtaxed herself. She was almost burnt out.

The tremors which shook the earth were strong in the southern reach. The moon hung dazed in her cage as branches crashed around her, falling from the spindly tops of the frailest trees into the black ferns below. In the aftermath of that trembling, the slime mold shivered, quaking as water does when disturbed, and starfish and toads troubled the surface of the ferns.

But no branches broke from the tree encircling the moon. Here was the cataclysm she had hoped for, but it did her no good. Instead, she was rudely bashed against the branches, scratched by their harsh bark.

She was alone. Maxwell was gone, dragged from his perch uncomplaining, swallowed by the fetid undergrowth below her. She felt a sadness deeper than words, and she realized with a shock that it had little to do with herself. Where had Deirdre gone? Maxwell had done nothing wrong, and in his absence, she thought not of her loneliness but of his pained uncomprehending final hours. She had kept her eyes closed, tried to block out the horrible sucks and slithers she'd heard, and not until long after they'd ceased did she look across to the empty branch on which the young raven once sat.

It was over, she knew. The sky darkened again, hours before nightfall. The owl had decreed this succession of events, and he'd been neither stupid nor pompous, simply right. With Deirdre missing, with Maxwell gone, she had nothing further to hope for. From the south, the faint intermittent keening she had heard for two days grew in intensity after the tremor ceased, as though the wails were her own.

She thought of all the time she'd wasted, sailing through the sky unmoved by the cycles of life and death which went on below her. She'd been too distant to notice, too uninvolved. Parents died and children struggled to fill their empty space, to do honor to their ghosts, to overcome them. She remembered the first words she'd spoken to Deirdre: *worms will shrink from your beaks and you'll fall dead from hunger and thirst. . . . You will be less than the rocks; you will rot to form leaf mold. . . .* She had learned, along with her other lessons, to hold her tongue.

* * *

Deirdre flew west into the darkening sky. She had no other choice but to go for help. If all was as she expected in the Deadwood Forest, there would be other ravens she could call on. But first she had to find them.

She crested the pass between the two imposing peaks, almost lost in the black swirls of descending cloud. The other side fell away, a glacier spilling downward to the rock, ledges, scree, the whole mountain crashing against the short plain which stretched until the forest began. Deirdre folded her wings and dove. It was a flashy trick she had learned from her mother, a way of outflying even the swiftest bird, and dangerous. She flattened herself into a bullet, and the wind whistled over her, scattering her short harsh breaths. Below her, the mountain sped, the ice of the glacier gave way to rock, and she spread her wings to slow herself down. She thought for a minute she'd made a mistake, gotten caught in an updraft, and her wings stretched as though they were being torn. In that instant, she remembered Maxwell.

There was nothing to do but continue her descent. The short stretch of plain swooped up at her, and she glided out over the top of the Deadwood Forest. As she flew, she thought of all those who now depended on her—the moon, the broken raven, and the three she had left stranded at the base of the cliff.

It was more than she could compass. Her addled brain tried to understand this predicament. In her excitement about the Keep, in her desire to tell Derin, she'd forgotten Maxwell, and now she could lose all. If she decided to fly south in an effort to save him, she might arrive too late, and by using her time in that manner, help might not arrive for Matthew, Derin, and Vera.

The recognition of her shortcomings sapped her purpose. She felt rotten, sick at heart. She, who had always held fast to the principle of loyalty, for whom a promise made was a promise delivered, had broken her own commandment. She had sworn on the graves of her parents to do everything in her power to bring the owl to ruin, and she had hurried on toward that end, unmindful of her other responsibilities.

Beneath Deirdre, the trees stretched their leafless branches, a bewildering net of circumstance. A thick ink pooled there, an ocean of regret. The ground accused her, as though the darkness were the massed forces of her clan who knew her failures, ignored her brave attempt to bring order and balance back to the Forest, condemned her.

The voices she heard were long dead, stories told by ancient ravens when she was just a nestling, among them the tireless voices of her parents who, day after day, had instilled in her the values by which she'd tried to live.

Maybe it wasn't that she'd done so badly. Perhaps it was simply that she'd tried to do too much. She wanted forgiveness, approval, mercy, but the only ones who could bestow their blessing had died long ago in the great wind. Inside her breast, she tried to locate their voices, a remnant of self-love she had carried with her from her earliest years. Ahead, she saw a crowd of ravens coming her way. They flew in tight formation, fiercely, spread in a wide-necked V. Unsure of herself, unable to tell the allegiance of the birds, she darted into the forest and hid, appalled by her sudden lack of courage. She sat quavering on the lower branches of a hemlock and tried to appear as inconspicuous as possible.

They had seen her, and when the ravens came to the place she had disappeared, the entire formation arrested its flight and hovered in the dark air. They settled into the branches around her, and every raven turned his red eyes upon her.

"Who are you?" asked one of them, his voice as hard as iron.

If there had been a time during the past week when bravery was needed, it was now. Deirdre sat silently and stared at them. A tiny flame flickered in her chest and as she waited, refusing to answer, it grew until it was a full-fledged fire, kindled by her anger and resentment, the knowledge of all she had done and tried to do. "And who wishes to know?" she replied. The ravens bristled, stuck their black-sheathed necks out further over her.

"Your name doesn't matter," the one who had addressed her said. "All we care about is your stake in this struggle."

Deirdre puffed herself up until she was larger than her usually imposing size. When she spoke, the fire blazed forth, and she was proud, forthright, herself again. "But it *does* matter," she said. "My name is Deirdre, the daughter of Orak and Ada, and until I die, I will oppose the owl who caused their deaths. I'm not afraid of you. You can do with me as you see fit, but you'll have quite a struggle on your hands, you toads."

"Deirdre!" the leader said, and she heard her name repeated by the others. It shimmered in the air like ripples on the surface of a pond. "You've come back."

"Of course I came back," she snapped, "but under different circumstances than I had intended."

"I'm honored to meet you," he said. "I'm sorry for my rudeness, but it's come to that. The forest is chaos. I don't know if darkness will disperse it or make it more intense. You've got to be careful. The owl has learned you're the one who flew east for help, and has sworn to hunt you down."

"That's only fitting," Deirdre replied proudly, "since it is I who earlier swore to hunt him down."

"Stay with us," he urged, the others clamoring behind him. "We'll protect you."

"Thank you," she said. "I can't. There's something I have to do. But there is a way you could help me, help us all. Right now, at the crest of the mountains, my friends lie almost buried in snow. A young boy, a satyr, and a fox, the three you've heard mentioned by the owl. If they're not rescued soon, I'm sure they'll die. There's no time. Go now, all of you. Directly east of here, where a large cairn of boulders sits, the mountains rise to twin peaks. You'll find them on the far side of the pass at the base of an ice cliff."

"Come with us," one of the ravens pleaded. "Show us where they are."

"I told you, I can't," Deirdre said. "I have another obligation I've forgotten."

"We're on our way," the leader said. "Don't worry, we'll find them. But remember what I said about the owl."

"I'll do my best," Deirdre said. "Now hurry. Good luck."

The ravens returned her parting words, and then they rose above the trees, disappeared in the darkness to the east. "At least that's settled," she said. "I hope."

There was still Maxwell to deal with, and she took a deep breath, steeling herself for the flight south. Perhaps her luck was still with her. Those ravens would rescue the three, and now she had time to take care of her promise.

She left her branch and flew to the top of the tree, settling there a moment to look around. The forest was quiet. If the skirmishes she'd just heard of were still happening, they were in a distant section of the land. As she looked across the tree tops, dissolving into blackness, she could see no other living creature. She breathed a sigh of relief, for her own safety, for the promise she'd made to Maxwell. Flying low over the trees, ready to plunge for cover if threatened, she headed south.

Condor followed her at a distance. He'd been among the ravens she'd just talked to, but out of fear and shame, he hadn't shown himself. After he left the inquisition, he had flown aimlessly until he'd found another group of ravens, the ones now flying east. They didn't know him and accepted him solely on the basis of his opposition to the owl. As the others flew to rescue the snowbound travelers, he circled back, vowing to counter his betrayal of Deirdre by staying with her, protecting her if he could.

She flew swiftly. Several times he was afraid he'd lost her, but he kept pace, staying distant enough so she didn't know she was being followed, but close enough to keep her in sight. Beneath him, the tree tops rattled in the aftermath of Deirdre's rocky path. Now and then, he almost flew straight into a tangle of branches, but all his senses were straining at their fullest capacity and he darted and wove among them.

Could he catch her? Should he? He didn't know what to do. More than anything, he wanted to unburden himself to Deirdre, explain what had happened, and ask for forgiveness. She was the wisest bird he'd ever met, and she would see that he had done nothing wrong, at least intentionally. Surely she'd made a mistake once and would understand.

But he'd said too much already. It was his stupid tongue which had gotten him into this in the first place, and maybe it would be better to let his actions speak, to come to her aid if she should need it, and prove his loyalty through deeds instead of words.

Ahead of him, Deirdre stopped in midair, and he caught himself up short. A wall of feathers had arisen, blocking her passage. She'd been so intent on her flight she hadn't seen the falcons hunched in the tree tops until they loomed in front of her, their leather hoods darker than the night. She cowered in their presence momentarily, and then tried to appear calm.

"Excuse me," she said. "I'm in a hurry."

"Where are you headed?" Hazzard demanded.

"To take care of my mother," she said. "She's very sick."

"And she lives in the southern reach?"

"No," Deirdre said. "Not far from here. I'm afraid she's dying."

"Perhaps she's already dead."

"Not yet," Deirdre said. "But she will be, if you detain me any longer." She attempted to mount above them, but they rose again in front of her, and she saw she couldn't circumvent them, would have to convince them to let her go.

"Your name?" Hazzard demanded.

"Gartrud," Deirdre said.

"Your mother's same?"

"Ada."

"And your allegiance to the owl?"

"I'm with him all the way. Now, if you'll excuse me."

"No," Hazzard said. "What's that white pearl on your left claw?"

Deirdre glanced down at the calcified ooze she'd carried since her first encounter with the starfish, and her heart stopped. They were not going to let her go.

She opened her beak and screamed, cawing wildly. She ducked her head, spread her wings, and took off toward the east, her tailfeathers quivering in the cold air. The falcons thundered up, their talons wide as their purpose. Hazzard hit her where her left wing joined her body. Condor watched it happen, and there was nothing he could do.

"It's finished," Hazzard said. The owl turned his haughty stare full on him and asked. "How was it accomplished?"

"With dispatch," the falcon said. "With flair."

"No matter," the owl said. "I don't need the details. Go, all of you, and wherever you find a raven who opposes me, tell him of Deirdre's death."

"You're making a mistake," Hazzard warned. "She'll become a legend."

"No, she won't," the owl replied. "This news will break the opposition. Those birds would not place anything before their own lives."

"As you wish," Hazzard said. He flew into the air, followed by the others.

When the last falcon disappeared from view, the owl realized how angry he was. He did not like to be contradicted, and Hazzard had been too snide, too forward. He would have to wait until they returned for what he had to say. Obeying meant giving no advice. Hazzard would be made to understand that.

Under the dark sky, the forest around him was still. He felt he was in the middle of a whirlwind, the light losing all luster, the night coming on in earnest and for good. After all his planning, victory clearly in sight, he wondered that he was plagued with this temper; it would not dissipate. He should have felt a hot rush of pride. He'd been powerful enough to challenge the sun. He'd usurped this territory, brought the animals west, and kept them under his thrall. But it was petty anger which filled him now.

He shrugged and slowly shook his head. He still had one thing left to do. His talons stretched, releasing mud from their grasp, his huge wings spread, and he rose into the darkness above the clearing. The Forest stretched placidly in all directions, his, all his. He headed south, to speak to the moon.

Below them, the snowfield rose to the eminence of twin peaks, and the ravens, still bunched in their tight formation, soared over the glacier's pass. They were bent on finding the three Deirdre had spoken of, and each bird stared downwards, looking for a sign.

Ahead of him, the lead raven saw something dark in the snow. He swooped toward it, and the rest followed, as though tied by invisible wires. It was Derin's pack, flung down when he jumped after Matthew. A raven picked up a bottom edge in his beak and shook it. Out tumbled a shirt, a blanket, the stone Derin had been given by the jay. The meager pile saddened them and they looked out over the spot where the mountain broke away. When had Deirdre flown back to the Forest? Had she left her friends only for the earth to fall beneath them? Even in the darkness, the snow gleamed, and the wind picked up little spouts, whirling like ghosts.

"She said we'd find them at the base of a cliff," a raven said. "Did she mean those mountains?"

"No," the leader said. "An ice cliff. Like this one."

He stared over the lip of ice. Something moved beneath him. "Look," he said. "Down there."

As they strained their eyes, a dark patch appeared on the snow, and they flew down to where the three lay. Matthew was still on his back, his breathing now regular and full. Against his side lay a figure with long white hair, and beside her, another thin body. As they stared, wondering at the strangeness of these two-legged creatures, Vera raised her head and sat up. Matthew moaned, deep in sleep, and the boy stirred and settled again. She ran her fingers through their hair. The satyr turned on his side, and as he reached out to her in his dream, to gather her toward him, his fingers closed on white fur and he felt the nuzzle of a cold nose against his face.

The ravens panicked. They flew into the air, cawing, astonished at the transformation. Vera thought they might not return. She called to them, using Deirdre's name as proof they had nothing to fear. Wary at first, the ravens stopped their circling and settled on the snow.

"Take them," Vera said, "Get them out of here."

"But what about you?" the leader of the ravens asked.

"I stay here," Vera said. "This is where I live. If you'll just help me to the top of the cliff I'll be fine. My lair's at the summit." She padded over to Matthew and stood for a minute staring down at him. His mouth was curved in a thin smile. She licked him, once, on the cheek, and he moaned again, didn't hear her whispered good-bye.

The ravens, with Vera's help, laid the bodies in two gauze slings. With a burst of wings, three of them carried the fox to the blue lip of ice and then returned to pick up the others. They left Vera behind; the pass receded beneath them, the snow fell to where the rock face began. Flying as urgently as they had on the night they'd stolen the moon, the ravens swept on to the Deadwood Forest.

Stunned by the motion through the air, wind whipping his face, Derin ascended from his dreamless stupor, until he opened his eyes. From that height, the earth looked like a toy, the rocks so much rubble, and in the distance, the trees were matchsticks, stuck awkwardly into mud by a child who'd grown tired of his play and abandoned them. He was weightless and the rumble of wings was music. He swiveled his head and saw Matthew behind him, borne by the dark wingspans of the other ravens.

"The creature was a nightmare of himself."

SATYRDAY

Out of the sky's abyss, the moon heard a noise approach. A thunderstorm, a rolling accumulation of sound, pealed from the farthest corners of the Forest and centered on her. It came crashing through the branches near her, not a storm at all. His wings outstretched, the owl descended, his size so great he could not slip among the twisted trees and so brought destruction with him.

Limbs were sheared off, taking other branches with them as they fell. The owl thudded into the ground, the echoes of his cadence reverberating through the forest, followed by the slowly ending crash as all the broken branches found the ground as well.

The moon drew a deep breath, and in her glow, she saw him sitting magisterially, unfazed by the route he'd taken into the Forest. His descent created such a wind the ferns had been blown clear of the circle on which he perched. Dirt surrounded him, the ferns cowered, and starfish, scorpions, the long pink worms could be seen dimly, writhing some distance from the owl's talons.

"Sorry for the racket," the owl said, fastening his golden eyes upon her. "I hope I didn't disturb you." She said nothing, turned away from him, but his voice boomed out at her. "Look at me!"

"I owe you nothing," the moon said. "There is nothing further you can do to me."

"That may be so," he said. "Still, there's one way I could be of help to you."

"And what might that be?" she asked, as proudly as she could. Her voice sounded pitiful. It had weakened, had none of its former hauteur.

"I spoke to you several days ago," the owl said. "I presume you've had time to consider my proposition."

"I don't know what you're talking about," the moon said.

"Perhaps you've been too distracted," he said. "I mentioned there might be a place for you when my plan came to fruition. Provided. . . ." He paused for a moment and stared at her. "I want to know where your sister sleeps."

"It doesn't matter any more," the moon said, giving up all pretense at dignity. "You've gotten what you wanted. It's plain you've been successful. Nothing I could do or say would have an impact on that."

"Then why not tell me what I want to know?" His voice was seductive, melodious. "I could use your help. The night is an enormous kingdom."

"Your flattery is worse than insult," the moon said. "I'd rather hear you curse me."

"I harbor no bad feelings," the owl said solicitously. "Quite to the contrary. You've been a model prisoner."

"She's still my sister."

"But as you've seen, she's failing without you. I hope that's given you some pleasure."

"None whatsoever," she said. "Her misfortune is no joy to me."

The owl considered the moon. She had become tattered and tarnished during her captivity, but her beauty was still plainly visible. Among the torn and broken trees, she shone like a treasure. "I have done all I can without you," the owl said. "I need your light. The creatures of these lands, even the ones who know only the night, can't live in total darkness. I'm not stupid."

"No, you're not," the moon said. "There have even been moments when I've been impressed with your thoroughness."

"Thank you," the owl said. "I appreciate that."

"But I haven't been impressed with your generosity," the moon said. "Until this afternoon, I had a young raven named Maxwell for company."

"Ah yes," the owl said. "My mistake."

"You had his wings broken."

"I admit it," the owl said. "The other animals might have learned from his example. My power is absolute, but illusory, much like your light. I assume those I rule won't understand my power is something which can be taken away from me."

"I hadn't known your penchant for the philosophical," the moon said. "But all the philosophy you could command can't change the fact of Maxwell's death."

"He was only one raven," the owl said.

"Yes," the moon said. "He was that."

"Tell me," the owl asked, "what this past week has been like for you."

"I have learned about humility and bravery," the moon replied. "And I learned that there are creatures in this world who care about something other than themselves."

"And who might they be?" the owl asked.

"One creature in particular," the moon said. "A raven named Deirdre."

"I've heard of her," the owl said mildly.

"She taught me something I hadn't known before. She taught me about love," the moon said, her voice rising. "She taught me it's possible to perceive the world as existing outside oneself, something you'd find difficult to understand."

"She's dead," the owl said. "She died earlier this evening." He watched the moon carefully, interested in how she would take the news. He'd kept this information as a trump, savoring it, knowing its impact would break her spirit. She slowly turned away, trying to keep herself under control. A sob attempted to leave her mouth but she fought it down, and with it, the tears.

"Tell me," he said soothingly, "where your sister spends her nights, and all this will be over, I promise."

"All right," the moon said, her voice shaking. "I'll tell you. But what will I gain from it?"

"Half the kingdom of night," the owl said. "The honor of all who live in the land."

"I had that before," she said stiffly.

"No, you didn't," the owl said. "You were too distant, too frosty. And you'll have your freedom. Your strength, your light, your beauty."

"She sleeps in a deep well," the moon said. "Beyond the western rim of the forest, in the darkness nothing penetrates."

"Ahhh," the owl said. It was a moan of sensual pleasure, throaty and deep. The moon swung in her cage to look at him. His great lids had lowered. The scarf of thick feathers around his neck bristled.

"Thank you," he said. "Thank you very much."

"It was nothing," the moon said softly. "Really."

Shivering, Derin looked up into an immenseness so black he could make out nothing. He felt he was floating in a sky devoid of light. The wind had ceased its whistle in his ears, but a roaring continued inside his head. He lay bundled under his blanket. Gradually, his eyes became accustomed to the dark, and the trees of the Deadwood Forest stretched away from him. He had the peculiar sensation of rushing backwards, watching the few reference points he'd settled on for stability recede into the distance.

He was the vortex of a whirlpool, the center of a storm. Around him, the ground slipped away. He was inside a shell, a lustrous curved slide of obsidian. He was whirling down its circular embrace toward a fixed point of purpose he hadn't suspected before.

Groaning, he turned onto his side and the spinning stopped. Next to him, Matthew lay silent. And behind them, the massed forces of the ravens who had rescued them stood guard. Their eyes blinked, a sea of pinpoints lending a strange majesty to the night.

The roaring in his ears faded and Derin began to hear the garbled voices of the birds, speaking in hushed tones as if in a language he didn't comprehend. Although he couldn't make sense of their sentences, an occasional word stood out like a touchstone. He heard them mention the owl and Deirdre and the words were like the names given to vast opposing forces, fire and ice. In this waking dream, Deirdre became for the boy much more than the loquacious raven who had been with him only hours ago. If she were a match for the owl, she loomed in his mind, a natural element like wind or rain. The owl was a mountain, and Deirdre the erosive power of weather, or Deirdre was a river and the owl a sharp acclivity of rock breaking the water's rush.

He drew his knees to his chest and hugged them until he was a tight ball, and in that position, whole again, he remembered what had brought him to this place. The avalanche, the snow, the sifting face of mountain came back to him, and then darkness. Derin got to his knees, then shakily to his feet. As he stood in the clearing, the ravens stopped talking. He stumbled over to Matthew and knelt beside him, could barely see the satyr's face wreathed in smile. His horns were hidden by the tangles of hair falling back from his forehead. His blanket had been placed over him so that only the tapered ends of his hooves were visible. Derin drew the coat from the satyr's chest and Matthew stirred, made a tentative grasp with his right hand. The boy reached out and shook his friend's shoulders, and the satyr groaned, tried to turn onto his side, opened his eyes. He stared up at the boy as if he'd never seen him before.

"Matthew," Derin said. "It's me."

The satyr closed his eyes, intent upon returning to whatever vision had so pleased him, but the boy shook him again, and this time the eyes focused and Matthew brought his hands to his face, drawing them down from his forehead as though he were wiping water from it. "I was dreaming of Vera," he said, looking around him. "What is this? Where is she?"

"We're alone again," Derin said. "She stayed on the mountain like she said she would. We're in the Deadwood Forest."

Perhaps the dissension was under tight cover; perhaps all the animals were asleep. For whatever reason, the falcons found no one to tell of Deirdre's death. Even for them, the silence was eerie.

Recrossing the forest from east to west, they came upon the owl. After he'd received his information from the moon, he left her stranded in her cage, left her to watch the ferns and starfish recover the ground he'd sat upon, like a sick tide coming in, and had returned north.

"Have you told everyone of her death?" he asked.

"Everyone we found," Hazzard replied.

"How did they respond?"

"As you would have wished," the falcon said.

"Good," the owl said. "Very good. There is one more thing I want you to do for me." The falcons waited, silent. "I've discovered where the sun sleeps. Before she wakes, I want her destroyed."

Hazzard regarded the owl blankly. "Tonight," the owl said. "Now. There will be no light tomorrow. Within a few hours, the kingdom of night will be completely mine. The moon has told me. She sleeps in a well to the west, out over the void where the furthest trees drop into nothing. Pour water down that well and put her fire out for good."

"There's been no water in this forest for fourteen years," the falcon said.

"It doesn't matter to me," the owl said vehemently. "Drop sticks and stones, drop that dead raven's body, I don't care." He had not forgotten the sting of the previous day when Hazzard had questioned his order, and now he was getting the same surly response.

"I've been meaning to say something to you," the owl said evenly. "Some words of advice. I've come close to the end of patience. This undertaking hasn't been easy. Up to this point, I've been grateful for your dedication and support. So don't question me now." His voice rose a tone or two and the feathers on the falcons' chests quivered in exasperation. "I wasn't pleased with your questioning yesterday. And your skepticism tonight is insulting. I don't care how you kill the sun. Just do it."

Hazzard swiveled and looked at the members of his patrol. All stared past him, totally impassive, their faces like chiseled stone. He was looking for a flicker in their eyes, but nothing shone back at him from the darkness. Slowly his head swung back until his gaze locked with the owl's. "We mean no disrespect," he said. "We'll do as you ask."

"That's better," the owl said. "I appreciate it. By this time tomorrow, the struggle will be over."

"Yes, my lord," Hazzard said.

"I want to see you as soon as it's done. I want to know every detail. Where the well is. What she looked like sleeping in its depths. What happened when you put her fire out."

Hazzard flew, the others with him, and he thought for some reason of the moon. On one of the owl's missions, he had seen her reflection in the ponds and lakes of the meadowlands. That night there were two moons, the one below a pale copy of the one above. Perhaps there was a message in this; perhaps if he thought about it long enough, there would be an answer, a hint as to how this latest order of the owl's should be followed. The Forest was as quiet as it had been earlier. He involuntarily shivered. Close behind him, he heard the thud and volley of the other falcons' wings.

"They will suffer for this," the owl said as he watched the falcons disappear to the west. "I'll have no further need of them once the sun has been dispatched." Deirdre dead, the sun extinguished, the ravens cowed; the moon still captive in the southern reach. It was all his, his alone. Yet he would be true to his word. He didn't need the moon's help—not as much as he'd led her to believe—but he hadn't lied. The kingdom of night was large enough to share. He would grant her some measure of freedom. Perhaps he'd use the falcons as her bodyguards. Perhaps he'd let them. . . .

It was a lovely idea, and the owl was so pleased with himself he might have crowed if there'd been anyone to hear him. The falcons would feel proud to guard the moon, would not see it as punishment. It would suffice until he thought of a safe and efficient way to dispose of them.

As for the moon, she would be slow to attempt an escape with the falcons surrounding her. Besides, there would be nowhere to escape. With her sister dead, with the world under his thrall, the moon would be powerless to do anything but go along as gracefully as she could.

How well everything was coming together at the end! It was better than the owl had hoped. As each problem had presented itself and been solved, the owl achieved a deeper sense of his own power. Now, he need only await the arrival of his three visitors—if they were not already dead.

He looked around him at the spindly trees whose upper branches disappeared into the inky darkness. Did they have a sense of how close he was to total victory? Did they remember how once leaves had grown and thrived, how songbirds had twittered in their branches instead of those lean predators or the ravens with their eyes like burning stars?

The owl slowly swung his head from one side to the other. That panoramic swivel took in everything: the trees, the scrubby leafless bushes, the rich mulch under his talons. His gaze had reached its furthest pivot to the right and started back when he felt the eyes watching him. They were out there, but he couldn't find them. They bored into his back like drill-mouthed snakes. He savagely turned to confront his attacker but nothing was there. Darkness—total, absolute—was all he could see.

"Who is it?" he screamed. "Show yourself." The Forest made no answer. "I won't allow this," he said. The echoes of his voice receded into the darkness. "Damn you," the owl thundered. "You will not do this. Who is it? *Who is it? You belong to me.*"

* * *

Like dandelions, thistle, chokeweed in untended ground, guilt thrives in the moist soil of the conscience. It is hardy and its taproot deep, reaching to a place where it can settle and take hold, subduing by threats and intimidation all other emotions. Thus it can overwhelm; but it can also transform.

Deirdre's death was a double shock to Condor. Her loss made him reel, and his complicity, unintended, made him momentarily crazed. When the falcons first hit her, he cried aloud, but neither aggressors nor victim heard his shrieks. The night air was torn by the bloody battle. He wanted to fly to her aid, to sacrifice himself, but he was overcome with dread. Forcing himself to leave, horrified by his own fascination, his first thought was to flee the Outer Lands, to put as much distance as possible between himself and Deirdre's death.

Through the messages his brain telegraphed, one stood out. He would do what he could to avenge her death. And if he alone were not sufficient to bring down the owl, he would find others and make them join with him, as she had. He flew crazily over the forest that night, searching for other ravens, but everywhere he went, he found the same deadly quiet. It was as though the ground beneath him had been uninhabited for years. Where was everyone?

Condor had never felt so righteous. All traces of doubt seemed to have died with Deirdre, as though he had inherited her mantle of power. But the exertion of his search and the intense emotions he felt combined to wear him out. He settled in the top branches of a tree and tried to think.

He heard the thudding of wings coming toward him before he'd even had time to catch his breath. Because the night was so dark, he couldn't tell at first from what direction the birds were coming, and he twisted, trying to get his bearings. He darted to a lower branch, keeping out of sight. The falcons, in tight formation, passed over him. Like the angel of death, they came and were gone in a moment, and the little bird felt the chill of their wings and talons even in their absence. It was only when he had flown stealthily in the other direction, away from the falcons, that he heard the words floating up to him from the Forest.

They will suffer for this. I'll have no further need of them. . . .

He tucked his wings, and like a dark arrow, headed for one of the trees. From the back, the owl looked like an enormous rock, egg-shaped and covered with feathers. The talons, sunk in the mulch, were invisible. As Condor sat there, he felt he could hear the owl think, but the words were not foreign to the young bird. They were the same thoughts crowding his head. *Deirdre, the moon, the falcons.*

He hopped from his branch to one below it as quietly as possible. The owl's head swiveled leisurely, moving to the right. For a moment, Condor had the peculiar sensation the head was unattached to the rest of the owl's body and would turn in a complete circle. When the owl turned suddenly, wrenching his talons from the soft ground, Condor froze. The voice booming out at him was the one which had so recently filled him with dread and hatred. "Who is it?" the owl thundered. "You belong to me."

It was too much. The memory of his humiliation in front of the other ravens, the pang of Deirdre's death, rose in his chest until his wings began beating. Before he knew what he was doing, he was flying straight at the owl, his back arched, his claws tight against his body.

The owl was startled by the clatter, and in his surprise, didn't see the tiny arrow hurtling toward his head. Condor thrust his wings out, braking himself, and his claws dropped, ripping across the top of the owl's feathered skull. The bellow the owl gave was more in shock than pain, but it filled Condor with courage. Before the owl could turn around, Condor twisted, this time raking him from back to front. The rage in the voice was unmistakable, no words, only the bewildered screams of wounded pride.

Condor fluttered in the air, paused long enough for the owl to see him. The great head reared back, the beak opened, the golden eyes fastened on him, fixing him momentarily in space. With a whipping motion, the owl spread his enormous wings and beat the air. Dirt and twigs, dried leaves churned under him, leapt from the ground. Condor tumbled, the puny motion of his wings insubstantial in such a heavy wind. He turned somersaults, borne upwards away from the owl, and when he'd barely righted himself, the owl's wings stopped.

In that vacuum, Condor fell toward the owl's open maw. Frantically, he spread his wings. Below him, the beak snapped shut, and given that second of timing, Condor tensed his claws, heading for the eye. The enormous head jerked to the left and Condor felt only space under him. The owl swung his head and caught Condor in midair, sending him spinning. As he was thrown, he saw the owl's wing unfurl and begin to close on him. With what little strength he had left, he flapped his wings, was caught again in the updraft the owl created, and tumbled away from the fierce embrace seeking to crush him to the barred chest.

Once he was truly out of reach, he lunged upward, into the dark air. He was nothing but a gnat to the owl, an annoyance, and yet he hoped the first blows he'd struck would be taken up by other ravens. Below him, the bellowing continued. Condor was bruised and battered, breathless, amazed at his own courage, and he was proud. Even Deirdre — for all her talk — had not drawn blood.

"No more chatter," Matthew said. "It's a wonder we're still alive."

"But we should. . . ."

"Hush," the satyr said. "They've been waiting for fourteen years. They can wait another few hours. Now try to sleep. We'll start as soon as there's light to see by."

Derin slumped under the coat and closed his eyes, leaving Matthew more alone than he could remember feeling. He changed his mind, started to reach for the boy, to make him sit up and talk, but stopped and lay down next to him instead. When he closed his eyes, he knew he wouldn't be able to sleep. He tried to force the image of his last dream — Vera — to return, but it was no use.

It was as though the night had swallowed all possibility of joy. Vera's absence had left him desolate. Although he was glad to be alive, he was not glad to be in the Deadwood Forest, and he had strong premonitions about the day that lay ahead. Was it possible the sun would not shine? It didn't matter if their arrival were two hours too late or two years. Once night had been established, it would be impossible to reverse.

Matthew felt the steady pumping of his heart, blood coursing through the intricate latticework of his body. Such mystery! How did it go on from day to day? He had barely met the fox and now she was gone. He thought about the boy, the man, sleeping at his side. The satyr closed his eyes, tried to remember Derin's face, but the features dissolved into his own.

He remembered kneeling by the side of a pond in the meadowlands, splashing his hair with water until it ran down his cheeks and dripped back into the pool from which it had come. Each drop sent reverberations away from its center, hundreds of intersecting circles punctuated by the silver bells of water hitting water. As he'd knelt in the stillness, the circles dissolved and the surface of the pond became perfectly opaque, clouds moved soundlessly across it, and staring up at him was his face, the eyes slightly narrowed in surprise.

It was a handsome face. The nose was aquiline, a bit off-center; pointed ears appeared from the black tangle of his curls. The face had character. But Derin? He'd known the boy for fourteen years, yet in this day to come, who knew how the boy would respond, for all the intuition Matthew could bring to bear? He might cower before the owl; he might find resources of courage which would surprise them both.

He moved to wake the boy. He wanted to lift his limp torso from the mulch and shake him. He wanted to look at his face, trying to read there some sign by which he would know who the boy was. But Derin lay on his stomach, his face twisted away from the satyr, his left arm bent as if broken, and something in the careless attitude of the body, this body he had seen ascend the ladder of years to its present fullness, stopped him.

Matthew caught his breath, felt the odd unfamiliar spider of grief spinning a web in his throat. It was not loss he was feeling, nor anger, nor disappointment. It was simply wonder at the complexity of his attachment to the boy, and his knowledge of how little he could affect the outcome of that other life.

Around him, he thought he heard the darkness rustle, as if it were a great snake coiled around the Deadwood Forest. The night seemed to undergo a muscular constriction, moving from behind him in a sweeping arc to either side. The trees barely registered the change.

And then the sun came up.

The falcons had flown beyond the reaches of the forest, out through the thick layer of cloud into the void they'd never seen. The air was thick as honey, and stuck in their feathers. Though Hazzard was filled with trepidation, he said nothing to the others and continued to stare beneath him looking for a well, the dim glimmer of the sleeping sun.

They circled and wheeled. They soared as high as they dared and swooped until there was no bottom, then pulled from their dizzying fall and regained a level altitude. Invisible to each other, they stayed together by an instinct for self-preservation. If one of them strayed, he would have been cast on the vastness of space, with no way of returning. Hazzard had almost lost his nerve, was about to pivot and fly back, when the first faint streaks of light reached him.

In formation, the falcons turned and looked. As the sun began to creep over the world's edge, over the clouds surrounding the earth, they could see her form, a lonely ellipse spinning in space, so beautiful even they were moved. The sun was a pale yellow, a wobbling yolk beginning to lose its center. The light was watery, cold, but even at that distance, the sun rose into the dark sky with unmistakable majesty.

Who were they to kill the sun, and who was the owl to give such an order? She had moved behind them without their knowledge, and now shone in the east when they had been looking for her in the west. As they returned toward the layer of cloud, preparing themselves for the passage through its moist folds, she moved higher in the sky, across the ocean of grey. Though the clouds absorbed her light, seemed to sap her strength, they still surged with a faint glow, like beaten gold.

Hazzard disappeared into them, leaving the sun behind as he was swallowed by the mists. This, too, was strangely beautiful to him. The night before as they had plunged into the clouds, had vaulted through to the blackness of the void on the other side, they had been able to see nothing, had simply felt the swirling tendrils seeking to drench their feathers and pull them down. Now they flew through an opalescent chamber whose folds opened before them, caught in a room of light, the luminous coupling of sun and water.

When at last the falcons broke through, the Deadwood Forest lay beneath them, its branches reaching for the sun. It was as though the entire world were vertical, stretching upwards in search of warmth.

They flew solemnly over the tops of the trees. Though the sun was weaker than she had ever been, though the light she cast through the layer of cloud that morning was wan, colorless, a dying gasp of heat, the falcons remembered her as she had appeared above the horizon, sailing free over the clouds, out of touch with the earth but still inviolate, imperial.

They understood without speaking, without saying a word to one another. The owl could fix the creatures of the Forest with one cold stare. He had talons, feathers, a mighty wingspan. The sun had none of those things.

She had a crown of fire.

"My lord," the old crone said, out of breath. "You'll want to know the strangers have arrived."

"Ahh," the owl replied. "Which one of my outposts has reported them?" His eyes gleamed. He'd been waiting for the news, stood poised to fly to the eastern perimeter to greet them.

The raven coughed, a spasm starting deep in her throat, wracking her. In the dim light of that morning she looked poorly. Her feathers were dull grey and a thin red film coated her eyes. "I'm afraid this spying has been too much for me," she said.

"Answer my question," the owl demanded. "Where are they?"

"They're in the forest now," she said. "No one knows exactly where."

"But how did they cross the eastern border?" the owl asked, drawing himself to his fullest height. "They should never have entered the forest without my knowledge."

"I don't know, my lord," she said miserably. "I've heard all this by word of beak. Everyone's speaking of it. The two. . . ."

"Two," the owl screamed. "Now there are only *two*?"

"That's what I heard," she said. "Two monsters — as everyone says — a satyr and a boy."

"They must be headed south," the owl said. "Surely you would know that."

"I don't, my lord. I'm sorry." The coughing spell returned so fiercely it almost threw her to the ground. The owl had an impulse to catch her in his talons and crush her.

"You must find these things out," he said menacingly. "You're outliving your usefulness to me."

"I'm very old," she said. "I can no longer catch my breath."

"You should have thought of that before you offered your services to me. Are you still intrigued by that post you mentioned?"

"Yes, my lord," the crone said, trying to recover as quickly as possible. "Should I live that long."

"Then go. Now. Gather every raven who remains loyal to me and bring them here. There are still many?"

"Yes," she said. "I should think so."

"Save your breath," he said. "I want to see them now."

"But where are the falcons?" she asked. "Surely they could tell. . . ."

"I don't need your advice," he said fiercely. The mention of the falcons enraged him, for he knew they had failed. They had not found the sun. The dim light made that abundantly clear. "Get out of here. Gather the ravens."

The crone nodded, only too glad to end the interview. She flew off, her tired wings flapping as hard as they could, her ancient heart knocking against the walls of her chest. The owl watched her go, trying to remain calm. He would have to be in control when the ravens surrounded him and it would take all the time before they arrived for him to master himself.

As the first thin light reached the rest of the Forest, Condor was exultant. He had waited for hours for the trees to assume their gaunt profiles. Now, at last, the ravens would come from hiding, from wherever they had been, and he would find allies. He had spent enough time looking for them; perhaps if he stayed in one place long enough, they would find him.

Condor was slightly surprised at himself. It was unseemly so soon after Deirdre's death to feel cocky, excited, happy. Yet he was doing what she would have wanted him to do, he thought, and all his energy would be spent avenging her murder. He would organize a task force, they would devise a strategy, they would fly at the owl and overpower him. But as he thought about this, he remembered only too vividly his own encounter. The owl was huge. Could any number of them truly kill him?

The cawing came from the east, and he burst from his branch to welcome them, but when the ravens swooped over him, he knew he'd made a mistake. He could tell from their eyes, from the cant of their tailfeathers, that these birds still believed in the owl. He wondered if they could see as clearly in him his desire to bring the owl to ruin.

One of them remembered him from the day before and looked at him suspiciously. "You're the one who revealed the traitor, aren't you?" she asked. "What's your name?"

"Condor," he said. He stared back at her, trying to appear as non-committal as possible.

"You disavowed the act, if I recollect," another said.

"Pardon?" Condor said.

"You were unhappy to have given her away," the raven said.

"No," Condor lied. "I was just confused."

"Then you'll be pleased to hear she's dead. The falcons killed her late last evening."

"Oh," Condor said. "I didn't know. That's good news."

"Death to all traitors!" a raven shrieked from a branch behind Condor.

"Ah, cut the rhetoric," another said. "I'm sick of slogans."

"Fly with us," the first raven said. "The owl has called a convocation of all those who side with him."

"I think I'll stay here," Condor said.

"You have to attend," she said. "It's required. Besides, you're safer flying with a group today. The strangers have arrived. The foreigners from beyond the mountains."

Condor tried to keep himself from showing any feeling. "They're monsters," the raven continued. "They walk upright on the ground. One of them is half-covered with hair."

"You've seen them?" Condor asked.

"No. But we've heard of them. They could be anywhere."

"I think they must be able to fly," another raven said. "How else could they have crested the mountains?"

"It's a bad sign."

"The owl will be furious."

Condor listened to the garble of voices as all the birds began talking at once.

"You won't come with us, then," the first raven asked. "It's your funeral."

"No," Condor said. "I'll follow in a moment."

They talked among themselves in voices so low Condor couldn't hear them. He felt his stomach contract, suddenly afraid, but then, nodding to him in farewell, they flew away. He watched them turn into small black specks finally swallowed by the blanket of cloud.

He had no time to lose. He would fly and find the strangers. They were the ones in whom Deirdre had put all her faith. They would know what to do. He would make himself subservient to them, as he had placed himself under Deirdre.

But then he had a better idea.

The sun changed the Forest's tones from black to grey, and Matthew felt his mood rising with the tide of light. Despair evaporated, like fog under the sun's glare, and left him with a measure of hope. They were not too late. The kingdom of night was not final, irreversible.

He woke the boy. Derin did not grumble or tarry, but threw off the blanket of sleep, ready to begin. He rose to his feet, a man in the first flush of his power. His eyes were clear, and he looked to Matthew, even in the ashen dawn, tanned and vital.

"The first light came from over there," Matthew said, pointing. "That should be east." The meadowlands, he thought, the mountains. "And this direction," pointing in front of him with the other hand, "is south." The moon, the Keep.

"Where's Deirdre?" Derin asked. "It would be good to see her."

"Soon enough," Matthew said. "She'll hear we've arrived and find us. I wouldn't give it another thought."

Side by side, they started for the south. They made their way through the Forest's rubble, rotting stumps, vines tough as rawhide, the tangled underbrush. Over them, the trees spread their emptiness. Nothing separated them from the dim sky. They moved quickly, as quietly as they could, aware that their presence was known, that the owl would be looking for them.

As they hiked, Matthew was renewed. He felt strong again, slightly wild. "What day is it?" he asked. "Do you know?"

"I don't have any idea," Derin said. "I don't even remember how long it's been since we left."

"I think it's Satyrday," Matthew said. "I can feel it."

"You're wondering why I called this convocation," the owl said, looking around him at the several hundred ravens gathered in the clearing. "Where are the others?" He looked up at the branch where the old crone sat, covered with dust. She wheezed, a thin piercing whine, filling the vacuum the owl's voice left.

"These are all I could find," she said, her voice hoarse and strained.

"Your best is no longer good enough," he said.

"If you will pardon me, my lord," a raven said from among the assemblage. "There are no others. We could find no one else who would come."

"Why not?" he asked.

"I don't know," the crone said. "I think they must. . . ." A coughing fit interrupted her answer. Her neck jerked forward with each spasm; her beak, slightly open, seemed to be in molt.

The barred feathers on the owl's chest bristled. "It doesn't matter," he said, his voice rising. "If you are all I have, you will suffice." He thought for a moment of how the trees had looked when all the ravens roosted in them, the empty branches taking on black leaves until the forest was luxuriant with their darkness. If that had been the height of summer, this was late fall. In their nervousness and fear, the ravens had scattered themselves so widely, they dotted the branches instead of filling them.

"Come here," the owl said, almost gently. "Gather around me. Close ranks." They flew, then, in short bursts until a tight cluster of black feather began at his talons and stretched away from him, a circle of loyalty. "That's better," he said. "Look how many of you there are."

It was true. When the ravens had massed their forces they felt stronger. They looked up at the owl, waiting for him to speak. Above him sat the crone, the only one who hadn't flown to the ground.

"You will have heard the strangers have arrived," he said. "They must be stopped. They are not monsters, although you will have heard they are. They are two creatures whose strength is nil. Though they can run, the antelope outrun them; they are no match for animals — although they swim, a fish of any kind is stronger; they cannot fly. And though they walk upright like bears, though one endures the halfness of a goat — though they are strange to you, you have nothing to fear."

The owl's voice gained in power, assumed a soft incantatory music, until the ravens swayed to the rhythm of his speech, entirely under his spell.

"They're headed south to free the moon," he said. "My friend above me will know where."

"But my lord. . . ." she cried. He paid no attention to her, his soothing voice a stream rising over its banks, engulfing everything in its path.

"She will lead you," he said. "Fly as you did when you captured the moon, with swift wings and silence. Swoop down upon them so suddenly they won't know what happened. Peck out their eyes, tear their faces with your claws. Bring me the boy's right hand, the satyr's hooves."

The ravens' wings began to twitch. They were ready to fly. A dark wind swept the ground at the owl's feet. "Lead them," he said to the crone. "When you return with your proof, you'll receive the post you want."

The crone took a deep breath and cawed, and the other ravens raised the cry until the small clearing where they sat rebounded with wave upon wave of their murderous screaming. The crone spread her wings. She felt her heart hammering within her, a furious rhythm bent upon the strangers' deaths. And then it faltered. A deep pain shot from her chest along the edges of her wings. Her eyes bulged, glassy and awful. She cawed once more, flapped her wings, and left the branch, fumbled in the air and fell, a dark missile, dead. She plummeted into the middle of the ravens, and they cawed in horror.

"Go!" the owl thundered. "Kill them! Kill them!" The ravens, leaderless, rose into the air and headed south in frantic disarray. On the ground below them, the owl, in fury, reached out a talon, kicked the body of the crone. All things lead to darkness; all things die.

They came to a section of forest where they could no longer walk abreast. Derin fell behind and followed Matthew through the narrow corridor of trees. The satyr's step was light and sure. He walked in a slight crouch, his shoulders hunched, as though he were stalking something. But Derin wasn't thinking of the satyr. He was preoccupied with what lay ahead. Since he'd heard about the Keep, his mind was centered on that. People, his people, the final mystery. He wondered if they would know him, if his life would change, in their presence, into something richer, more profound, if finally he would feel at home.

Ahead, he saw Matthew step sideways behind cover of a large maple. The satyr had a finger over his lips, and with the other hand, motioned the boy off the trail. Derin turned sideways, letting the thick trunk shield him. "What is it?" he whispered. "Shh," Matthew said.

Derin heard a rustle in the underbrush, and as he watched, a line of skunks moved across the path, headed east. One of them stopped, confused, and sniffing the air, decided to continue. They threaded past and disappeared among the remnants of underbrush.

"There *is* life in this forest," Matthew whispered. He slipped back on the trail when he was sure they were gone. Overhead, a group of five ravens flew and the two froze in their tracks, hoping the birds would not notice. The air was thick with their cawing, and Derin searched among them, expecting to see Deirdre, but the ravens were too far away, were gone too quickly. "Everyone's headed somewhere, and in a hurry."

Matthew decided they had to be even more careful. He slipped from tree to tree, darting between them so fast he was a blur. How far ahead was the moon, and where? He knew she was caged in the south, but the

Forest was immense. She could be anywhere—in the southeast or southwest—and they might never find her. Why hadn't Deirdre given them clearer directions?

The trees melted into one another as the ground receded behind them. From the bushes where they hid, they watched squirrels and foxes headed east. The sky was crossed by more small bands of ravens, flying in the same direction. Of all the creatures in the Deadwood Forest, Matthew and Derin seemed the only ones moving south.

The light was beginning to wane when they saw the moon. She hung between the thick branches of a tree, far in the distance, and the sight of her filled them both with such excitement they forgot themselves, shouted, started running. In the gathering darkness, her dim glow was a beacon.

They were still hundreds of yards from her when they ran into the ferns. Waist high, the black fronds waved around them. Matthew felt something grip his hoof, begin to climb his leg. He grunted in horror and retreated. A starfish, leaving a trail of silver ooze, glistened on his knee. He grabbed it, wrenched it free, and hurled it to the ground, stamping it under his hooves. Derin, behind him, was luckier, escaped without feeling the creature's grasp.

What could they do? Matthew crouched and saw the toads, their red eyes blazing, the long pink worms, gathered at the ferns' edge, awaiting them. He realized nothing would entice Derin to try to reach the moon.

"Hey," he screamed, waving his arms in the dark air, dancing like a fool. "We're over here; we've come to help." The moon gave no sign of having heard. Matthew wanted to address her directly, but how do you talk to the moon? He yelled louder, cupping his mouth with his hands. "We're Deirdre's friends," he screamed. Slowly the moon swung in her cage and looked at him, trying to focus.

From one end of the Forest to the other, the animals were feverish. It was clear their lives were in danger. The air was stained with the black streaks of ravens and the word had spread of the monsters' arrival. Many who had, until that day, paid little attention to the drama being played out in the Forest, who had not seen the owl since the night he had demanded their obeisance and who wished never to see him again, were fleeing with their families. Though the mountains bordered the Forest completely, shutting it off from the Plains beyond, they were headed east, whole clans, as if something deep in their blood urged them to move.

Snakes wound through the mulch, often under the cover of leaves, occasionally poking their diamond heads into the air, red tongues flickering like flames to test the atmosphere, the heat of day. Squirrels and chipmunks, long since accustomed to silence, moved stealthily from branch to branch, or on the ground itself, never chattering, afraid of being apprehended. Even the larger beasts smelled disaster in the air and hurried to escape the Forest.

The flurry of activity put Condor in immediate touch with large numbers of ravens who sided with him. Every time he met a group, he persuaded its members to rest a minute, and he told them his idea. It was so simple, so practical, none of the birds could believe it hadn't been thought of before. It required no convincing for them to hear Condor's plan and embrace it.

Each group he told went in search of others, and by late afternoon, Condor found himself at the head of an army of thousands of ravens. They'd decided to meet at the eastern edge of the Forest. Below them, the animals huddled. The hoards, who had streamed from the Forest all day, now cowered in the shadows of the great mountains they were afraid to cross.

So the two groups faced each other, the ravens darkening the crossed branches of the trees, the scores of other animals on the narrow plain beneath, staring up with fear and desperation. Condor took to the air from time to time and circled the ravens, keeping a rough count, waiting nervously for all those coming to arrive. They flew from the north, south, and west, coming toward the plain as if it were a magnet and they small metal filings.

If the animals could have seen through the layer of cloud, they would have watched the sun touch the western perimeter, and with a dying sigh, slip below it. What they did see was the hovering ghost of night steal down the slopes of the mountain, an almost liquid thickness threatening to drown them. As the blackness deepened, Condor arose one final time from his branch and hung in the air, arrested in space. The other ravens, waiting for that signal, knew the time had come and as one they also rose, so it seemed to the animals watching from the plain that night ascended to meet night, blackness descending and rising at once.

At the moment they met, the ravens screamed. It was a stunning sound, deep as an earthquake, fearless, determined, dedicated to the survival of them all. A week before, the ravens at the owl's command had flown to capture the moon. Now, under Condor's leadership, they were flying to set her free.

She'd hung in her cage, exhausted, since the owl had left her in the previous darkness, and now as another night descended, she was sure she would not see the light of a new day. Although she'd lied to the owl, she knew her sister could not hold out much longer anyway. Her light was almost spent. Now she would have to deal with the owl's rage when he discovered there was no well to the west.

All of it seemed so useless. Why did the owl want this power, this kingdom of darkness? What did he expect to gain from it? Before this madness had begun, he'd enjoyed the obedience, even the reverence of the animals who lived in this forest. Wasn't that enough? Or wasn't it true? Perhaps there had been no love at all, only fear. But if that were so, why had she expected differently from the creatures of earth? She had been aloof, disdainful, and vain. Now she knew better; she could be worthy of them. Instead, she was condemned to a final withering in this tree.

The moon fell asleep and in her dream she saw herself hanging in her cage, exactly as she was. As she watched, a small speck appeared, drew closer, landed on one of the limbs of her oak. A small male raven, one she hadn't noticed before, looked at her imploringly, wanting to help.

"What can I do?" he asked.

"Nothing," she said. "Just leave me be."

"Can I get something for you? What do you want?"

She stared at him for a long time, recognizing in his youth the opportunities now denied her. She thought of all she could tell him, of how beautiful the earth looked from far away, how fragile it was, given to deep tremors within its core, huge waves upon its seas. She could tell him about loyalty and trust, how friendship blossomed in the soul's desert. She could teach him about love. But she was in no condition. In her dream, she was old and wrinkled and ugly. Her shining surface was pocked with age and care, and dark furrows marred her brow. She took a deep breath. He had asked and she would tell him.

"I want to die," she said.

Through the haze of her sleep, she heard someone else calling to her, someone more distant than the small raven now no longer with her. She saw the satyr and the boy, the strangers Deirdre had spoken of, standing waist-deep in the ferns, waving their arms.

"Go away," she groaned. "Leave me alone." How cruel dreams can be, she thought, offering in unconsciousness what life denies.

"We've come to help," she heard them say. "We're Deirdre's friends."

"You've come too late," the moon said. "Deirdre's dead."

And then, as though time were elastic, she heard, coming from the distance, the sound which had interrupted her tenure over the earth. Like the gathering rumbles of a thunderstorm, like a tidal wave rising from the surface of the sea, like all the elements of nature joined in one last fury of destruction, the noise approached.

It was well before midnight, and the air was filled with wings.

The crone's death and the owl's fury had thrown the ravens into a panic. Though they flew south, as they had been told, their course was erratic. Without a leader, the group was at the whim of whomever flew first, and as one raven tired and another took his place, they swung from the southeast to the southwest and back again.

Nervous and frazzled, no longer confident of the owl's mastery, the group was prone to argument. They roosted in trees, disagreeing violently about direction and method. Some of the group favored swooping down upon the boy and satyr as quietly as possible, as the owl had said. Others thought fear would be their greatest ally, that they should attack full-throated, claws ready to shred.

As the daylight waned, the ravens realized all their petty talk had wasted valuable time. They appointed one of their members to guide the way, and she flew silently and swiftly at their head. Under her, the trees grew darker and night came on. How would she find the monsters in the dark?

In the distance, she saw a mirage, the first new light in a week. She flew toward it, expecting some connection between this apparition and the monsters, but soon she stopped, hovered in the air, and the other ravens, caught off guard, thudded into her. The air was filled with their angry squalling, but all she did was stare, oblivious to their words, as she watched the moon rise in the evening sky. The sight of her horned face silenced them all, and then, without a word to one another, they fell apart, flying in all directions like a whirling circle which has lost its center.

The moon awoke with a start. The nightmare was the worst she'd ever had, and she couldn't seem to shake it off. The air reverberated with that chilling *cr-r-auk* which had entered her head a week before. But it wasn't a nightmare. The owl had sent the ravens back. She was being moved once again, and she couldn't stand it. She'd been discovered as a liar. What would happen to her?

"No!" she screamed. "Let me be. Leave me here to die."

The ravens were determined. It was so familiar to the moon by now she could have directed the action. Numbers of ravens clustered on the branches surrounding her and pulled them apart so another group could fly inside. They swirled around her in a dark wind, covering her with the gauze.

But this time it was different. The ravens took care not to tangle the net in her horns. They were gentle with her, and although she couldn't hear what they were saying, their voices were soothing.

She looked through the gauze and saw, perched near her, a young male raven. He stared at her as if she were his personal prize, but his eyes were flooded with tears.

"Deirdre!" he cried, and the call was taken up by other throats until the name of the dead raven reverberated through the Forest. She looked out across the ferns and saw there, dim in her light, the figures of a satyr and a young man. So it hadn't been a dream.

And then the moon felt herself rising. Above her, ravens pulled back the branches, a circle of wooden bars, and she ascended through them until she hung suspended above the trees of the forest. Still, the name rang from the ravens' throats. And she was floating upwards, away from the forest.

As the moon saw the earth recede, she was filled once again with wonder. What was happening that she should be given, even for one final time, a glimpse of this place she had taken for granted? She breathed deeply, and felt a surge of power. Over her, the ravens gave off a blue-black light.

To her side, the young raven she had seen before was flying, the only one not tangled in the net. He was gazing at her as he flew, and when their eyes met, she felt a bright flash of recognition. He darted as close as he could, trying to scream words at her. But the roar of the ravens' wings swallowed all sound. "My debt is paid?" he seemed to ask, and she wondered what he could mean. Still, she nodded at him and he flew upwards to where the other ravens held the net.

Suddenly, the gauze dropped away below her; the ravens separated, flying to either side. She felt herself falling toward earth, brighter than she'd been in a week, but plummeting toward destruction.

She was free! There were no branches around her, no net, nothing but the clean sweet air. As she realized that, as she tried to stabilize, she felt herself climbing. Below her, the earth became more distant, until the gentle curve of its surface could be seen again. She didn't understand, but she wasn't about to ask questions. The sky was hers and she rose as quickly as she could, taking deep draughts of the night air. The details of the surface of earth became visible, vaguely lit by her pale fire. Above her, the clouds shone, luminous and strange, and she stopped her ascent.

Everything was lopsided and irregular. She wasn't where she should be for this time of night, if she could even remember. She had to find her orbit again. She had to find her sister.

The animals on the plain were filled with awe when the moon rose over them, seeking her distant orbit. Used to her earthbound captivity, to nights without her light, they had forgotten how beautiful she was, and in her escape, she seemed to have grown in stature. A curve of shine, a paring of light. Antelope and beaver, muskrat and mink stared upwards, privy to a feeling the first animal must have had when the primeval shrouds of mist cloaking the earth disappeared and the full glory of the evening sky was revealed.

What would the owl do now that his hold on them had been forcibly removed? The moon had been the symbol of his power. If he could wrench her from the sky and keep her, who were they to question his omnipotence? Now she rode on the harsh strains of a night breeze. It gained in velocity as she mounted the sky, and she became a symbol of another sort—an image of what the world had been like before the owl's iron talons clamped down on it. She was eternal variety, the balance between fullness and emptiness Deirdre had spoken of so many days before.

The animals remembered the moon's moments of fulfillment, when as a perfect circle, she shed her light freely, without thought of return, and the Forest was illumined as if from within. Or now, tonight, only a crescent moving toward dissolution, her light pale and delicate, she reminded them of all they yearned for and never found, the necessary move toward darkness before the light could be restored. In her waxing and waning was contained all they knew of the mystery of life. Just as a snake shed its skin and grew another, the moon lost everything only to gain it again. Though the moon rose in the sky like the thinnest curve of an antler, she gave promise through her dimness of a surfeit to come.

The falcons had settled on a group of trees in the center of the Forest, and they looked on the moon's rising with the same wonder with which they had witnessed the sun. It was as though they were listening to a transformation the earth had undergone.

Miles from them, the owl burst from his sequestered clearing. Puffy with rage, unable to vent his anger, he thought he would explode. The uneven racing of his heart pushed the blood so quickly through his body he was feverish. His bib glowed with crimson fury; his claws clenched and unclenched in spasms. His wings, ribbed in the moonlight, rippled like a stormy sea.

He was determined to consolidate his power; he would recapture that traitorous moon. He was certain now she had lied to him; wherever the sun was to be found, it was not in a well to the west. How stupid he'd been to believe her! To have come so close to perfection and to have fallen short! This time, no mercy would be shown. As soon as he had her back in the Forest, he would torture and kill her, and he would make the animals watch.

Like an alien planet, the owl soared over the surface of trees, and then he rose in the air. Over him, the moon's crescent was a wicked smile. He saw the animals dimly, covering the plain to the east, the feathers and claws and scales stretching from the Forest's edge to where the mountains surged skyward. At last, a cry escaped him, an anguished ululation which echoed back and forth across the evening air.

The animals heard the cry, and turning from the moon, they saw the solid form of the owl shooting toward them. He thudded to earth so fiercely, his talons sank into the ground, fixing him there, his forward momentum so strong he almost lost his balance. But the enormous wings flurried, pushing him back until he settled to rest, yellow eyes blazing, his throat parched and ravaged from his brutal outburst.

"You are still mine!" he screamed. "What you see above you is a poor trick of light! The moon remains my prisoner in the southern reach!"

Suddenly, another thrash of wings was heard. The falcons flew swiftly from the west, their leather hoods glinting in the pale light. The owl spread his feathers to welcome them. "Kill them all!" he shrieked, sweeping his wings over the plain.

The falcons broke formation and fanned out across the sky, a wall of beak and talon as they reached the edge of the tree line. They swirled in the air, a deadly whirlwind, and plummeted toward the plain.

Like bullets, the falcons fell, and Hazzard hit the owl in the back of the neck. The owl's head jerked in surprise and pain, and his golden eyes glassed over. He was suddenly wearing a brilliant red scarf. In succession, they thudded into the enormous body, their talons tensing and releasing. After each blow, they staggered back into the sky. The great beak opened and snapped shut, but no sound was heard by the animals, nothing but the wings, like the monotonous clapping of hands, and the swooping hits punctuating the attack.

The owl spread his wings with great effort and snared a falling falcon in the plumage. But the falcon struggled free and ripped from the wing large greyish-brown feathers which fell from his talons like drifting leaves.

Covered with blood, the owl faltered. He attempted to fly, but he was too damaged. The wingspan quivered in the rising wind; feathers fell from his body, his eyes opened and shut as though he were trying to awaken. He couldn't get loose from the ground. His talons, deep in the plain's soil, released, but he had no power to pull them free.

And then cascading like a waterfall, Hazzard dove from straight above the owl and tangled the talons deep in the owl's chest. The bright bib overflowed, the wings dropped to earth, and the owl fell backwards like a toppled tree, hitting the ground with such force it trembled. Hazzard still rode him until the beak stopped moving, and the talons, released at last from the ground, ceased their grasping. The eyes stared vacantly at the brightening sky, and then lost their sheen.

As if waiting for this moment, the wind, building since the moon was freed, ripped loose from its moorings and tore the clouds apart. The black vault of sky appeared, and behind it the stars, bright, unwinking, flecking the darkness. Shreds of cloud made smaller and smaller by the wind scudded into the distance until there was nothing as far as the animals could see, nothing but night and the promise of sunrise.

The moon rose magisterially into this perfected blankness. With a slight shock she settled into her orbit, and *did she shine!* She vibrated with light, the pleasure of her return so obvious, so loving that the ground below thrilled to her joy.

In the meadowlands, the streams began slowly to trickle and the grasses lifted their heavy heads and whispered to the night air. The winds, from the eastern sea to the edge where the Forest dissolved, died to a calm waft, and the world seemed cleansed, fresh. The drooping leaves of maple and oak tensed again as sap started to flow. The Swollen River calmed. And if Deirdre had been alive to return to the seacliffs where she had been born, she would have heard the first faint lapping of the waves as the ocean regained its rhythm.

The falcons surrounded the body of the owl, hiding it from the animals' view. They were inscrutable until they removed their leather hoods. And then the numinous sound of thousands of wings was heard, and all eyes turned up. Coming toward the plain, from the air itself, the ravens who had freed the moon flew high above the earth, and in the moon's light, they looked like silver-black meteors coming home.

Matthew and Derin watched in amazement as the ravens wrapped the moon in gauze and lifted her from the tree. The birds strained against the branches, bent them back, and her curved flicker swung under them, free at last of the owl's grasp. They stared at the slow ascent, saw the black veil fall away and the moon's crescent steady itself and rise in the evening sky.

The beauty of her passage from captivity stunned them, buried their grief, until the ferns at their feet shriveled in the pale light, the starfish and scorpions disappeared, and the Forest spread before them, swept clean as if by a furious wind.

It was then the full meaning of the moon's last words descended upon them and Derin sat on the clear dirt floor and wept. He cried for the death of Deirdre and the glory of the moon; he cried for the fourteen years of life he'd left behind him and the years which lay ahead. He cried for the parents he had never known.

The satyr stood beside him quietly. He looked up at the blur of moon, refracted through his tears, and saw the clouds rip open and the deep vault of night appear. Condor dropped from the sky, another shadow, and landed on the satyr's shoulder like a leaf.

"You were friends of Deirdre's," Condor said. "I saw her die."

* * *

Together the three moved south, headed for the Keep. Condor rode the satyr's shoulder, rising in the air from time to time to fly ahead. In disconnected fragments, he told what he had learned of the owl's death, how he lay on the northern plain, his life's blood drying in the moonlight. Derin wondered at the tale he heard. The night before, the falcons, acting on their leader's orders, had killed Deirdre; tonight they had turned against the owl himself. Somehow the two deaths mirrored, cancelled one another, as if the raven's absence had been answered by the echo of the owl's.

Matthew caught the first glimpse of the Keep. It rose from the forest floor abruptly, shrouded in shadows. In his surprise, he gave a low whistle and turned to Derin. "Do you see it?" he whispered. Derin stopped. In all his thoughts about the Keep, he had never entertained the possibility of fear. "Come on," the satyr said. "We're almost there." But Derin held back, and when Matthew moved to grab him, the boy reached out and pushed against the satyr's shoulder.

Condor hurtled into the air, aggrieved, and his cries turned the silence in the Keep to chaos. The air filled with muffled shouts, rough grunts and moans, a garble of voices. "Hush," a single voice called, harsh and guttural. "Deirdre, is that you?" To Derin, the voice was a growl, and yet it had a level of inflection like his own. Inside the Keep, the noises ended. Matthew nodded to Derin, but the boy couldn't speak, stood trembling beside his friend. "Deirdre, is that you?" the voice repeated, and the hand the satyr laid on Derin's shoulder freed the boy.

"No," he said. "She died last night."

"Whose voice is that? What's happened to the owl?"

"My name is Derin," he replied. "The owl was murdered by his falcons."

The Keep echoed with the screams of the People. Startled by the confusion, Condor darted into the air. As the jubilation leveled, Derin heard the voice again, cutting through the celebration. "We've been waiting so long," it said. "Let us out."

Derin walked hesitantly to the Keep, picked up a rock, and began chipping at the mud walls. The sound of the fortress falling drove the People into a frenzy. Matthew stood and watched the boy grow more agitated as the wall crumbled at his feet. "Help me," he yelled to Matthew, but the satyr shook his head. He backed away, his leg muscles tensed, ready to run. "Derin," he said. "Stop that. Come away with me."

"Are you crazy?" Derin said. "What's the matter with you?"

It took a long time, and as Derin hammered, furious at Matthew, the howls and screaming never stopped. The wall was several feet thick, baked hard by fourteen rainless years, but he finally broke through, the last heave of rock cracking the clay, throwing a pool of moonlight into the Keep.

Derin crawled through the opening he had made and stood up. The stench was overpowering; he almost fainted, and unearthly reverberations made his head spin. It was unbearably hot, and he backed out, tripping in his haste. Something was after him, he could feel it, some demon he would never shake loose if it caught him. He turned quickly in the rubble he had made and on his hands and knees scrambled back to where Matthew crouched, waiting. The satyr stood and Condor flew into the air, cawing. Matthew's eyes were wide with fright, and a strange rasping echoed in his throat. The hair on the back of Derin's neck bristled.

"Did you see anything?" the satyr asked.

"No," Derin said. "It was too dark. The smell was awful."

And then the Keep was utterly silent, and the night was quiet, so quiet Matthew and Derin could make out a strange shuffling coming toward them from within the Keep. The creature groped his way along, emerged through the hole Derin had made.

Matthew closed his eyes and turned away, overcome, but Derin stared in open-mouthed horror at the apparition he saw. It was vaguely shaped like him; the remnant of a head rested on a body so emaciated it was more skeleton than living being. It hunched over, its front legs hanging to the ground. In the dim moonlight Derin could see the white hair, the shriveled genitals, the ghostly skin, the wild blind eyes. The creature, shut in darkness for so long, was a nightmare of himself. Tentatively, it pawed the air in front of it, crouched low, sniffing.

Derin screamed at the thing to go back, but Matthew clamped a hand over his mouth, silencing him.

"Where are you, boy?" the creature said, almost tenderly. "Come here."

"He can't," the satyr said, uncovering Derin's mouth. "He belongs to me."

"Who's that?" the creature asked.

Derin looked from the misshapen form before him to the satyr. "My family," Derin said. "He raised me from a boy."

"Your parents died fourteen years ago," the creature said harshly, "when the owl seized power. You dishonor your family name."

"I honor it," Derin said. "Those you love are your true family. You are a stranger to me."

"I know little of love any more," the creature said. "Suffering does not ennoble the soul, but diminishes it. From what you've said, I expect you'll leave us again?"

"Yes," Derin said. "I've done what I came to do. The owl has been killed, the moon released. You're free of the Keep. I can't stay here with you."

The creature shuffled backwards into the Keep and then reappeared, carrying something in his arms. "This is for you," he said. "It's the only legacy you have."

"Put it down," Derin said, "and go inside. I'll take it after you're gone."

"Just once I would have liked to touch your skin."

"No," Derin said, "I can't."

The creature didn't say another word. When he had disappeared, Derin ran to the hole he had made and then with a sigh so deep it seemed the wind had made it, he picked up the baby at his feet, the baby who, just then, for no reason, started to cry.

In the east, the stars faded and disappeared, and the first hint of color in a week, dark grey fading to peach, was visible. Slowly the sky took on strata, a rainbow sweeping from the horizon to the dark blues and blacks of heaven's height. Then the sky flooded with light as if a pitcher of milk had been spilled. Pale blue became cerulean and, like a crash of trumpets, the sun's first evident rays shot over the world's edge, flaming the clouds. The surface of ocean changed from black to green, and pockets of water glistened like fish scales. Waves caught the tip of light and tossed it skyward, dissolving in foam.

The brightness hit the beach's sand and grains of mica and quartz glittered, hoarding the heat and spreading it. Light rose over the sea cliffs where Deirdre was born and flooded the trees of the meadowlands. The blue jay hopped on his limb, screaming "Hopscotch! Haberdasher! Happy New Year! Hallelujah!" The badger came from his burrow to feel the sun, warm and silky on his coat, while sparrows flittered in the maples bordering the pond.

Like a ruler dividing the living from the dead, the edge of daylight moved across the swamp, streaking the grooved trunks of the cedars. When it reached the Swollen River, fish leapt high in the air. It crossed the Plain and burned its stamp upon the sand. Heat hurtled in shimmering waves and ran like water to the west.

The sun rose higher in the sky, its light climbing the mountains' summit, turning the snow to burnished copper. It swept across Vera, standing on the highest peak, her white fur glistening in the early morning. It spilled down their western slopes and crossed the short plain, where the owl lay dead, until the Forest was drenched with light. It seeped among the twisted wreckage of the Forest, covering the ground as if the tawny spangled leaves had only recently floated to earth.

And then the sun's incandescence climbed the trunks themselves. They glittered, made of wire and tinsel. The world was on fire.

Matthew was consumed with joy. He leapt in the forest, hugging trees and bushes. Condor sat on a limb above him, cawing wildly. Derin held the baby in his arms and the light brought a flush to her cheeks. She lay sleeping, a little thing like a rose bud.

The three of them stared at the sky. As they watched, a raven crossed the blinding circle of sun and hung there a moment, eclipsing the glare, her black feathers rampant against the cadmium red, a silhouette, portent and memory both, and then was gone. She left in her wake the full strong light, hot enough to burn, crossing the sky's deep field of struggle toward another night.

About the Author

Steven Bauer is a graduate of Trinity College and the MFA program at the University of Massachusetts. His poems have appeared widely in such magazines as *The Nation, Massachusetts Review,* and *North American Review. Satyrday* is his first novel. He has received scholarships and grants from the Bread Loaf Writers' Conference, the Massachusetts Council on the Arts and Humanities, and the Fine Arts Work Center in Provincetown. He is currently a lecturer in English and Creative Writing at Colby College in Waterville, Maine, and is working on his second novel.